I0688604

Havoc Rises

Havoc Rises

A Havoc in Wyoming Story

Millie Copper

This is a work of fiction. All characters, places, and incidents are products of the author's imagination or are used fictitiously. Any resemblance to actual people, places, or events is entirely coincidental.

Technical information in the book is included to convey realism. The author shall assume no liability or responsibility to any person or entity with respond to any loss or damage caused, or allegedly caused, directly or indirectly by information contained in this book of fiction. Any reference to registered or trademarked brands is used simply to convey familiarity. This manuscript is in no way sponsored or endorsed by any brand mentioned.

Copyright © 2020 CU Publishing
ISBN-13: 978-1-7353101-1-4

All rights reserved.

No part of this publication may be reproduced, stored in a retrieval system, or transmitted in any form or by any means without the prior written permission of the author, except by a reviewer who may quote short passages in a review.

Written by Millie Copper

Edited by Ameryn Tucker

Proofread by Light Hand Proofreading

Cover Design by Dauntless Cover Design

Also by Millie Copper

The Havoc in Wyoming Series

When a series of coordinated attacks devastate the United States, the people of Bakerville, Wyoming, must come together to survive. Unfortunately, not everyone has the town's best interest at heart. Some are striving for personal gain during the apocalypse.

The Montana Mayhem Series

A group from Bakerville, Wyoming strikes out on their own while searching for the desires of their heart. Unfortunately, the road will not be easy, and sometimes the heart is hardened and deceitful. When things don't work out as they hoped, will they become stranded in the wilderness? Or will each be able to find their way home?

The Dakota Destruction Series

After a series of coordinated attacks devastate the United States, Katie and Leo sacrifice everything to help their country. But some things aren't as they seem. Is it time to go home and start fresh, or can something good come out of this terrible situation?

The Lights of the Collapse Series

As martial law descends and society crumbles, families must band together to survive, finding strength in their unity amidst the chaos. But with danger lurking around every corner and the very fabric of reality seeming to unravel, they discover that the greatest threats might be closer than they ever imagined.

In The October Fall World

In the blink of an eye, an EMP changed everything for Lauren and her family. Now they are in a fight for survival, trying to keep their loved ones alive as society collapses around them. Their once peaceful town of Cody, Wyoming has turned into a powder keg. And with law enforcement a thing of the past, evil lurks around every corner.

In The As The Light Dies World

Lisa Bentley thought having her daughter attacked and left for dead was the worst thing that could happen. She was wrong. She and her family lived an ideal life operating a bed and breakfast in the perfect Wyoming town. That world came crashing down when her daughter was attacked.

Nonfiction Books

Millie has penned seven nonfiction, traditional food focused books, sharing how, with a little creativity, anyone can transition to a real foods diet without overwhelming their food budget. Many of her books also include preparedness and food storage tips.

Find these titles at:
MillieCopper.com

Join My Reader's Club!

Receive a complimentary copy of *Wyoming Refuge: A Havoc in Wyoming Prequel*. As part of my reader's club, you'll be the first to know about new releases and specials. I also share info on books I'm reading, preparedness tips, and more. Please sign up on my website:

MillieCopper.com

Chapter 1

Carefully avoiding my eye makeup, I wipe the back of my hand against my forehead. I've been at this forever. Punctuating my assessment, a drop of water runs down my nose. *Ugh.* I swipe again, this time using my forearm. I probably just streaked everything. I'll fix my face if I ever finish this sinkful. Everything takes longer since the electricity went out, especially the dishes.

It's only been five days since the attacks started, but things have changed in those days. It's like we're now living in a third world country. First the planes crashed, then bridges were blown up—which caused a crazy mass panic—and then, on Saturday, the cyberattacks started. At first, we all thought Prospect might be spared. The reports of lights going out and phones not working started several hours before we had any troubles. I was at work when the lights flickered. After the third flicker, they didn't come back on.

Around the time the lights went out, the phones started messing up. Grant and I had intermittent service into the next day, but eventually all the cell phone carriers and landline providers succumbed to the cyberattacks. Even the traffic lights in Prospect stopped working. Everything computerized was targeted.

The front door rattles. I stiffen. Is someone breaking in? Not bothering to dry my hands, I grab for a butcher knife and quickly move toward the sliding door. Grant's mom gave us a fire escape ladder for Christmas so we could get out of our second-floor apartment. Will I have time to use it? My throat tightens, and I feel my shoulders lift toward my ears.

With a squeak, the door cracks open. Grant sticks his head in. "Hey, Shelby." His smile immediately falters. "Whoa, babe. What's going on?"

"You . . . you scared me. I didn't—we need a code. I thought you were a robber. Or worse." My hand goes to my throat; my breath is shallow.

He moves inside and sets a five-gallon water jug on the floor, then retrieves the second jug he had to put down to open the door—and to scare the life out of me!

"Sorry, babe." Moving quickly toward me, he takes me in his arms. "Relax. I'm sorry. I didn't think."

I cough several times. "We really need a code. You weren't gone very long. Is everything okay?"

"Everything's great. You okay? Do you need a treatment?"

I cough again and wave him away. "Why was today quicker?"

"They added a new water station."

"A new water station? Where? You went there?" The city officials have been pumping water out of the nearby creek and putting it in portable cisterns, then taking it to various locations on our end of town. On the other end of town, they're doing the same thing but pumping from the river, which skirts the east side of Prospect.

He gives me a patient smile. "I went to my usual spot at the hospital, but the line was shorter since other people went to the new one."

"That's great. Any news?" I ask, returning to my dishes.

"Nothing new. No terrorist attacks today. Not yet, anyway."

"So maybe it's over?"

"Maybe. But it's still early. Sometimes we don't hear about them until later," Grant says, grabbing the jug of bleach. The water in our apartment stopped working within a few hours of the lights going out. Within a day, it was out everywhere and the water stations were set up. Even before the water stopped working, we had to purify what came out of the tap because of E. coli and typhoid fears, due to other towns' water supplies being sabotaged.

"Way to be a Debbie Downer. If there's another attack, I really want to talk about— "

"Not now, Shelby."

I give a curt nod.

"Are you okay on water?" he asks.

"I'm fine, just about finished."

"Don't forget to save the rinse water."

I shoot him a look. The day after the power went out, we managed to do some serious shopping. Grant and I both work at the SuperMart—or maybe *worked* is the right term. We don't know when or if the store will reopen. When the power went out on

Saturday, we were sent home with instructions to show up for our regular Sunday shift, whether the lights were back on or not. Our managers set things up so we could help people shop by letting only a handful of people in at a time and one of us escorting them through the store and recording the cost of their purchases.

The process worked well the first hour or so, then there was grumbling in the line and a couple of arguments in the store. Those issues were handled, and things kept on an even keel. Even so, the tension in the air was almost palpable. With each passing moment, the calm seemed to unravel, like pulling a loose thread on a sweater.

Grant and I helped a couple who were doing some serious purchasing. They, the man especially, seemed to think the power would be out for a long time. They were also kind enough to suggest things we should buy. And after we helped them out with their shopping, they gave us a huge tip—over five hundred dollars!

Grant was due for a break, so our manager let him shop without needing to wait in line—a rarity since we're not even supposed to shop when we're on our shift, break or not. It's a good thing he did because the shelves were emptying out fast. At that point, our manager started limiting purchases. No more than two like items per family, except for produce. He thought it best to not limit those purchases since they're perishable and he'd prefer people buy the produce rather than it rotting in the store.

Most items in the meat and freezer cases were already pulled out, due to health codes, before we opened. A generator kept one case working where the eggs and butter were displayed. Sometimes I wonder what happened to the meat and frozen goods. Did the managers take them home? I hope someone was able to use them instead of them all going to waste.

As soon as it was my break time, I also shopped. Neither of us could pay until the store closed, so we kept our carts in the backroom. Things completely fell apart when someone pulled a gun in the line outside. The situation was controlled and the person pulling the gun apologized, saying she'd just lost her head for a moment. But the shopping was halted. Our manager said they'd try it again the next day but would put different rules in place.

Our shopping followed the same rules as regular customers, as far as the cost being written down and sticking to limits, which we all did as we filled our carts. We paid in cash. Those of us working were promised double-time pay for the day, but our manager also gave us each a hundred-dollar credit. He didn't offer anything for the time we are owed toward our pay period, saying corporate will take care of that when the power returns.

Just like there were unhappy customers about our shopping process, there were unhappy employees. Several thought we should get whatever we needed, or wanted, simply for the fact we're employees. There was a lot of grumbling, but nothing changed. In the end, how employees felt didn't really matter.

As we were finishing up, the chief of police showed up with the mayor and said they were confiscating everything left in the store. They did allow us to take our purchases, but everything else is now city property to be doled out in some manner yet to be determined. At least that's what we think will happen. So far, the process has yet to begin. The two other grocery stores were also taken over. There are still a few businesses open in town, but for the most part, all of Prospect is unemployed.

Grant made many brilliant purchases on our crazy shopping day, including a couple of rubber dish tubs. These we set in the sink when we do dishes to help us conserve water. The rinse water is reheated to become the wash water next time. It's gross, but it makes sense. Hauling water isn't easy.

"You want to— " Grant stops midsentence as a shot rings out. He shakes his head. "I figured it wouldn't be long until they started shooting the town deer."

Four more shots follow. "How many deer are they shooting?" I ask.

Then things are suddenly crazy, with too much gunfire to even count the shots. "Get down," Grant says, pulling me to the ground.

I put a hand protectively over my stomach. "What's going on?"

"Nothing good," he answers.

"Where are they? Are they shooting at us?"

"I . . . I don't know. I don't think so."

"Then who?" My breathing is labored, and I'm suddenly feeling sick.

"Stay calm, and watch your breathing. I think maybe it's coming from the hospital," he guesses, then croons, "We're okay."

"The hospital! Who would shoot at the hospital? Besides, that can't be right. They put up those gun-free signs. You can't take guns to the hospital."

He gives me a look.

"Oh," I say, realizing the signs aren't much of a deterrent. We huddle close on the floor, me gasping for breath.

"Are you okay, Shelby? Do you need your inhaler?"

"I'm okay," I say, catching my breath. "I'm just scared."

He nods and pulls me closer. "We're okay. I think it's almost over. The shots are spreading out."

"You mean slowing down?"

"Right. I think it'll stop soon."

"Then what?"

He pulls me even closer in response. I feel myself calming as we shift into a sitting position. He kisses my cheek, the stubble from his chin brushing like sandpaper, then lays a hand across my growing stomach. "We'll stay here until we're sure it's over."

Chapter 2

"Is it done? Can we get up?"

"Maybe," Grant answers with a shrug. "Let's just wait another minute or two."

He pushes a hank of bleach blond hair off his forehead. While he's been working toward Wyomingizing his look by removing his lip and tongue rings, he's yet to give up his surfer hair or laid-back attire. Last time we saw his grandpa, he made a point of saying Grant is finally starting to look like the wholesome boy he remembered. He followed that with, "Now, it's about time you make amends with your dad."

I take a deep breath and caress my stomach. There's a strange smell, like burning wire. The stench causes my stomach to flip.

"Pee-yew. What's burning?" I ask.

"Could be from the shooting," Grant says. "The gunpowder."

"I don't think so."

Like a Labrador, Grant sniffs at the air. "You're right. There's a fire."

"In our building?"

"Maybe. Let's go." He stands and offers me his hand. Getting to my feet, I teeter slightly as I struggle to get my glossy-black platform pumps under me. As soon as I'm stable, he delivers a quick kiss. I stare at him as he says, "We're okay. Breathe easy." Then he moves quickly to the kitchen, returning with a damp dish towel. "Use this over your mouth," he says. "And grab your purse. You have an inhaler in it?"

"Our stuff," I say, gesturing at the things we've collected over the last few days. "We need these things or else . . . "

"I'll get you outside and safe, then deal with that. Your inhaler?"

"Yes, I have it."

He grabs our two duffle bags loaded with essentials, packed by Grant in the days since the attacks, using the shoulder strap for the large bag and the handle for the smaller one. Even though Grant looks scrawny, he's strong. At the door, he puts his palm flat against it. "Checking for heat," he says.

"Is it okay?"

"Yeah, I think so." Then he gingerly touches the knob. "We're good. Let's go."

In the hallway are several neighbors. The woman from next door has a baby on her hip and is holding her toddler by the hand. "Is our building on fire?" she asks with barely concealed panic.

Grant shakes his head. "Don't know. Best to get out just in case."

"Can I take your little one?" I ask.

She glances at my swollen belly and shakes her head. "We're okay. We'll follow you down. Right, Mason? Let's follow our neighbors."

The toddler makes a noise I assume is an agreement as we start down the hall. There's a bottleneck at the staircase with slight pushing and shoving.

"Hey, let's calm down," a voice booms in the small space.

"Mind your own business," a nasally man responds.

The space seems to tighten around me. We're halfway down the stairs when the baby screams.

"Quiet down, kid," Nasal Voice says.

Mason follows with his own yell as the crowd crushes closer. I didn't even realize so many people lived in our building. I feel my chest starting to constrict.

"We're almost out," Grant whispers. "Almost there. You're okay, Shelb. Hang on."

The stairwell is full of people jockeying toward the exit. Someone is holding the door, calmly saying, "Just keep walking. Get out of the building and move away. Just keep walking."

Finally, we're out. I remove the towel from my mouth and suck in a breath of air, immediately regretting it. The smoke is thick. Grant ushers me to a tree. "Sit down. Lean against the tree and get your breathing under control."

My asthma started when I was young. Then, when I was eleven, it seemed to go away. I was completely symptom free until the last few months. Now I have a rescue inhaler to use for emergencies. So far, the symptoms aren't severe enough to use a daily steroid inhaler. My doctor said it's not entirely uncommon for asthma to leave at puberty and return later in life, especially during pregnancy or a time of emotional upset. While I'm now excited that we're going to have a baby, I wasn't at first. It was a time of emotional upset. And with everything going on now . . . I practice my breathing. My baby needs my oxygen.

"You good?" Grant asks, worry painting his face.

"Better." I attempt a smile, letting out a wheeze at the same time. "I don't see any flames."

"Me neither. I'm going to walk around the building to look for flames or smoke."

"No need," Nasal Voice responds. "It's not us. Look." He points behind us toward the hospital where smoke and flames are pouring out. With our attention now drawn to the hospital, the commotion is apparent.

"Shelby, are you okay here?"

"What do you mean?"

Gesturing toward the hospital, Grant says, "I'm going to help."

"I'll go with you," Nasal Voice says.

My neighbor with the children says, "I'll stay with her."

I nod. "I'm okay. Be careful, Grant."

He gives me a quick kiss, then he and Nasal Voice trot off to the hospital.

Sitting down and pulling Mason onto her lap, my neighbor says, "You seem to be breathing a little better. I was concerned when we were heading down the stairs."

"Asthma," I say with a hand wave.

"Sure." She nods. "My brother has asthma."

"I'm Shelby Wayman—I mean, Cameron."

"Are you newlyweds?" she asks with a furtive glance toward my stomach.

"We've been married eight months, but I've always used my maiden name. Now, with the baby coming . . . " I shrug.

"Children are a blessing from the Lord."

I try not to roll my eyes. "I know we've seen each other in the halls, but I don't remember your name."

"Oh, sorry. I'm Kirstin Lewis. This little guy" —she nuzzles the baby's neck, eliciting a giggle— "is Caleb. You've met my big guy, Mason." At the sound of his name, he looks up from the stem of grass he's examining.

"Hi, Mason. Are you finding something interesting?"

He smiles his response and returns to his investigation.

"Mason is a man of few words," Kirstin says, "just like his dad."

"Where's your husband?"

She gives a sad smile. "My father-in-law died last week, before all this mess started. The funeral was Friday. I spoke with Ethan—that's my husband—on Saturday before the phones stopped working. He was trying to figure out a way home. Now . . . " She shrugs. "I don't know."

"Where was he?"

"Vegas."

I nod. She must be totally freaking out, here alone with the children. We sit in silence as we stare at the hospital. I feel my chest loosening. After several comfortable breaths, I ask, "Are you still working?"

She shakes her head. "I do a little freelancing, but I stopped working when Mason was born. In fact, I should be getting some pictures. Can you hold the baby for a second?"

She hands him to me and takes her phone out of her pocket, then starts snapping photos of the fire. "This is terrible. But do you think they're gaining on it? Do the flames seem less?"

"Umm, I'm not sure. Maybe?" I squint slightly, thinking it might help me discern exactly what's happening. She might be right. They may be getting it under control. "Yeah, I think they are. That's good. I was afraid it would burn to the ground. Whew."

We watch as the bucket brigade continues fighting the fire. "So my husband, Ethan, he used to work at the lab in Cody," Kirstin says. "He was among the first group of layoffs. We were fortunate he was able to find a job here in Prospect. He's working at the landfill. Kind of a step down, but he's happy just to be working, happy to be able to stay here. Thought we might have to move home."

"To Vegas?"

"Nah. His dad moved there last year. We're from a small town in Idaho you've probably never heard of. But with his job and the little bit I make from a blog and writing articles for the Prospector Peak Press—have you read it? It's an online newspaper."

"Uh, yeah. Sure. There's often articles linked to it on social media."

"But you don't subscribe?" she asks.

I shake my head.

"Oh, well, that's okay. Anyway, we make do. How about you? From your slight accent, I'd say you're not from here either."

"True. I'm from Kentucky, but Grant's from here. His family has lived outside of Prospect since" —I shrug— "forever, I guess, like the 1930s."

"It's nice you have family here." She puts her phone away and reaches for her baby. If she only knew the truth of it, she might not think it so nice.

"You moved into our building when? Early May?" she asks.

"End of April. But we moved to Prospect last fall. We were renting a studio apartment in a house, but we wanted a little more space."

"So how did you meet?" she asks. "Over the internet?"

"Ha. No. Galveston. We were both working there for a season."

"Sounds like that might be an interesting story."

"Not really." While we've been talking, I've kept my eyes on Grant as he makes his way to the hospital. He's been helping people who were sitting near the building move away. He has his arm around a man, helping him walk. I watch as he sits the man down, then gestures toward the building. *Oh, no.* He runs toward one of the entrances.

Kirstin gasps. "Oh, the building, it's . . . " She pauses and shakes her head. "I thought it was going out. The fire, it's . . . it's completely out of control."

"Yes," I whisper, "and Grant just went inside."

Chapter 3

"Please, please," I whisper, eyes glued to the door Grant rushed through. It's an eternity before I catch a glimpse of his bleached hair at one end of a hospital gurney. I let out a breath.

"Is that him?" Kirstin asks.

I nod as he passes the bed off to someone else. He and the other person who was handling the bed dart back inside. I chew on my top lip.

"He'll be fine," Kirstin says with a nod.

He repeats the exit and reentry procedure several times before Kirstin says, "The smoke is changing. I think we need to get farther away. It's getting worse."

"I don't—I want to be able to . . . "

"Sure." She gives an impatient wave of her hand. "You want to be able to see him. Let's walk over to the City Hall Park. The wind might not be blowing that direction. And I can get more photos from a different angle."

I nod and start to stand.

"Shelby? Shelby, I'm so glad I found you!" I'm engulfed in warm, strong arms, causing me to almost lose my balance. The woman pulls me tighter, righting me, keeping me stable.

"You're here?" I hug her. "What are you doing here?"

"We saw the smoke. At first, I thought it was your apartment. Where's Grant? Helping?"

I nod as tears fill my eyes.

"I knew he would," she says, her voice filled with pride. "Now we need to find someplace else for you. This smoke is bad. Not at all good for you or our baby." She gives my stomach a light pat.

"We're going to the park," Kirstin says.

"Probably fine," my mother-in-law, Pamela, says. "I imagine the smoke inside your building is even worse than out here."

"It was pretty bad when we came out. Like you, we thought it was our building on fire. I guess we should've realized it was the hospital, especially after the shooting." I feel my chest start to tighten.

11

Pamela notices and says, "Let's go. Once we're relocated, you can tell me what this is about a shooting."

"Lots of bullets," Mason says. "*Pow, pow, pow.* They go bang for a long time. Scare mommy and Mason. Baby cry."

"I bet that was scary. But you're okay, right?" Her round face breaks into a large, kind smile.

He nods and smiles in return.

"Mind if I carry you, young man?" Pamela asks, as she straps the larger of our duffle bags across her body. I pick up the smaller one and my purse.

Mason glances at his mom before lifting his arms. "You're tall," he says, as Pamela hefts him into the air.

"Why, thank you. You'll be tall someday soon too."

Even with holding Mason and the duffle bag, Pamela wraps a protective arm around me. Since Grant and I moved here last fall, Pamela has gone out of her way to make me feel welcome, to be a part of the family. We meet for lunch at least once a week and have even gone up to Billings on a shopping day. We had another shopping day planned for baby things, but now, with the attacks, I don't know when—or if—we'll ever be able to do that. The one thing we don't do: we don't go to Pamela's house. The home Grant grew up in is currently off limits to me.

"There now." Pamela sets Mason on the ground. "It's much better here." She guides us to a good-sized tree.

"Everyone else must think so too," Kirstin says, gesturing at the large crowd of people.

"I think some of them are hospital patients. They're still in hospital gowns." Pamela squints her eyes. "Yes, I think it's a triage area. I recognize a doctor and several nurses. Are you okay here, Shelby? I'd like to see if I can help."

"I'll help also."

"No, dear. Please, please stay here with your friend. I'll feel so much better knowing you're out of harm's way."

"Pamela, I— "

"Oh, I know you're fine. Please just humor a worried mom. Besides, I'm sure your friend could use the help."

"Kirstin. I'm Kirstin Lewis, and I'd welcome Shelby's help. My little guy is ready to eat and . . . " She gives a shrug.

"All right." I hold back my sigh. "You be careful too."

Pamela gives my shoulder a squeeze, then hustles off to a group nearby.

"So that's your husband's mom?" Kirstin asks.

"Oh, gosh. Please forgive my terrible manners. I didn't— "

"Don't worry about that at all. Now's not the time to be concerned with something so trivial." Kirstin takes a couple quick pictures before putting her phone away and shifting positions. In full baby talk, she says, "Are you ready to eat? I bet you're hungry. Nom, nom, nom." He coos and giggles his response. Quietly and in an almost cheery voice, she says, "Can you do me a favor, Shelby?"

"If I can."

"Maybe we can keep our talk kind of light? Mason and Caleb— "

"Oh, yes. Sure."

"After Caleb eats, he'll go to sleep. Mason, are you sleepy too?"

"Not sleepy," he says with a hand to his eye. "Want to play with bugs."

Tears sting my eyes as I watch Kirstin with her boys. My baby is due in November, on Thanksgiving. The only hospital in Prospect is burning to the ground. Where will I have my baby? I take a deep breath, wipe my eyes, and straighten my shoulders. "So, you're a journalist?" I ask in the lightest, cheeriest voice I can manage.

Kirstin gives me a grateful smile. "I know it probably seems pretty morbid to be taking pictures. I'd like to think I'm a journalist. But I'm not really. I have a blog, and occasionally Milena Maynard will buy one of my stories. Do you know Milena?"

"Well . . . " I don't want to tell Kirstin how I've heard things about the woman but don't actually know her. My eyes wander to the hospital. *Where's Grant?*

Kirstin lets out a small laugh. "That's right. You work at SuperMart. You probably know about the tiff she got in with her former boss's wife, right there in the produce department."

I catch a glimpse of Grant and let out a sigh of relief. "It happened before I moved here, but it's part of the training on how to handle escalations between shoppers." And *tiff* isn't how it was described to me. *Knock-down, drag-out fight* was what I heard.

"Oh, I bet it is. I didn't live here when it happened either. We were still in Cody. But I had met Milena when she worked for the Prospect Record. I was trying to get my foot in the door there, and she was nice to me. But Richard Majors, the owner, wasn't a nice

13

guy." She gives a small shudder. "I can understand the trouble Milena had with him."

I expect her to say more, but she goes back to talking with the baby.

I alternate my gaze between watching Grant at the hospital and keeping an eye on Pamela as she helps the injured. They're loading people into cars and pickup trucks, whisking them away. She catches my eye and gives me a sad smile. I should be helping. I should be doing something other than just sitting on the grass while this craziness goes on around me.

It's only a few minutes until Kirstin asks if I can hold the now-sleeping baby. She wants to run back to the apartment and grab a couple of things. Mason is also asleep, using my leg as a pillow.

"Maybe the smoke won't be bad and we can go home," Kirstin says.

"Want me to go with you? I can carry Mason."

"No, let me check it out. It's better for you here, in the fresh air."

I nod my agreement. I'd rather stay and watch Grant anyway. A few minutes ago, he stopped going inside the building. Everyone stopped. The hospital is fully engulfed and beginning to lean to one side. Now everyone is part of the bucket brigade, trying to wet down the nearby buildings to prevent the fire from spreading, in case the wind shifts. There's a large parking lot and then a small green space between the hospital and our apartment building, so our place should be fine. Even though the wind is still blowing in that direction.

Chapter 4

Kirstin returns much quicker than I expect, loaded down with blankets and bags. She flicks a large, thin blanket out on the ground, then we gently move Mason so he's on it.

"Here, Shelby. Lean against the tree."

I nod and position myself to use the tree as a backrest. She sits next to me and puts the baby on the blanket, letting him stretch in his sleep. Taking out her camera, Kirstin glances at the hospital. "Oh no. It's going to collapse."

"At least they've moved everyone back." I bite my lip, knowing my statement is only part truth. How many people were they not able to get out? "How is the smoke in the apartment?"

"Bad. I opened our windows, but I don't know how we'll sleep in there tonight. If you want, I can go back and open your windows, for all the good it'll do."

I consider giving her the keys to our apartment, then decide against it. As nice as she is, today's the first day I've ever really talked to her. We say hi when passing in the hallway or the parking lot, but I don't know her. And I don't think I want her to see the stuff we've managed to acquire in the last few days. "I'll probably need to walk around soon. I'll do it then."

She keeps snapping pictures. "Doesn't look good, does it? I hope they were able to get everyone out." She pauses. "I guess that probably didn't happen." Sitting her phone on the ground, she whispers, "It's pretty obvious they didn't. The smoke— "

"It's going to be pretty bad."

"Pray with me, Shelby?"

"That's not— " I hesitate. Why not, if it brings her comfort? "Okay, I will."

She takes my hand and bows her head. "Our Dear Heavenly Father, as this tragedy unfolds before us, we know that You are our hope. Please, Lord, please wrap Your loving arms around us. Be with those who are injured; heal them in Your mighty way. Be with those who may have— " She lets out a small cry, and I watch as tears drop to her lap. "Please, Lord, be with those who may have lost a loved one in

15

this tragic event. We know we'll have troubles in this world, but we also know You're with us to help us through these times. Be with Shelby. I suspect she's thinking about her baby and wondering what the loss of the hospital means for her baby's birth. You're a faithful God. You'll be here to help her, to help us, to meet our needs." She gives my hand a squeeze. "Thank you, Lord, for all You do. We pray these things in Jesus' name, amen."

I'm surprised to feel tears in my eyes. What's this about? Pie in the sky religion does nothing for me. My mom taught me that if I want to get anything in life, I'm the one who makes it happen, not some fictional being playing us like puppets. That's one reason Grant and I get along so well.

While he grew up in a Christian household, he shed that fake news and now lives his own life. Pamela understands this and accepts us as we are. Grant's dad is another story. He's just like the other people I've met who claim to be Christians but are judgmental and hypocritical.

My mom told me all about *those* people. She made sure to protect me from the embarrassment she felt when she made the mistake of going to church with my dad before they were married. She'd never been to church before; her parents didn't go. They never talked about God or anything in the home she grew up in, so she didn't know what to expect. Dad told her she'd love it, that it'd be uplifting and wonderful and her heart would be filled with joy.

None of that was true. Instead of being welcomed with kindness, a few women gave her dirty looks. They pointed at her and then covered their mouths and laughed. Were they making fun of the way she was dressed? Her hair? What exactly was their problem? I can only imagine what those snooty church people would think of me. I have no doubt they'd laugh me out of the building.

Mom made it through that awful service, not once feeling anything Dad told her she'd feel. All she felt was uncomfortable and out of place. She refused to return. Dad wanted to get married in the church, but Mom said no. They took the Justice of the Peace route, just like Grant and I did. Dad continued to go to church, but even after I was born, Mom never went and she forbade him from taking me or mentioning anything to do with religion in the home. When I was twelve, they were both killed in a car accident. I went to live with Grams and Gramps, my mom's parents.

"Are you okay, Shelby?" Kirstin asks, squeezing my hand again.

"Oh, yeah, sure." I wipe my eyes. "The smoke was bothering me, I guess."

She gives me a smile. We watch as people start quickly moving away from the hospital. "Something's happening," Kirstin says.

"It's getting ready to go," I whisper.

"What? Oh!" She grabs her phone and takes several more pictures.

I glance down at Mason and Caleb; both are still sleeping. We watch as the building continues its lean to one side. There's a huge commotion as the bucket brigade moves away. I search out Grant's shock of blond hair. When I finally find him, he's staring at me. He lifts a hand and then turns to watch the building as it gives a dramatic shudder. The entire south side collapses, leaving only skeletal remains.

"Sixty-eight minutes."

"What?"

"It took sixty-eight minutes from the time I first smelled the smoke," Kirstin says. "That's longer than it took the South Tower to collapse but less time than the North Tower."

"What are you talking about? The World Trade Center?"

"Right. I'm being morbid again." She starts tapping on her phone. "I'm just taking a few notes, even though I'm sure Milena is around here somewhere. How could she not be?"

"True. It looks like everyone in town is here."

We sit quietly for a few minutes before she says, "Do you feel comfortable watching the boys for me?"

"Umm . . . are you going back to the apartment?"

"I thought I'd help. I see a nurse I know. I'll keep looking over here, and you can signal if you need me."

"How?"

"How what?"

"What signal do you want me to use?"

"Just wave at me—like, frantically. Or if I hear one of the boys scream, I'll come back."

I bite my lip. Do I want to be responsible for these two little boys? "Sure, yeah. Go ahead."

Kirstin stands up. "The diaper bag has supplies and snacks."

She makes a beeline for the main group, then veers off to a woman helping load several people into a car. After she finishes, she looks in my direction and gives me a thumbs up. I move my fingers in a gentle wave, making sure it doesn't look at all frantic. She turns and helps someone else.

I hold and cuddle the baby while he sleeps. Mason stirs slightly but doesn't awaken. I'm almost enjoying the sunshine and snuggling with the children, but the muffled cries of the injured and the smell of death in the air punctuate what is happening. Kirstin chose a good spot. It's close enough to see what's happening but far enough we're not right in the middle of it. Still, I'd rather be any place else.

I take out my phone and find a song to play. Music has long been a wonderful escape for me. It's amazing how the right song can reach out and speak to me. Usually I play music with an app on my phone, but it stopped working after the cyberattacks. Now I'm limited to the eight songs I have downloaded on my phone—songs that helped me get through a rough patch after losing both my Grams and Gramps within weeks of each other. I still love the songs, but sometimes they remind me too much of those days.

"Shelby?" I turn my head at the sound of my name.

"Hey!" I say quietly, so as not to wake the boys. "I didn't know you were here. Your mom didn't tell me."

"All of us are. We all came into town when we saw the smoke," Grant's younger brother Bryce says. "I was helping at the other apartment building—you know, the one on the backside of the hospital? We tried to keep it from burning."

"Did you? Keep it from burning, I mean."

He shrugs. "Mostly. The siding closest to the hospital melted. Someone said it probably has some structural damage and serious smoke damage. They won't be able to go in there until it's checked out. I need to go back and help again, but Grant asked me to open the windows in your apartment. It smells pretty bad in there."

"Thanks for doing that."

"Who's kids?" Bryce asks, nodding toward Mason and Caleb.

"My neighbor's. She's helping. Your mom is over there too." I point at Pamela. Kirstin is staring at me, so I give her a small wave and a smile. She returns with a thumbs up sign.

"She left her kids with you? I didn't even think you liked them."

"Umm, Bryce, you do know I'm going to have a baby, right?"

"Yeah, but that's different."

I shake my head. "I like kids just fine. Besides, she thought she might be able to help. And your mom won't let me help."

"That sounds like Mom."

I smile and say, "So Dax and your grandpa are here too?"

"Yep. At the apartments. Dad too." His eyes meet mine, an unspoken acknowledgment of the troubles between his dad and Grant, and by proxy me, is relayed in his gaze. "Um, do you have a mirror?"

"What?"

"Your makeup is . . . not quite right."

"Oh!" I put a hand to my eye.

"The other one," he says with a small smile. "Don't worry, though. You're still beautiful." He gives me a wink and a wave as he turns away and trots toward the area of destruction. At almost sixteen, Bryce is the most like his mom—open and warm, going out of his way to include me in the family. Even a bit of a flirt, in a completely harmless way.

Dax, three years older than Bryce, is more reserved. While never hostile, he isn't overly affectionate either. Grant says he's the same as always, even before the family troubles happened. But sometimes I think he looks at me weird, like he doesn't approve. Just like Grant's dad does. I know he doesn't approve. He even refused to come to our wedding last October. Pamela, the brothers, and Grant's grandpa Paul were there.

And this past week, with everything that's happened, Grant's mom or grandpa made sure to check on us. Paul gave an ominous warning for us to "stay on your toes."

Prospect was a mess those first couple of days. Many people were on the road, away from their homes. This just compounded the troubles. We had an influx of travelers, people who were exiting Yellowstone and other local vacation spots. Some people were stranded here. In fact, I seem to remember hearing about a soup kitchen being operated out of the hospital. Maybe the soup kitchen people had something to do with the gunfire.

I fish in my purse for my compact. Bryce was right, I'm a mess. I do a quick repair job, which isn't easy while holding a baby. It's not great, but it's better than before.

Chapter 5

Completely useless, that's how I'd describe myself right now. While the entire area is abuzz with people helping the injured, I sit against the tree holding the baby and playing with Mason. He woke up from his nap, concerned where his mom might be. After a few moments, he settled in. Thankfully, he's a calm child, and the toys his mom had in one of the diaper bags seem to be enough to occupy him for the moment.

He does look over at the triage area occasionally. Once, when someone is crying out in pain, he says, "They have owie. Need kisses." Later, when baby Caleb loudly messes his diaper, Mason—in perfect adult sounding enunciation—says, "Mark my words, that's going to be a bad one."

A loud laugh escapes me, causing the baby to cry out in fright. A few minutes later, with Caleb kicking and screaming the entire time, I determine Mason is correct. It's a bad one. After not only a diaper change but a full clothing change, he's put back together and finally happy. Mason, however, makes it clear he would rather be at his own home playing with his toys. He settles for digging a book out of the diaper bag.

After Mason reads the board book about trucks and a second one about trains—many times—then takes short walks around the area and plays with the few toys he has, Kirstin shows up to feed Caleb.

"There's food for Mason in the bag. Feel free to have some also," Kirstin tells me.

I dig out a snack for him. "You want something?" After she asks for a breakfast bar, I rifle through my own duffle for food. "How is it?" I ask.

"It's fine. Blueberry's my favorite."

"I meant the . . . the people."

"Oh, that. No, that's not good. I'm glad you have the boys over here."

"We can still hear. You know, the louder ones."

"I think the ones who are severely injured have all been transported. There were some who . . . " Her voice fades off as she stares into the distance. With a slow nod, she says, "It's really not good. There's still a lot of minor injuries. Some will go to other hospitals, but most are just going to be treated on the lawn and sent home."

"Do they know what happened?"

"There don't seem to be any complete answers. There was a fight that escalated into a shootout. What do they think we are? The wild west? Anyway, how the fire started is a mystery."

"Is there a— " I bite my lip and tilt my head.

She shakes her head in response. "Not yet. A lot. Many of our doctors and nurses. Patients not ambulatory and unable to get down the stairs. Did you know people like Grant were carrying the hospital beds down the steps? They saved many lives, but someone said possibly a hundred patients, doctors, and other people didn't make it out." I had heard rumors that, since the attacks, there's been many people in the area admitted to the hospital for injures or illness, to the point they were past capacity. And the hospital had meeting rooms and their auditorium being used as sleeping space for displaced people. "There are a few people going around and trying to find those they know should've been in the hospital when it started."

"A hundred deaths? That's . . . that's terrible."

"You're still okay with the boys? I'd like to go back and see if I can be of further help. Oh, and I was right. Milena is here. She still wants to look at the pics I took, though, and asked me to write something. We'll collaborate on an article."

"That's good." I want to ask about her payment for writing. Things have gone so crazy so quick, there's not much to buy even if you have the cash to buy it. And with not only the SuperMart but also the Albertson's and a small, locally owned grocery store under the control of the city, purchasing food isn't happening. Grant still goes out every day, looking for things we can use. We've tried to be thoughtful, to take only things we need. But I've heard people talk. There's a rumor going around that the mayor will start going door to door and taking stuff from people who he deems have more than they need. Nobody seems to know what "more" entails.

"So, you're okay then?" Kirstin asks.

"We're fine. Your timing was about perfect for feeding Caleb, so if you can do that again . . . "

"Oh, yeah. No problem. My body tells me when he needs to eat, just like his body tells him. We're a team. Aren't we, cutie?" she coos, snuggling him a little before handing him to me. Wrapping Mason in a hug, she tells him, "You be good for Shelby. Help with your brother."

"We go home soon?" Mason asks.

"Soon. The fresh air is good for you. But stay under the tree so you don't get too much sun."

"K, Mama. Mason help with brudder?"

"Yes, just like you always do."

Another hour passes before I see Grant walking toward me. His bleached hair is darkened from ash, his face and clothes covered in soot. Dax and their grandpa Paul are walking with him, looking about the same. Bryce is slightly dirty, but not to their degree.

I try to smile. "How you doin', little lady?" Paul Cameron asks.

"I'm okay. Wish I could be of more help."

"I suspect watching the young'uns is a help. Besides, in your condition, you don't want to be near the mess. Too much stuff burning. Wouldn't be good for you to breathe it."

"And her asthma," Grant says, giving me a small, sad smile.

I shrug. "Sure."

Paul lifts a hand in greeting to someone across the park, and I turn my head to see who it is.

"Is that Chaplain Rick?" Dax asks, lifting his chin toward the man sitting on the bench. "I thought he died?"

"Heard that too," Paul says with a nod. "Guess the rumors of his death were greatly exaggerated."

I smile at the misquote while Bryce says, "That doesn't make any sense."

"I'm going to talk to him. Dax, Bryce, you coming with me or staying here?" Both agree to go with him.

Grant sits on the grass, making sure to not touch the blanket.

"Dirty," Mason says, acknowledging Grant for the first time since he returned.

"Definitely. I need a shower."

"Shower broken," Mason says.

"Yeah. I'll figure something out."

Mason returns to his toys while Caleb starts to doze off.

Grant quietly says, "Bryce said the apartment's pretty bad. The smoke— "

"I know. Maybe it'll be okay. What are you doing now? Are you finished or taking a break?"

"A break. I'm going back in a couple of hours to relieve the people who stayed behind. We're pretty sure the fire won't spark up again, especially since the wind is better, but we'll have to monitor it for . . . I don't know, days maybe."

"Did you see your dad?"

Grant narrows his eyes, then looks away.

"Did you talk to him?" I persist.

"Not now, Shelby. Being over there, so close to all the . . . the death, was one of the hardest things I've ever done. I don't need to be reminded of the rest of my failings right now."

It's nearly dusk when things start calming down enough that Kirstin and Pamela feel they can stop helping. After getting most of the soot and ash washed off, Grant, his brothers, and his grandpa helped with the minorly injured, mostly driving people home. Now Grant and Dax are taking a shift monitoring the still-smoldering fire.

Because of the damage to the apartment building nearest the hospital, residents aren't allowed to stay there tonight. A short while ago, the mayor called people together at the amphitheater. He looked perfectly pressed in his suit, not a hint of ash or soot anywhere. Did he help with the fire? If so, he sure cleaned up in the time since.

City Hall Park is a large greenspace in front of Prospect's administrative buildings. The mayor's office, planning and zoning, building permits, and other city services are housed in this building. The park is also home to an amphitheater for summer concerts, a farmers' market, and more. Our apartment building is just across a side street from the park. The proximity to both the park and the hospital was one of the reasons we chose the apartment.

Today, the park was used to triage the injured and will now be a campground for the newly homeless. While many can stay with friends or family in Prospect, there's still a considerable number of people camping out. The mayor hands out new tents, still in boxes, probably from the SuperMart requisition. There's not enough, so plenty are simply sleeping under the stars on this pleasant June evening.

"Let's see about your apartments," Pamela says to Kirstin and me. "Bryce, pick up the duffle bags, please."

We make sure Kirstin and her children are settled in their apartment, which does have a strong smoke odor but is better than I expected, before going into my place.

Bryce lets out a whistle. "It amazes me how much stuff you guys bought. When I was in here earlier— "

"Bryce," Pamela cautions, "you don't need to advertise it."

He shrugs and drops the duffle bags onto the couch. "What did you do? Buy out the SuperMart? You should see all the stuff Grandpa got. He went to his friend's— "

"That's enough." Then, in a whisper, Pamela says, "Paul went to the restaurant supply store his friend Angelo owns."

"Traded fuel for food," Paul says with a nod. "Looks like you guys did pretty good. Smart. I'd expect nothing less." His smile lights up his round face.

Paul and his son PJ are both big guys and obviously father and son. Grant's dad, Dusty, was adopted and is the opposite; he's skinny as a rail and shorter than I am. Paul and his wife, Kathleen, had PJ and then tried for five years for another child before adopting Dusty. Grant takes after his dad in stature, but his brothers, Dax and Bryce, are both taller and heftier, thanks to Pamela's genes.

Pamela and I are very similar. We both married men we not only tower over but considerably outweigh. I try not to feel self-conscious about that. It's not easy, especially with the pregnancy and my rapidly changing body. I've never been skinny, but not obese either. I used to call myself plump. Grams told me I had a beautiful face and could have been a pinup model. Now, I play that up by making sure my makeup is perfect and that I dress the part. And I no longer call myself plump, now thinking of myself as voluptuous.

Picking up a box and shaking it, Bryce says, "You sure bought a lot of cereal. How are you going to keep the milk from spoiling?"

"No milk. We'll eat it dry. Except the oatmeal and shredded wheat. They'll be fine with just warm water."

Bryce makes a face. "I thought Grant had a thing about having too much stuff around the house?"

"You mean that 'live in the moment' mumbo jumbo he's always going on about?" Paul asks.

"Right." Bryce nods. "What's up with that, Shelby? Doesn't he have a fit about all this, just like with all your clothes? He's always talking about you having too much stuff. I can't imagine he's happy

24

about all this food and"—he pauses a moment before continuing— "other things you have laying around."

I tilt my head. "He's definitely a minimalist."

"Have to be after living in his car for all that time," Paul scoffs.

"True. It's just, you know, things seemed different all of a sudden, with watching the grocery store shelves empty and knowing there were no trucks coming to refill. So, the day after the cyberattack, we did some shopping."

"Looks like crazy shopping," Bryce says. "And nuts? I didn't even know Grant liked nuts."

"Right, crazy shopping day. Those nuts are not his favorite," I reply with a shake of my head. "But by the time we were able to start shopping, our choices were limited. And we wanted to buy things we could eat without much preparation. Grant is concerned about cooking odors."

"Cooking odors?" Bryce asks. "Who cares about that?"

"Well— "

"Smart boy," Paul jumps in with a nod. "I don't know if I would've thought about that. He learned that when he was living on the street?"

I bristle at the way Paul says *living on the street.*

"Now, now." Paul smiles. "I didn't mean anything by that. Other than he learned some skills that might come in handy now."

"I guess maybe his time away will be of a benefit," Pamela says. "Of course, the best thing to come out of that time is you, dear." She gives me a look of love. "And our grandchild. You were such a natural with your friend's children today. I just know you'll be a wonderful mom."

My eyes fill with tears. "The . . . the hospital . . . what am I . . . where . . . ?"

"Now, now." Pamela wraps an arm around me. "We won't worry about that today. Each day has enough trouble of its own."

"Wise words from our Lord and Savior," Paul says. "Besides, come November, things might be just fine and it won't be a problem to go to Cody or even up to Billings to have your bub."

Bryce hands me a tissue from the box on the coffee table. "That was the last one. Do you have more?"

"In the bathroom," I say, trying to control my blubbering. "We might need it for toilet paper. That was one thing we couldn't buy— the shelves were empty. We got a couple rolls of paper towels and three boxes of tissue, along with a package of napkins. Then, when that's gone, we have a big box of shop towels from the automotive department."

"Jeez. That all should last forever," Bryce says.

I give a snort, not wanting to tell him I use the bathroom more than any human should. Ever since I found out I was pregnant, my bladder has seemed to shrink in size.

"Shelby," Pamela says gently, "you know you and Grant could always come out to the ranch."

I shake my head. "You'll need to talk with Grant about that. Or, more likely, your husband would need to. You know how it is."

"They're both just being stubborn," Paul says. "Neither wants to admit he was wrong and apologize to the other. You women both need to talk to your husbands and tell them— "

"Paul, that doesn't help anything," Pamela says. "Besides for being my husband, Dusty is your son. You could talk to him too."

"That boy hasn't listened to me since he was sixteen!"

Pamela gives him a knowing look.

He raises a hand in defeat. "Fine. Fine. Point taken. But know this, Shelby. Whether they figure out their issues or not, you and Grant are to go immediately to the ranch if you ever feel unsafe."

"Absolutely," Pamela agrees.

"Thank you both. I'm sure if things ever got too weird here, we'd do just that."

Chapter 6

Last night was terrible. I was so wound up that I couldn't relax. As we lay in bed, I flopped and turned, trying to get comfortable. I finally sat up and told Grant I needed to talk. He was already asleep, and even though he did wake up briefly, he wouldn't stay awake. I was so irritated with him. I turned over in a huff, making sure I made plenty of noise, expecting him to say, "Hey, what's wrong? Are you okay?" Nope. Nothing.

I must have finally fallen asleep because the next thing I know Grant is touching me gently, saying, "It's a dream, Shelby. Only a dream. You're safe."

The stench from the fire doesn't help any. As soon as the sun begins to rise, I crawl out of bed. Grant is already dressing. The awful smoke smell isn't much better today than it's been since I came back to the apartment. How long will this lingering stench be around? I'm suddenly struck with guilt. How can I be concerned about the smell when so many people lost their lives in the fire? What kind of person does that make me?

"I heard some things yesterday," Grant says while we sit on the couch. He sips coffee while I start on my water for the day. Staying well hydrated helps keep the asthma under control. Apparently, there's a link between dehydration and asthma. There's also a link between stress and asthma. I take a long, calming breath.

"What kind of things?"

"Not only has the mayor taken control of the grocery stores and the Rite-Aid, but also the other pharmacy in town and Angelo's restaurant supply place. Of course, thanks to my grandpa, that place was pretty much empty."

"Did you hear anything about when they'll start handing out food? Kirstin didn't say anything, but I got the impression she and the boys don't have a lot."

"Not really. The rumor is they're taking inventory now and then they'll figure out what to do. There's a secondary rumor . . . " His voice fades off as he stares out the patio door, watching a bird on the railing of our balcony. As it flies off, he says, "There were more rumors

27

of them going door to door, taking any food and supplies deemed excessive."

"They can't do that! How is that right?" Just thinking about this gets my blood boiling every time.

"I wouldn't think they could. And I honestly can't imagine it would be a smart thing to do. Knock on the wrong door and bullets would start flying."

"It's just a rumor, though, right?"

He shrugs. "Maybe. Maybe not. My guess is, it's probably part of their plans but they'll do other things first. I think we should expect it to happen at some point."

He returns to his coffee while I pick at my thumbnail, smoothing the decal near the cuticle. This is my favorite design: glossy white with red cherries. And one nail on each hand has plain red.

Nail stickers are an amazing invention. I'd never be able to afford hand-drawn designs at the nail studio, but for only a few dollars, the stickers give me a high-end look. I move on from my thumb to my pinkie while I wait for Grant to continue. After several minutes, I say, "I understand helping people. We've talked about it— "

"Right. Exactly. But we talked about helping people on our terms. Not being forced by someone else to give up our things. I won't risk your health or the health of our baby. We've talked about hiding things so it's not all out in the open. We need to do that, but I think we need to *really* hide things too."

"Where? This place isn't that big. And don't you think, if they did do a door-to-door search, they'd look in the closets and under the bed?"

"They would. But I have some other places in mind."

I wait for him to continue. When he doesn't, I ask, "Such as?"

"What if we took a piece of the drywall out?"

"Uh. No. We rent, remember? Our deposit— "

"I could fix it when everything gets back to normal. They'd never know."

I shake my head. "How would that help anyway? Don't you think the—what do we call them? The people who would go door to door and take our things?"

"Thugs? Thieves?" With a shrug, he stands up. "I'm going to get more coffee. Want anything?"

"I'm good. I'll make us breakfast in a bit. I thought we could have pancakes and the rest of the eggs. Are you sure the eggs are still good?"

"It's probably best to finish them up." Grant walks to the kitchen and opens the freezer above the fridge. On Saturday, after the power went out, he went to his grandpa's filling station. A short while later, he returned home with several blocks of ice. He put ice in our fridge, turning it into an icebox. This gave us several days to use the food in the fridge. What little ice and food we had left was then moved to the freezer, and we started working on that.

"I think we'll need to start our stealthier cooking before too much longer," Grant says. "In fact, let's look over the things we separated out and see what we really need to use."

"Your grandpa was pretty impressed with your stealth food plan."

"Was he? I wish coffee didn't smell so good. I'll hate to give that up."

"We have a whole canister of coffee plus the opened one. Maybe things will still be fine and it won't be a concern."

"Maybe. But starting tomorrow I'm going to cut back. I've had caffeine headaches before, and they're not pleasant. I should've never started drinking it."

"The Mountain Dew wasn't any better."

He tilts his head in acknowledgment before sitting on the couch. "But at least you can't smell Mountain Dew throughout the entire apartment building."

"Go back to telling me your plan for the hole in the wall—which I happen to think sounds a little ridiculous."

"Just a hole in the wall would be ridiculous. But a strategically placed hole in the wall, say, behind that painting" —he gestures toward my beloved Charles Lee lithograph my Grams bought at an auction on a cruise ship— "might be smart."

I narrow my eyes. "You mean like hiding a safe behind a picture? Wouldn't they know that trick?"

"Maybe, but I still think it's worth a try. And we could put a hole behind each of your posters in the bedroom."

"I don't know. I can't imagine how that would work. The painting and the posters are too high. You wouldn't be able to get things out."

"I have a plan for that too. But that's not all. We'll stash things outside of the apartment."

"What? Like in the community laundry room?"

29

"Did you know my grandpa made me promise we'd go to the ranch if things got bad here?"

"He told me the same thing. No matter what's happening between you and your dad— "

"Right. And as much as I don't want to, I will, for you and our baby. We'll go there."

I feel the sting of tears. Not trusting my voice, I bite my lip and nod.

"Oh, hey, don't cry. It won't be that bad if we have to go there. I mean, it won't be like living on our own, but it won't be terrible."

"I'm not crying about that. I just—I don't know why I'm crying. Just thinking about having to go and you wanting to keep us safe, it just . . . overwhelms me." I wipe my eyes on the sleeve of my robe.

"You need a tissue?"

"No, I'm okay. Besides, the box is empty."

"It's not like I can't go get the box out of the bathroom." Grant stands up, heading that direction. A moment later he returns, peels the top off the box, then hands me a tissue.

"Thank you," I say before blowing my nose.

"So, I think we should stash some things between here and there."

"Between here and where? The ranch?"

"Right. I told you how I knew guys that did that? How they'd keep things in different sections of town in case they needed to relocate in a hurry?"

"You told me, but weren't they using bus lockers or something like that?"

"Not usually bus lockers. They only let you leave things for a short time, like twenty-four hours. So those weren't good options. And since I had my car, it wasn't something I did. But others would hide things in abandoned buildings or even dig a hole in the park."

"What about mice and rats? Didn't they get into things?"

He shrugs. "Sure. Sometimes. So they'd have more than one stash. And besides, usually they were stashing their booze, so it wasn't a hot commodity for the vermin."

"Okay, so you're going to dig holes to put our stuff in, hoping the rats or whatever don't get to it before we do?"

"Something like that. Yeah."

"Honestly, that doesn't sound any more secure than letting the thugs—or whatever we've decided to call them—take our stuff."

"I think it would be. Plus, if we have to leave here in a hurry, we'd know we at least have some supplies to get to the ranch. It's only fifteen minutes if we're driving, but it'd take longer if we had to go overland."

"Overland? You mean walk?"

"Right. If we had to leave in a hurry and couldn't take the cars, we'd probably skirt the creek. That'd be the most hidden route. I don't think we could make it in a day. It'd probably take two."

"I think I'd rather drive."

"So would I, but if we can't, we should have things in place. I'm going to prepare for both possibilities."

"Whatever you think, Grant. I'm going to get dressed."

"Um, Shelby?"

"Yeah?"

"About that. You know I love the way you always look so . . . perfect, right?"

I can't help but smile. "Sure. You tell me often." I turn to head toward the bedroom.

"I do. I really do. But— "

I spin around. "But what?"

"I think maybe you should wear your work clothes. You know, just for now. Tone it down a bit," he says quietly.

My hands instantly go to my hips. "Tone it down a bit? What's that supposed to mean?"

"If we did need to leave in a hurry and walk the river, you'd be better dressed for it in the clothes you wear for your SuperMart shift than your—than your *you* clothes."

"Isn't that what the duffle bags are for? We each have tennis shoes and workout clothes, along with food."

"Yes, but what if we didn't have time to grab our bags?"

"Then I guess you'd better add some ugly clothes for walking the river to the stash. Because if we're here, I'll dress the way I always do."

I stomp into the bedroom and shut the door with considerably more force than necessary. What makes him think he can tell me to tone it down? What does that even mean? *Tone it down. Ha.* I'll show him how I tone it down.

I pick out my favorite nautical dress, which has a high waist perfect for my changing body, then put my long hair into a side twist. I use an extra heavy hand with my makeup, finishing the look with bright

31

red lipstick and platform pumps to match. Striking a pinup girl pose into my full-length mirror, I give an air kiss. "How about *that* for a toned-down look?" I whisper.

In the kitchen, Grant is rinsing out the camp stove coffee pot. "Hey." He gives a small smile. "Look, I messed up. I didn't think about what I was saying, or how I was saying it. I love the way you look—all the time, even in your SuperMart garb—so I didn't even think it might— "

"Hurt my feelings?" I snap.

With an earnest nod, he says, "You're always beautiful. It doesn't matter what you're wearing. Even in that ratty old robe, you're amazing."

I lift my hand. "Then why say anything at all?"

He shakes his head. "I get scared, too, you know. Everything is changing—changing faster than I can keep up. I want us to be ready if things change again. That's all."

I put my hands on my ample hips. "I can't be someone else. I'm just me. I'm not one to want to wear sensible shoes like Kirstin or your mom."

A small smile plays at his lips. "I'm not asking you to be like Kirstin. And I don't want you to be like my mom. Let's just forget I brought it up." He slides over to me.

I purse my lips and narrow my eyes, then pointedly look away.

He caresses my arm. "Okay?"

"I can't be someone other than who I am."

"I'm not asking you to be anyone else. Honestly. I was just thinking different shoes would be easier for you. It's no different than you buying the flat shoes to wear when you're more pregnant."

"More pregnant?"

"You know." He puts his hands in a sweeping motion in front of his stomach, emulating a large round belly. "When you get big."

"You should probably just stop talking. You're not helping yourself."

He lets out a breath. "I'll start making breakfast."

"Thanks, Grant. But I said I'd do that this morning."

"I know." He gives my arm another rub before returning to the kitchen.

Chapter 7

The hospital fill station is now closed, so Grant has started going to the park for water. Someone decided the apartment building damaged in the fire was not safe to live in. The mayor and his crew were able to find housing for everyone by moving them to empty apartments in other buildings and even a couple of empty houses.

One couple moved into our building. I overheard my building manager arguing with someone about it. The manager was upset because he is expected to let them live here without a deposit and without collecting any rent. I'm not sure how he expects to collect rent, since the banks have been closed since the cyberattacks started. Credit cards and ATM machines stopped working, we can't go inside the bank to get cash, and checks—for those few who still use that archaic method of payment—aren't worth the paper they're written on. I don't even know how we're going to pay rent when it's due at the first of the month. Will we be kicked out of our apartment?

Some people still have cash, but these last few days store owners don't seem as interested in accepting cash. Grant's taken to trading items we think we can do without for items he thinks we need.

His Thursday water run seems to be taking much longer than it should. I never thought of myself as a worrier, but now it seems worrying is all I do. I'm so concerned that at one point I go outside and look around.

There are several people using rakes in the still smoking rubble of the hospital. The western view from my apartment complex has changed dramatically after the destruction of the hospital. Now, instead of a multistory building, there's a panorama of the mountains.

Prospect sits on the edge of a mountain range, close to what Grant calls the foothills—a section of small hills graduating upward in height leading to the mountains—and several huge rock outcroppings. The oldest section of Prospect where we live is flat. To the south is a flattop hill terraced with houses, with more houses on the butte; that section of town was developed in the mid-1950s. The newest section of town is to the east, just beyond the river. There are no mountains on that side of town. Instead, it opens to a large expanse of arid desert.

A decent-sized year-round creek is on the north side of town. It's flat for several miles beyond the creek before there are a few rolling hills leading up to Prospector Peak, rising high above the valley. The creek joins up with the river, making that part of Prospect almost seem like an island.

Grant's parents' ranch is west of Prospect, partway up the mountainside, nestled alongside the creek. They're at the edge of the wilderness area, with part of their acreage forested and part arid. It's so odd to me that there can be so many different environments in proximity. I prefer town or the mountains. The rest is too much like the desert, with sand and even small cactus. Grant took me hiking up to Prospector Peak a few times. While it's beautiful from the top, the hike up was anything but fun as we dodged boulders, cactus, sagebrush, and had to watch out for rattlesnakes.

I'm just about ready to go back inside when I see Grant weighed down by the large water jugs, slowly walking toward me. I lift a hand in greeting. He smiles and lifts his chin.

"You want me to take one of the containers?" I ask.

"No need."

I hold the door to the building and then open our apartment.

"Whew. That'll build up some muscles." Grant purifies the water, and after several minutes, he says there's a rumor going around that the sewer system on the other end of Prospect is failing.

"Failing? Like people can't flush their toilets? Don't they just add water like we do?"

"Adding water isn't the issue. The sewer is backing up and coming up into the bathtubs and showers."

"Ewww. That's disgusting. Can they use a plunger to fix it?"

"No, it's the entire system. The mayor is telling them to close off the bathroom and dig a latrine in the backyard."

"Like an outhouse?"

Grant nods his response and then returns his attention to the water.

"The SuperMart? Is its sewer failing too?"

"I suppose so, since it's on the far east end of town."

"What about our toilet? Is it still okay?"

"For now. We're on the original part of the system. This area is fully gravity fed, leading toward the treatment area south of town. The east side of town needs pumps to connect it to the treatment area since they're a lower elevation."

"But will ours stop working?"

He shrugs. "No one knows for sure. But it's possible. I guess we'll know if it starts to stink."

"Great. That's just great."

"Hey, hey." Grant moves toward me. "We'll work it out. Let's not worry about something that isn't happening yet."

"You sound like your mom."

He gives me a half smile. "Well, it's good advice. Served me well for several years. When you only think about the moment, it helps keep things in perspective."

"Okay. But it's not easy. None of this is easy."

"C'mere." He opens his arms and holds me for many minutes until I start to squirm. "Our normal life is suddenly upside down. The unknown can be scary. But one thing I know for sure is we're together. We have each other."

"But our baby? What if things are— "

"What if things are fine? We don't know."

I bite my lip and melt into his embrace.

Chapter 8

Friday and Saturday pass without any new disasters—in Prospect, anyway. We heard there was some trouble in the nearby town of Wesley. An apartment complex was attacked, and several people were killed. There was also a sheriff deputy killed in an unrelated incident. I've visited Wesley a few times; it's an unbelievably cute little town, and the people are really friendly. It's hard to imagine such bad things happening there.

Our toilet seems to be working fine, of which I'm exceedingly grateful. When the wind blows exactly right, we can smell the sewer system from the other end of town. I can't even imagine what it would be like to live with that. The smoke smell is bad enough. Thankfully, that's beginning to subside.

We still don't know exactly how many lives were lost in the fire. It was so crazy that trying to account for all the patients—many who were here from surrounding towns—was impossible. Especially without computers to track who was there, and with all the paperwork lost to the fire. We do know many of the hospital's nurses and doctors didn't make it out. They were trying to save their patients and lost their own lives. The smokey pile of rubble is now a makeshift memorial.

Grant hasn't mentioned my choice of clothing or shoes again. Even so, I've replayed the argument over and over in my head. The same way worrying is new for me, fretting over the past is also new. Could he be right? My stiletto heels and pencil skirts are not made for hiking. They're not made for much except looking and feeling magnificent. Is my pride over my appearance putting me in danger? Putting both of us in danger?

Grant put his plan for having stashes—or as he calls them, caches—into action. He made me go hiking with him on Friday (yes, I did wear actual hiking clothes), so I could see where the first cache was, the one that has my ugly clothes and a small backpack with food. He hid a tan plastic tote in a section of rocks near an old falling down cabin, then added additional rocks until it was fully concealed. I never even noticed it until he pointed it out. He also pointed out various landmarks so I could find it again. He thinks the plastic tote should be fairly varmint proof, plus the food is in a metal case as a second layer of protection.

His grandpa Paul gave him the key to the service station so Grant could use anything he thought he might need from there. While Paul took the snacks and other items sold near the check stand, there were still several containers and boxes Grant put to use.

We've also been visiting the pawn shop, thrift stores, hardware store, and antiques stores for usable items to help not only with creating our caches but also to use in our apartment. All places have been well picked over, but Grant has a way of looking at things that seem like total junk and finding a use for them.

Getting to the hiding spot was a challenge. The terrain was rugged and uphill. The fallen down cabin was just off the creek in an area Grant refers to as the foothills, where the mountain range is beginning. His family's ranch is about halfway up the mountainside. Another reason that it'll take us some time to get there, even though it's not many miles to the ranch, is because going uphill is not my strong suit.

"Remember," Grant said as we were hiking, "you can follow the creek up the mountain to reach the ranch."

"Sure. But it's not like I'm going to go there without you. You'll be able to show me all of your secret ways."

"The creek is a direct way, not that much farther than going overland."

I stopped walking.

He took several steps before he realized I wasn't next to him. "Why'd you stop?" he asked with his hand on his sidearm, looking around.

"Why are you telling me how to get to the ranch?"

"Because it's important for you to know."

"Why?"

He walked back toward me and placed his hands on either side of my face. "It's important for you to know how to get there in case we get separated."

"We're not going to get separated."

"I know." He gave me a quick kiss. As he pulled away, I grabbed onto him.

"Promise me."

"Shelby."

"Say, 'I promise we won't get separated.' Say it, Grant."

He let out a sigh. "I can't promise that. There might be a reason you need to leave before I do. I might need to—I don't know, but something might require us to separate. You need to know how to get there. The creek is an easy landmark. The way we hiked here is a little confusing, so I'm going to show you another option on the way back."

I begrudgingly followed behind him. I knew he was right. I should know how to get there in case we're separated. But I didn't like it. The other route was a slightly muddy drainage ditch that we walked along the top of.

"This isn't deep right now, but if it rains, it'll have more water in it. I like it because if you're in the ditch, it's deep enough that you're hidden. It might be a little slick, so watch your footing."

"Where does this come out?"

"You know that culvert under the highway near the fairgrounds?"

"No."

"Oh. Well, there. You can go under the culvert and then about fifty feet later there's a decent spot to get out, right by the elementary school. You can't miss it. From there, you'll be able to see the hospital."

"You mean the rubble."

"Right. You'll want to try and stay in the trees and behind the buildings while you're getting to the ditch. There's about fifty feet where it'll be wide open when you cross in front of the school. That's the most dangerous section for being spotted."

More and more, I'm wishing we would've already gone to Grant's family ranch.

We've been spending time with Kirstin and her boys. Last Wednesday, when her phone started ringing, we were all surprised. She didn't recognize the number, and no one was on the line when she answered, but that was the first indication things might be returning to normal. Kirstin tried to return the call, but it never connected.

After that, others reported their phones were working. None reliably, but we're all very hopeful. She's tried her husband many, many times but has yet to reach him or any of his or her family.

Pamela and I have been able to talk on the phone several times. While we both think this is an indication things will be fine, the electricity is still out and the grocery stores are still under city control. Plus, as far as we know, trucks aren't on the road to bring new food and supplies. She thinks we should continue our efforts in case things don't return to normal as quickly as we think they will.

Grant agrees with Pamela, saying we're better safe than sorry. Over the past few days, he's even started carrying a sidearm. Not always, but at times when he thinks he might encounter danger. I'm no stranger to guns. They were plenty abundant where I lived growing up; my dad had a couple of rifles and so did Gramps. And it's completely common to see people wearing a pistol here. But not Grant. He's never carried a gun. When I asked him where he got it, he said Grandpa Paul had it locked up at the service station. It was one of the things his grandpa wanted him to be sure to grab. A shotgun was also kept in a locked closet off the employee bathroom. It's now in our bedroom closet.

Even though I grew up around guns, I've never shot one, and I have zero desire to do so. While I love video games, real guns hold no appeal. Before the attacks, I often played *Call of Duty* with an old friend from home. Online gaming is as close to shooting a gun as I intend to get.

Today we're taking the afternoon off. Kirstin and her boys will go to church, then the five of us are having a picnic. She invited us to join them for church. Ha. Like that's going to happen. I tried to be gracious in my refusal, telling her I had several things to do before we took off. She smiled and said, "Maybe next time."

The knock at the door interrupts my lunch preparations. I'm making tuna salad for our picnic. We don't have any bread, but we still have tortillas and crackers to perch the tuna on.

"Hey there," I say, opening the door.

"Wow, that's an amazing dress," Kirstin replies. "Did you change your mind about church? You look ready."

I give a little twirl to show off the full skirt. "No, it just feels like a special occasion. Like we're celebrating the return to normalcy."

"And not a moment too soon. Before the phones came back, I was really starting to worry. Another week of this and I'd be struggling to feed Mason. But now . . . " Kirstin lets out a sigh. "Now it feels like we'll be okay."

"It does, doesn't it? The phones coming back on is huge. I'm sure the electricity will be next. And we'll soon see trucks delivering again.

I can't believe I'm saying this, but I'm looking forward to getting back to work. Grant, though, the way he's acting . . . " I shake my head. I'm not sure why Grant doesn't realize things will be fine soon.

"I just wish I could reach Ethan. I'm sure he's on his way home, but it'd be nice to know exactly where he is."

"Did you want to come in?" I open the door a little wider. Now that we have all the food relocated, having her in our apartment isn't the concern it was on the day of the fire.

"Can't. I left the door open to my place so I can hear the boys. I just wanted to tell you we're getting ready to leave. Did you still want to meet here afterward?"

"Sure. Grant is off filling our water right now."

"I know. He took care of mine also. I meant to ask him about our plans then, but with Mason and Caleb, it slipped my mind. I made a salad."

"A salad? Like a lettuce salad?"

"Don't I wish! No, it's out of canned black beans, green beans, and corn. They're marinated in a vinaigrette. I tasted it, and it might be the best thing I've ever made."

"Oh! Kind of like Texas Caviar?"

She gives me an odd look. "I don't think so. It's— "

A loud *beep, beep, beep* sounds from Kirstin's phone. My phone, sitting on the kitchen counter, sounds in unison.

"Oh! That scared me." Kirstin reaches for her phone. "It never rings like that."

"Was that the emergency system?" I ask, rushing toward my own phone.

"No. Please, God, no," Kirstin cries, running from my apartment door. I grab at my phone.

BALLISTIC MISSILE THREAT INBOUND TO UNITED
STATES. MULTIPLE INBOUND MISSILES DETECTED.
SEEK IMMEDIATE SHELTER.
THIS IS NOT A DRILL.

Chapter 9

As soon as the alert on my phone goes off, the public warning siren sounds. Kirstin immediately reappears at my door with Caleb on her hip, Mason at her side, and a frantic look upon her face. There's a lot of commotion with the several other neighbors in the hallway. "We're going to the laundry room. It's probably the safest place in the building," Kirstin yells over the siren, hefting her large diaper bag higher.

"That's probably good. I need to find Grant."

"Come with us. Leave him a note or try to call him on the way."

I scrunch my eyes closed and let out my breath. There's a pressure on my chest. "Just give me a minute."

"Shelby, we have to hurry."

"Please."

The siren stops and a computerized voice sounds through the public address system, *"Shelter in place. Shelter in place. Shelter in place."* Then the siren resumes its blare.

Shaking her head, Kirstin ushers Mason inside and closes the door. I've barely finished writing the note when the door bursts open.

"You're ready?" Grant asks, rushing to the bedroom.

"We're going to the laundry room," Kirstin replies.

"There's a basement under City Hall," he yells from the bedroom. "We should go there." Grant rushes back into the living room. "Kirstin, where's your backpacks?"

"Oh! I forgot. I'll get them." She thrusts Caleb toward Grant.

He takes him, saying, "Shelby? Can you?"

I take the baby while Grant grabs our duffle bags. "We should go to the ranch," I say.

"No time."

Kirstin returns with the backpacks Grant put together with her over the last couple of days. She's already wearing her pack and helps Mason put on his child-size one. The tiny blue backpack covered in trains, planes, and trucks seems much too cheery for a missile alert. Kirstin slings her diaper bag across her body; Grant also looked through this

41

bag, adding a few things and removing others. His time living out of his car really did help him discover what's essential and what isn't.

"Mommy!" Mason cries, lifting his arms to be picked up.

"Are you okay with Caleb?" Kirstin asks, stooping over to retrieve Mason.

I lift a hand in acknowledgment.

"Shelby," Grant says gently, "we're going to be moving quick."

I nod my agreement, fully understanding he was right the other day. Today I'm wearing ballerina flats because they look so perfect with my dress. They'll also be better for "moving quick" than my usual high heels. The siren stops and the computer voice returns.

"I'm ready. I can carry him," I say, as the wail of the siren resumes.

We're down the steps and out the building, moving quickly as Grant promised. When we reach City Hall, there's a dozen people at the door.

"What's going on?" Grant asks.

"They won't let us in," a lady screeches, as several bang on the door.

"They have to let us in," someone else cries, looking toward the sky. "They're bombing us!"

"Shelby," Kirstin says quietly, "pray with me."

"Pray with you?! Now?"

She reaches her hand out to me, covering my arm and making sure to also touch Caleb. "Wrap us in Your loving arms, Father. You alone are our portion and our cup. You are our refuge and our strength. Fill us with Your presence and give us peace and understanding. Show us the way and lead us to safety. In Jesus' name we pray, amen."

"Amen," Grant echoes.

I narrow my eyes. *What is he doing?*

The door to City Hall opens, and a lady I recognize as a SuperMart shopper says, "Hurry, hurry."

More have joined in the few minutes since we arrived; there's jostling for position as everyone tries to crowd through the door at once.

"Calm down, everyone," someone yells above the din. "Let's just get inside."

"How much room is there?" Grant asks the lady who opened the door.

"It's a full basement. Space isn't the problem, but we only have things set up for a hundred or so people."

"One hundred? There's almost ten thousand people in Prospect."

With a pinched look, she gives a shrug. "We've done what we could."

Running toward us, a man calls out, "How many do you have? Everyone, go to the staircase and make your way down. Someone will check you in at the bottom."

"This way," another man yells over the ever-present siren, motioning us with his arm to hurry. He flicks on a flashlight and aims the beam toward the stairwell. I pull out my cell phone to use as a light. There's more jostling and pushing as we make our way down the stairs. Kirstin and Mason are first, baby Caleb and I are in the middle of our little group, and Grant is right behind us. About halfway down the steps, Caleb lets out a bloodcurdling scream.

"Great! Just what we need," someone says. "Holed up with a screaming brat."

A wave of protectiveness rushes over me. "He's just scared," I say over Caleb's cries. "We're all scared."

"Yeah, well, shut him up. And someone shut the stupid siren up too!"

Before I can say anything else, Grant puts a hand on my shoulder and whispers, "Ignore it."

At the bottom of the stairs, people are being checked in: name, address, if they brought food and water, and if they're carrying a weapon. Those that do have weapons are asked to remove them; the weapons are being held until this is over. I turn my head to look at Grant. He gives a barely perceptible shake and puts a finger over his lips. The siren finally silences as we reach the bottom of the steps.

Once checked in, another guy directs us toward a room at the end of the hall. There's several battery-operated lanterns set up on various surfaces, and he hands out flashlights so each family has one. By the time they close the door to the room, there's over two dozen wide-eyed people sharing a decent-sized conference room. A long, rectangular table is pushed against one wall, and a dozen wheeled office chairs are lined up along the edge. I watch as an elderly man walks a similarly aged woman to one of the chairs. He helps her sit, then bends over and gently kisses her forehead. Others start filling the chairs. Many are crying, but some have completely empty looks.

With a click of the lock, the guy who showed us into the room turns and looks us over. He's older, late fifties or early sixties, and short. Taller than Grant, but not as tall as I am. But he's not scrawny like Grant, he's beefy like a wrestler. Even his face reminds me of the wrestlers from high school. He's ruddy and puffy, his nose seems too large for his face, and one ear is misshapen. In a moderately deep, slightly monotone voice, he says, "I'm Harry English. I guess we'll be getting to know each other well over the next several days. So let me lay down some brief instructions. We have food and water. There's a toilet off the room."

"What's happening? Are we being bombed?" a large sweaty guy asks.

Harry shakes his head. "We don't know anything more than the alert said. We have someone on the radio, trying to find out."

"How long will we be locked in this room?" a pale, shaking woman from my apartment building asks.

"Don't know that either. Except, you are free to leave. If you do leave, we can't let you back in until after the crisis has passed. Well, after *today's* crisis has passed." Harry shakes his head. "Let's get settled in. While this isn't going to be The Ritz, we'll make it as comfortable as possible. Those of you with children, there are some toys and a couple of playpens in the storage room. How about a few of you help me, and we'll start setting things up."

Within a few minutes, Harry, Grant, the sweaty guy, and the one who told me to shut Caleb up have pulled out the playpens, several camping chairs, and a large pile of blankets. In addition to Caleb and Mason, there's a little girl of about six, a boy around twelve, another girl about Mason's age, and a tiny baby who can't be more than a few weeks old. Those of us not helping with the setup stare at each other. There's tears and hand wringing combined with grim silence.

"Do you know what time it is?" the lady from my apartment building asks.

I pull my phone out and hit the button to light up the screen. Nothing happens. That's weird. It was working fine as a flashlight only a short time ago. I know it had plenty of charge.

"No, sorry. My phone must have died."

"Mine did too," the lady says.

"My phone's not working either," Kirstin says.

What had been grim silence is now complete chaos as each person in the room determines their phone no longer works.

"I don't understand," Kirstin says. "I know I had a full charge. I made sure of it."

"Okay, folks," Harry says, holding up his hands. "I'd like to say I'm surprised by this, but we feared it was a possibility. Now, I don't want you to freak out— " As soon as the words are out of his mouth, that's exactly what happens. Everyone freaks out.

"What's happening?"

"Did you do this? Are you blocking our phones?"

"Are we prisoners here?"

Lifting his hands again, Harry calmly says, "Let's keep it down so I can answer a few questions."

The muttering continues for several seconds until Harry gains control. After a deep breath, he says, "We're not blocking your phones. And, no, you are not prisoners. It's possible—*possible*—we've just experienced an electromagnetic pulse."

"Nope, not true," the big sweaty guy says. "The flashlights are still working. An electromagnetic pulse would've wiped those out."

"Maybe. Maybe not," Harry replies. "There's theories going either way. At this moment, the phones seem to be off and won't turn on, but the flashlights are still working."

"I'm glad they are!" the lady from my apartment yells. "I'd hate being here in the dark."

"What exactly is an electromagnetic pulse?" the elderly lady sitting in the office chair asks.

"You know, what North Korea planned to do to us," Sweaty Guy says. "In fact, it's probably him—that little weasel! He's using this opportunity, when we're at our weakest, to wipe us out. That's his plan, you know, to kill us all and then take our land."

With that statement, the pandemonium returns. Harry shakes his head and lets it go for several minutes. When it finally seems to start decreasing, he continues, "So we knew this was possible. And I could be wrong—I'm only assuming it's an electromagnetic pulse."

"An EMP," Sweaty Guy says. "They call them EMPs."

"Right," Harry says. "They do. Again, it's an assumption, that's what we're dealing with."

"But what is it?" the lady from my apartment asks in a screech.

Grant reaches for my hand. I glance in his direction. His jaw is clenched tight and he looks pale. I lean close. "What?" I whisper. He shakes his head.

"I don't know for sure, Lucy." Harry walks over to my neighbor and lays a hand on her shoulder before calmly continuing, "I'd really like to wait until we have more information. The mayor will be here shortly. He'll have the latest news. Okay?"

She nods and, in a shaky voice, says, "I suppose."

"Is that really the best you can do?" Sweaty Guy asks.

"Sorry." Harry shrugs. "It doesn't change much for us in the here and now. Let's just settle in and make the best of it. There are a few other rooms set up in a similar manner. Like I said, the mayor should come around in a few minutes. He'll update us. Then, three times a day, someone will come around and check on how each room is doing."

"How long do we have to stay in here?" someone asks.

"Again, you don't have to stay in here. If you'd like to leave, there's a protocol for that. We'll help you get out, while making sure everyone else is safe, but you won't be able to return."

"I heard someone say only a hundred people are down here. What about everyone else?" a lady I don't recognize asks.

"We have provisions for a hundred and fifty for those nearest City Hall, like the apartment buildings. For everyone else, you heard the intercom, shelter in place."

"But if we're being bombed—isn't that what's happening? A missile is a bomb? Then shouldn't people be underground? Isn't that safer?"

"We don't really know what's happening," Harry says patiently.

"Humph. I would think someone who works for the city might have a clue as to what is going on."

Chapter 10

There are plenty of tears and even raised voices while we wait for the mayor to show up. I try to focus on staying calm, controlling my breathing.

Grant leans over and says, "Your neck is red."

"I–it was itchy."

"Are you having an attack?"

"N–no. I'm trying to keep it under control." I physically lower my shoulders, which seem to be around my ears. The pressure in my chest eases slightly, and I let out a hacking cough, which garners me several looks.

The lady who thought the city should have a clue says, "You'd better not get me sick!"

"She has asthma," Kirstin snaps.

The lady shakes her head. "So you say."

I stare her down as I pull out my inhaler, give it a shake, then insert the mouthpiece. Taking a deep breath, I press down on the medicine canister and continue to inhale, not breaking eye contact. Removing the inhaler from my mouth, I hold my breath, letting the medicine do its work. I gently exhale and try to smile at the lady.

She huffs and shakes her head. I get it. She's scared. We're all scared.

I take a breath and evaluate whether I need a second dose or not. Deciding I'm okay, I put the cover back on the canister.

There's a knock at the door, and Harry hustles to it, cracking it open. He opens it fully and steps aside as the mayor walks in. As always, he's well put together. His usual suit is replaced with slacks and a polo shirt. His loafers have a high shine on them, and his hair is perfectly coiffed. As he glances around the room, he tries to meet each person's eye and deliver a confident smile.

He starts with a simple greeting but is interrupted with, "Are we being bombed?"

"We have no evidence of that."

"But what about the alert?" Sweaty Guy asks.

"We have not been able to reach anyone by radio to verify the alert."

"What's that mean?" the guy who yelled at Caleb asks, his booming voice from before replaced with an edge of fear.

"Only that we don't know anything more than the alerts went off. Our town alert system also went off. We assume these were legitimate warnings, but without being able to reach anyone by radio . . . " He shrugs. "Folks, we're guessing here. We do think there was some sort of an anomaly that attacked our cell phones. And— " He lets out a big breath. "We know most cars stopped working about the same time."

"I knew it. I knew it," Sweaty Guy says.

Grant squeezes my hand. When I look in his direction, his eyes are glued to the mayor.

"With the phones and cars not functioning," the mayor continues, "we believe this could mean there was some sort of an event that short-circuited things. This may be only temporary. We just don't know."

"It's not temporary," Sweaty Guy snaps. "We're done. Newt Gingrich said 90 percent of us would die if an EMP was detonated. It's a nuclear bomb let off in the atmosphere, you know. Can't survive stuff like that."

"What?"

"Not true!"

"You lie!" Several other exclamations of disbelief, along with many expletives, fly around the room.

Sweaty Guy yells, "Hey, I'm not making this stuff up. It's science . . . or something. Don't you watch the news? Everyone knows about it."

"Well, I don't know about it," Lucy from my apartment building says through her tears. "I don't know about any of this. What will you do, Mayor Stringer?"

Lacking his confident smile, the mayor says, "We'll do the best we can. Now, are there any other questions right now?"

"When will we get radiation?" a homely woman asks, so quietly I strain to hear her.

"What did she say?" an older man asks.

"Annette asked when we'll get radiation," Harry says.

The older man nods. "Good question. I was wondering that myself."

"If it is an EMP, we won't. Even though, as Philip said, it is a nuclear bomb detonated in the atmosphere, it's very high, up to one hundred miles above the surface. And without a surface detonation, there won't be radioactive fallout. Now— " he takes a deep breath and continues " —that's not to say there won't be other detonations. But if this is all, then we're good as far as radiation goes."

"But Newt said it will kill us!" Sweaty Guy, otherwise known as Philip, says.

The pandemonium returns. Grant's still holding my hand. I look to Kirstin; she has Mason asleep across her lap and Caleb in her arms. She kisses the top of his head. She must feel my eyes on her because she looks at me and attempts a small, wobbly smile.

"Wait a minute, folks," Mayor Stringer says. "I know this is a lot to take in. I should have been better prepared before I came in here. You're the first room of townspeople I've visited. I should have realized you'd have these questions. Let me start again."

"Hey, you all hush up now," Philip yells. "Let's hear what our mayor has to say."

As the room silences, Mayor Stringer gives Philip a single nod. "Let me start at the beginning. You all received the alerts over your cell phone and then the public alert system sounded, right?"

There's nods and agreements.

"Okay, then. At that point, we knew nothing more than you did. We immediately got on our radio and tried to reach other towns to see what they knew. Sherman Issacson reached his counterpart in Cody. They knew nothing more than we did. He tried several other towns but couldn't connect. Then, about half an hour after the alert, the radio went dead. It happened at the same time our cell phones stopped working. Sherm suspected an EMP and went outside to try and start his car."

"Wasn't he scared?" Lucy asked. "To go outside, I mean."

"I suspect he was. But when his car didn't start, he came back in for keys to mine and two others. When none would turn over, we discussed it and concluded we'd likely been struck by an EMP. Now there is a chance it's a solar flare, but with the alert for the incoming missile," he says with a shrug, "we assume an electromagnetic pulse.

"As I already said, the EMP is caused by a nuclear detonation in the atmosphere. We won't have radioactive fallout from it, but we're still recommending sheltering in place until we can determine there will be no additional attacks. It's not like Prospect is a likely target for attack, but better safe than sorry. Now, what questions do you have?"

"Will 90 percent of us die?" Lucy asks, looking around. Ninety percent of the less than thirty people in the room . . . only three of us will live? I suck in a breath. No, that can't be right.

The mayor gives her a patient smile. "I'm going to make sure that doesn't happen."

Once Mayor Stringer answers all the immediate questions, he leaves, telling us he'll return in a few hours after he's checked on everyone else. In the meantime, we should try and make the best of things. He also says not to be surprised if we hear the city alert system sound. Now, it seems the EMP may have affected it, but Sherman is working on it in hopes of fixing it. If they can get it going, he'll make announcements several times each day so the entire town can know what's happening.

Grant wraps his arm around me, pulling me close.

"What do you think?" I whisper. "Is he right? Will most of us die?"

"I think that was a generalization. You heard the mayor. He said the EMP reports said some areas could see a large population reduction but not everywhere. I think we'd have a lot fewer deaths in Prospect than somewhere like Chicago."

"Chicago was already bad," Kirstin says. "You saw the news reports before the power went off? There was rioting and craziness. I can't imagine it stopped after the cyberattacks."

"True," Grant says. "Things have been good here, for the most part."

"Yeah, well, they're not going to stay good," Philip interjects himself into our conversation. "You just wait until people realize the power is out for good. Things are going to fall apart when that happens."

Philip's statement brings on a new wave of loud conversation. While it's civil, for the most part, there's no denying the underlying anger—and fear.

Harry gives the conversation a few minutes to run its course before he brings things back together.

"Friends, we're all scared. None of us really know what's happening. Like the mayor said, we'll know more as time goes on. Let's look at the bright side for now. We do not believe there have been any ground detonations that will result in us receiving fallout. This is good news. Anything else that may happen, we'll deal with it.

Shoot, the power has already been off for several days. We're already learning how to live without electricity."

"Yeah? Well, how many people have already died?" Philip asks. "The hospital burnt to the ground because we didn't have the water pressure to put the fire out. How many are dead in the nursing homes that needed electricity to keep their machines going?"

"True." Harry gives a sad nod. "And I'm not saying things will be easy. I'm saying let's just get through these next couple days. Right now, we're sheltering here for our protection. Let's try and make the best of it."

The grumbling continues for several minutes but finally subsides as people settle in. Even though a few things were set up for our sheltering, the accommodations are rather sparse. While there are chairs, blankets, and the playpens, there are only a few sleeping mats, so many of us will sleep leaning against the wall.

The size of the room is not large enough for the number of people. And with the lack of showers over the last week since the running water stopped working, it stinks. I can only imagine how terrible it'll be after a few days pass. Part of me wonders if we really need to be down here. From the sounds of it, the EMP isn't dangerous, so we could easily stay in our apartment. Well, not immediately dangerous. I've heard plenty more from Philip about how the 90 percent death estimates are within a year. That doesn't make me feel much better, but at least people won't be dying while we're in this tiny room.

Chapter 11

My neck is stiff and my back hurts something awful. While I was one of the lucky few able to use a sleeping pad to stretch out last night, I'm still a wreck. Thankfully, we brought our duffle bags, which did make things a little better. I have extra clothes and a sweater to roll up as a pillow. There are only a few other people who brought bags with them. I caught a few snarky comments from others about how we should be required to share whatever we brought into the room. Harry, who's one of the few people with his own supplies, nipped that in the bud immediately.

Last night's dinner, provided from the shelter supplies, was crackers and assorted canned meats or peanut butter. I went with the peanut butter. Meat spread in a can holds little appeal. This morning we're having breakfast bars. I'm already looking forward to lunch. Harry says it'll be MREs the city had on hand for emergencies.

Seems a few years ago there was a city council meeting in which the new Homeland Security representative suggested the city emergency supplies were woefully inadequate. Plans were put in and purchases were made then. But when the Homeland Security guy moved on to a new location, his replacement didn't put the same emphasis on preparedness, so things fell by the wayside.

Harry says it's only in the last few days, since the attacks started, that they put these rooms together. And much of what's in here is merchandise they commandeered from the SuperMart and other places. Games and books were thoughtfully added to the supplies, which helps, but the day still passes beyond slowly.

Thankfully, they've also stashed plenty of bottled water in the basement. Grant mentioned he wasn't sure if the generators they've been using to pump water from the creek and river will still work. He's afraid the EMP may have affected them. I'm trying not to think about how much worse things would be if we don't have the ability to get water easily. Will we need to haul water from the creek?

When Harry suggests a Bible study, most of the group responds favorably. I even catch Grant nod his head. Which reminds me how he added an "amen" at the end of Kirstin's prayer yesterday.

"You're not going to join in on that stuff, are you?"

Grant lifts one shoulder. "It's not like I'm going to step out of the room while they do it."

"So . . . what? You're okay with it? Don't you think it's wrong of them to force their beliefs on us?"

"Not any more wrong than preventing them from pursuing their beliefs because we may not like it."

"Humph. Well, I think it's wrong. I don't believe I should be subjected to their fantasies just because I'm locked up with them."

"What are you going to do, Shelby? Hang out in the bathroom while they have their study?"

"I just might," I say with a huff. I make a point of turning away from the group. At least I have a book I can focus on. I wish my phone was still working so I could listen to music. When will I hear music again?

While Grant doesn't actively participate, he doesn't seem to mind their preaching and carrying on. The longer the service goes on, the more uncomfortable I feel. My book isn't holding my interest like it should, and I keep sneaking glances. Everyone else seems to be having a grand time. The guy who yelled at me in the stairwell to shut Caleb up, who introduced himself yesterday as Ellis, seems to have the most to say and even goes into a long story about how he knows God lives in him because of all the good he does. *Ha. Typical.*

"Thanks for sharing, Ellis," Harry says. "What was it that Paul said? 'Nothing good lives in me.' Let's see." He flips through his Bible. "That's from Romans, right?"

"I'm not familiar with that one," Ellis answers. "As I was saying— "

"Here it is," Harry cuts Ellis off. "Romans 7. I'll start at 14. 'We know that the law is spiritual; but I am unspiritual, sold as a slave to sin.'"

I go back to my book while he continues his little speech, but I glance at him when he says, "Boy, can I relate to that." He looks around the room, meeting people's gazes with a small smile.

"I'm going to skip down to 18. 'For I know that good itself does not dwell in me, that is, in my sinful nature. For I have the desire to do what is good, but I cannot carry it out. For I do not do the good I want to do, but the evil I do not want to do—this I keep on doing. Now if I do what I do not want to do, it is no longer I who do it, but it is sin living in me that does it. So I find this law at work: Although I want to do good, evil is right there with me.'"

Harry stops once again and looks around. Forgetting my book for the moment, I can't help but follow his eyes around the room. Several people, including Kirstin, are nodding. A few even have tears in their eyes. Harry gives a nod and then returns to his reading.

"'For in my inner being I delight in God's law; but I see another law at work in me, waging war against the law of my mind and making me a prisoner of the law of sin at work within me. What a wretched man I am! Who will rescue me from this body that is subject to death? Thanks be to God, who delivers me through Jesus Christ our Lord!'"

"Amen!" several voices cry out.

There's silence for several minutes, until a voice begins to sing, *"Create in me a clean heart, O God, and renew a right spirit within me."*

Soon other voices join in. I try to focus on my book but fail. While not the music I had in mind, it's still music. Their voices, many out of tune and plenty flat, share such fervor. Several have closed their eyes. A few raise their hands in the air. Annette, the lady who when she speaks is so quiet we can barely hear her, has a beautiful voice that rises above the small crowd. She has both hands raised in the air, as if trying to reach out for the mythical God himself. I've never seen anything like it.

After the song, Harry starts to pray and then others take their turn. While Grant doesn't say anything, he does close his eyes and finish with an amen. Grant's never been a follower. I'm not sure why he's participating in this . . . stuff . . . now. It makes zero sense.

Though the Bible study seems to lift people's spirits, there is still much discussion on what exactly is happening. There are tears and plenty of entertaining worst-case scenarios. Could Philip be right? Could 90 percent of Prospect die within the year? Ninety percent of Wyomingites? Ninety percent of Americans?

The mayor stops by after dinner with another gourmet selection of crackers, canned meats, and peanut butter. "So in this case, no news seems to be good news. We have not detected any radioactive fallout. At this point, we think we should remain sheltered through tomorrow. Then we can start talking about what happens next."

"Is the rest of the town still sheltering?" someone asks.

"Good question. For the most part, yes. We couldn't get the public address system working, but Sherman and I did drive through town this morning. We used the old bull horn and asked people to continue to shelter in place. We saw a few people out, but they agreed to return home. Again, this is only a precaution. There is no immediate danger."

"What will happen next?" Philip asks.

Mayor Stringer gives a confident smile. "We survive. It'll be a long time until Prospect is the town we knew before the attacks started. But I'm confident we'll all work together and make the best of it. Wyoming people are a special breed— "

"They say that no matter where a person lives," Ellis says. "We said the same thing in Georgia when I was living there. Kansas, Oklahoma, everyone thinks their hometown or state is special."

There's rumbling through the crowd. He's right. We said the same thing in Kentucky. Several others agree with him, mainly those like me who are here from somewhere else—transplants. But there's also many who say the mayor is right. Wyomingites are a breed apart.

I don't know who's right, I just know we're all in for a huge change. All those hopes Kirstin and I had when the phones started working again, those were shattered in the blink of an eye. The more I learn about the EMP, the worse it sounds. Of course, I think a lot of what Philip says borders on fear mongering, but Grant seems to know quite a bit and so does Harry. Even so, what I wouldn't give to do a Google search so I can find out exactly what is happening and what we can expect. Knowledge is powerful. And I put my trust in the tangible.

"That may be, but I know this town," Mayor Stringer replies. "I know these people. You've been here a few years now, right, Ellis?"

"Sure. Almost four."

"I remember that time we had coffee together at Patty's Cafe. You said you've lived a lot of places, but Prospect is special. You remember that?"

Ellis reluctantly bobs his head to one side. "Maybe."

"Well, I definitely remember it. Because you were right. Prospect is special, and what makes it special are the people. We've come together as a community many times in the past. This will be no different."

"But— " Ellis starts to interrupt.

"I know these people, Ellis. We'll continue to be a community. We'll not only survive this, we'll thrive. We'll recreate our lives."

The room fills with applause. There's plenty of *Attaboy*, and, *That's right!* and, *You said it, Mayor.*

I want to believe him too. I do. But somehow, it feels too much like a pep rally or a campaign speech. I raise my hand.

"Yes? Did you have a question?" the mayor asks me with a nod.

"Thank you, Mayor. You know, that sounds all well and good, but what is your actual plan? Where will we get supplies? Food? We don't even have a hospital."

His smile only slightly falters. "Thank you for your question. The truth is, it won't be easy. We'll all have to work together. We'll plant gardens and raise livestock. You're Paul Cameron's granddaughter, right?"

"By marriage."

"Right, right. People like Paul will be instrumental. We'll rely on the farmers and ranchers to teach the rest of us what they know. Have you heard of Victory Gardens?"

"They planted those during World War II," Lucy says.

"That's right. And we'll be planting them again. In fact, as soon as we know it's safe to leave, we'll start the gardens."

"And the hospital?" I ask.

"Do you know the big warehouse by the bank? The one they held the swap meet in last summer? We're setting that up to use as a hospital."

"But we lost so many doctors and nurses," someone says.

"We did." Mayor Stringer nods. "We lost many good friends, many valuable members of our community in the fire. I've been talking with Dr. Rick Brown, and he's putting his team together. I'm positive we'll have the hospital ready soon—well, before your baby arrives, anyway." He gives me the confident smile he's so good at.

"What about the food?" Ellis asks. "You got any seeds for planting a garden?"

"We do. As soon as things started to look" —he pauses and looks up to the ceiling— "*interesting*, we made sure to set aside seeds and tools for gardening. And Harry suggested salvaging produce and using the seeds."

"They might not all grow." Harry raises his hands in the air. "But it's something."

56

The mayor claps Harry on the shoulder. "I promise you, folks, we have a plan."

The mayor seems so sure of himself. I hope his confidence is genuine and not just a political show.

Chapter 12

The smell in here is unbearable. Almost thirty people crammed in a tiny conference room after more than a week without showering . . . ugh. I can't even begin to describe the stench. Ellis took his shoes off last night, and I swear my eyes started to water. And I wasn't the only one. The feedback from the room prompted Harry to pass an order requesting everyone who has shoes on must leave them on. Those of us barefoot, like me, were welcome to leave our shoes off.

I'm thankful I was wearing easy on, easy off ballerina slippers. I'm also thankful Grant made sure I had a pair of wool socks in my duffle bag. They, along with my yoga clothes, have made a huge difference in my comfort level. I've also focused on staying calm and hydrated, so my asthma hasn't been an issue.

Grant was so smart to set our duffle bags up for us, even though I argued with his choice of what to pack. I did tuck in a cute skirt and top, but it's much too chilly in the basement to wear. Plus, I've been sitting on the floor using my sleeping mat as a cushion—not exactly the best scenario for a dress. Even though I'm totally casual in my clothing, I still have a travel makeup kit and do my best to keep myself presentable. I'm much too unattractive to go bare faced in public, no matter what Grant says.

Few others brought anything with them into the basement. The couple with the newborn have his diaper bag. The family who has the toddler and young girl have bags like we do, with changes of clothes and few other things. Kirstin, Grant, and I also have food and water in our bags, but so far, we've been eating the same as everyone else.

Grant's handgun is also in his bag, tucked at the bottom in a holster. He makes sure the bag is always right next to one of us. We can't risk one of the children getting into it. Or one of the adults. Tempers are starting to get short. I now see why they were taking weapons away before we entered. Did anyone else sneak their gun in?

"So you don't think my car will work?" Kirstin asks Grant for the tenth time since we heard about the EMP.

His usual patient response now sounds strained. "I'll be surprised if it does. I'd be surprised if any of ours do."

Grant still drives the Nissan Pathfinder he lived in those years he spent on the road. I bought a used Jeep Compass a few months ago. The first couple of times Kirstin asked, he went into an explanation about the computer systems in cars and how the EMP would fry them. Now, he doesn't bother explaining. And I think we all know Kirstin isn't asking to be annoying, more it's disbelief and boredom. Boredom.

Shortly after lunch, Ellis slides over by us. "So, Grant, now that you're back in Prospect, are you going to be joining in the family business?"

Grant lifts his hands in an *I don't know* gesture. "I'm not sure there is a family business now. My grandpa's filling station shut down the day after the cyberattacks started."

"Right, right. I was referring to the outfitter's business. Did you know I worked for your dad and uncle PJ two seasons ago? They had me guide for them a couple of times. I loved it. But, of course, my wife hated it, so when they asked me about doing it last year, I had to pass."

"Yeah. That's one thing that's always been an issue. Not all wives are okay with their husbands being gone a week or two at a time."

"Where's your wife now?" I ask, not having noticed him with anyone while we've been locked in this room together.

"Well . . . " He scratches at the stubble on his chin. "There was more than just me doing the guiding that she didn't like. She took off in early March. I'm not exactly sure where she went."

"Sorry to hear that," Grant says.

"I was sorry, too, but now I've come to accept it's for the best. Hopefully, she's someplace safe right now and can ride this thing out. I tried to call her when the phones started working again, but I got a notice saying her number was disconnected. Kind of thought she might come back when the attacks started. Now, with the EMP, I guess it's too late. From the sounds of things, her brand-new car is nothing more than a giant paperweight."

"I'm afraid we're almost all in that same boat," Kirstin says.

"Yeah. By the way, I owe you folks an apology. I was rather rude to you when we were making our way down here. You were right to call me out on it. The baby was scared. I was scared. But they've been great while we've been locked up. Hardly a peep out of them."

59

"Thank you," Kirstin says. "They have been great, but like all of us, they're more than ready to get out of here and play outside. Especially Mason. Right, kiddo?" She ruffles his hair.

"Play outside?" Mason asks, starting to stand.

"Not right now, but soon. Maybe tomorrow."

Chapter 13

Early afternoon on Wednesday, three days after the alerts sounded, the mayor tells us they believe the immediate threat has passed and he is lifting the shelter in place order.

Not a moment too soon. Everyone is testy this morning. Even Caleb, who as Ellis said yesterday had been incredibly quiet, let loose several times this morning, screaming at the top of his tiny lungs. That earned him many angry looks and under-the-breath reprimands, including several from Ellis. It also earned us an open door and the ability to roam freely around the basement. The other rooms opened also, and we were able to visit.

Kirstin was extremely happy to find her friend Milena Maynard, owner of Prospector Peak Press, among those sheltering in the basement of City Hall.

"Milena, this is my friend Shelby and her husband Grant. I told you about them. They live next door to me."

"Nice to meet you, Shelby, Grant," Milena says, extending her hand.

I've worked hard to keep myself somewhat pulled together in the couple of days we've been sheltering in the basement. My makeup, while not to my usual standard, isn't terrible. And I changed back into my sundress and ballet flats when Harry said we'd be getting out today. Even so, I'm under no illusions I look good. There are dark circles under my eyes, and my dress is a wrinkly mess.

Milena, with beautiful red hair and a smattering of freckles, is wearing no makeup, has on jeans and a T-shirt along with tennis shoes, and looks amazing. She is fresh and vibrant. Even her voice has an excited lilt to it, like she truly is happy to meet us. I can't decide if I like her or hate her.

Five minutes ago, we made our way out of City Hall and back toward our apartment. I'm carrying Caleb while Grant is lugging our bags. We're several feet from the entrance to the building when Grant abruptly stops.

"What's going on?" I ask.

"The door's broken."

"What?" I ask, rushing forward.

Grant puts out his hands and grabs my arm. "Wait. Let me check it out. Probably whoever busted the door is long gone, but . . . wait here and I'll find out."

Several others from the building who were sheltering at City Hall are now gathered around.

"Someone broke into our building?" Lucy Fleming asks.

Grant is bent over the bag, retrieving his handgun, when another guy who wasn't sheltering in our room but that I recognize from the hallway, says, "Want me to join you?"

"If you'd like," Grant answers, sticking the holstered revolver on his belt.

"He had that with him all this time?" Kirstin asks in a whisper.

I tilt my head in response as Grant and the guy disappear inside. Within a few minutes, the guy with Grant comes running out. He barely makes it beyond the threshold of the door before he vomits.

The waiting group recoils, with many people commenting. A few throw their hands over their own mouth and quickly step away. I take several steps back from the mess in hopes of avoiding the smell. I feel a tightness in my chest as I try to take a breath. *Relax, Shelby.* Now is not a good time for an asthma attack.

"What's that all about?" Nasal Voice asks.

"Dead. They're dead," Grant's helper says.

Kirstin and I both gasp.

Grant appears at the door. While not in the same condition of his helper, he's noticeably pale.

People yell out *What's happening?* and *Who's dead?* and more.

Grant searches out my eyes and gives a grim shake of his head. "Can someone go after the police or sheriff?" Grant asks. "We don't know what happened. We found— " He visibly swallows. "There are at least two people dead."

Someone yells they'll go for help. The nasal voiced guy who helped fight the hospital fire with Grant, and was sheltering in a different room in the basement, asks, "Who is it?"

Grant shakes his head.

The other guy who went in with him says, "One of them was Jesus Trujillo."

There are several cries of disbelief. Kirstin leans toward me. "Did you know him?"

I bite my lip. "I think he is the one—*was* the one who always made a point of holding the door. Drives a red Toyota?"

"Oh! He's such a nice guy. What about his wife?"

I shake my head. The person next to us must have heard us because he yells out, "What about his wife? I think her name was Babbie."

"There was another man," Grant says. "I'm not sure who it was. We didn't go beyond the hallway, though."

"We should check," Lucy says. "People may be injured."

"Here comes Mayor Stringer," Kirstin says, pointing toward the mayor, Harry, Milena Maynard, and several others running toward us.

"You've found a body?" Mayor Stringer asks, gasping for air.

"Two!" Lucy cries. "Did you bring the sheriff?"

"We're looking for him. We're probably more likely to find one of the city police. I sent several people that were still at City Hall out to the officers' homes. Who found the bodies?"

Grant and the other guy both say it was them who went in. The other guy—who says his name is Todd Berringer, but everyone calls him Toad—goes into more detail on what they saw than his previous reactions seem like he should have. Milena Maynard is taking handwritten notes while he talks. Grant, standing next to me and holding tightly to my hand, adds little to Toad's spiel.

While Toad continues taking questions, I lean in to Grant and whisper, "What happened?"

"Nothing good," he whispers back. "It's . . . it's bad, Shelby."

I squeeze his hand. "Are you okay?"

"Not even remotely."

After many minutes, another guy walks up. I recognize him as being in the police department. He was with the mayor and chief the day they took over the SuperMart.

"Mayor? Have you gone in?"

Mayor Stringer has a surprised look. "N-no. Figured that was a job best suited for you or Chief Daniels."

"People could be injured," Lucy says. "Someone needs to check."

"Here comes the chief now," Nasal Voice says, pointing toward the street where an old Ford Mustang is heading toward us.

"I guess it's good some cars are still working," Kirstin says. "Wish mine was one of them."

63

"Yeah, makes me wish I had an old muscle car like that," Grant says. I think about his Grandpa Paul and the old truck and Jeep he has. Are they still running?

After Chief Daniels parks and is updated, he asks us all to move to the other edge of the greenspace while he and his office clear the building. Harry asks if they need any help, but they decline. They're gone for several minutes before Sheriff Spieth arrives. Mayor Stringer catches him up on the situation. After announcing himself at the door, he goes inside and joins the police.

After many minutes, Chief Daniels comes out and asks to speak with the mayor. Then, after only a minute or two, Mayor Stringer nods and the chief goes back inside.

The mayor lowers his shoulders and turns to face us.

"I'm sorry to say but they found several more. There are remains of several people in the building. This is currently a crime scene, so we'll need to find you alternative lodging for tonight."

As the crowd rumbles, the mayor raises his hands. "I know that after the last several days this isn't what any of you want to hear."

Grant gives my hand a squeeze, as the mayor continues, "Chief Daniels said they will allow small groups in to gather a few things. They need a few minutes before that happens."

"You're not going in," Grant whispers. "Tell me what you need, and I'll get it." He turns to Kirstin. "I'd be happy to go in for you, too, if you'd rather not."

"You don't think I should go in?" Kirstin asks.

Grant shakes his head. "I don't think you should. Let me do it for you. I'll get whatever you and the boys need."

"Where do you think we'll stay?" I ask.

"Tents? Back in the shelter?" Grant shrugs.

"Let's go to the ranch."

"I don't think we need to. It's just one night. We'll be fine here."

As the gathered crowd continues to discuss the situation, Grant asks Kirstin and me if we want to go sit down. Might as well try and be comfortable while we wait.

We move over near one of the trees. Once we're seated, Kirstin asks, "What do you think happened?"

Grant looks at his lap. I watch as he moves a hand over to a blade of grass and plucks it out. He runs a finger along the edge. "I think they were attacked."

"Attacked? Who would do that?" Kirstin shudders.

Grant shakes his head. "I don't know."

"When you go inside, can you get my car keys?"

He gives her a look before finally nodding.

"I have to try it," she says. "I have to know for sure that it doesn't work."

Grant looks over to the parking lot. Several people are trying their cars. Many have the hoods up. I don't hear any vehicles running.

"I know, Grant," Kirstin says, a small amount of heat in her voice. "But I have to know for sure. Aren't you going to try your cars, too?"

"I'm with Kirstin," I say. "I want to know for sure."

"Yes, of course. I'll grab our keys also."

After a little while, several people show up with tents and camping gear, and Mayor Stringer walks over to our group. "Would you folks rather camp or go back into the shelter?"

Simultaneously, Grant and I say, "Camp."

"Me too," Kirstin adds.

"I wanna camp," Mason says.

"Two tents!" the mayor calls out, raising two fingers into the air. Harry and another guy bring us tents and bedding.

With a wink, he hands me a sleeping pad. "We'll make sure you folks have dinner too. A hot meal for a change, even. Several of our town folk heard about what happened and are taking care of that."

"Do you know what happened yet?" Kirstin asks.

"Not yet, Miss. How about I send your newspaper friend over? I think she's getting the most up-to-date info. Did you hear she said she's going to start putting out a paper, even if she has to handwrite every copy?"

"I did." Kirstin smiles. "I offered to help her with the copy work."

"Did you, now? Then you'll probably be happy to hear I just might know where there's a tabletop printing press."

Kirstin's eyes light up. "A manual one?"

"Yep. From the late 1900s. Not sure how well it'll work for putting out a newspaper, but I'd love to help you two figure it out."

"Is it your printing press?" I ask.

"It was my brother's," the mayor says. "He was what you might call a collector. Or a hoarder. Depends on your perspective. Anyway, when he passed, I got his stuff. There's probably lots more we could use now that the lights are out for—well, anyway. Sad thing that happened today. You folks need help setting up?"

"We'll be fine," Grant answers. "Do you know anything about the water situation? Are the generators still working?"

"I'm not sure yet. We have someone checking on them. Chances are good the larger ones are done for. But there's several smaller pull-start ones we have in storage. Those should be fine."

"Okay. Is there anything I can do to help?" Grant asks.

"I'll let you know. Right now, we're okay."

While we're setting up the tents, Milena comes over. Without being asked, she immediately starts helping while she tells us what she knows.

"How many?" Kirstin asks.

"Eight was the last number I was given, but" —she takes a deep breath— "it's only the men. There are no women, no children. And we know there should be."

"Where's the women and children?" Kirstin asks, going completely pale. I'm sure I'm also pale. The women and children missing, that brings so many terrible things to mind.

"Why didn't they go to City Hall and shelter with us?" I ask.

"Don't know. Mayor Stringer says they took in everyone who showed up. They even checked the doors several times. There were a few gathered at the outside basement entrance to City Hall right after the EMP hit, but no one new showed up after that first day."

"They probably did what we were going to do," Kirstin says. "Figured they'd just find the safest place in the building."

"Maybe," Milena says. "A couple were in the main hall—probably the ones you found?" She lifts her chin toward Grant.

"Yes."

She waits for him to say more. When he doesn't, she says, "I interviewed that Toad guy. Would you like to add anything?"

"Not particularly."

"Okay. There were a few in the laundry room. And the rest were in apartments. And" —she leans in— "I can't get confirmation on this, but there may be at least one dead who didn't live there."

"Like a visitor?" I ask.

"Or one of the assailants," Grant says.

Chapter 14

The very quiet lady we were sheltering with at City Hall, Annette, who every time she spoke we had to strain to hear what she was saying, cautiously walks over to us. She's changed her clothes, and her hair is damp. I feel a rush of envy over her ability to clean up after being in lockdown for several days.

In her quiet voice, she says, "Is there anything I can help you with?"

"I think we're okay," I answer. "You don't live in our building, right?"

Her answer is lost on the breeze.

"Pardon?" I say.

Slightly louder, she says, "I have an apartment above the sporting goods store." She motions to the hiking and camping store less than a block away. Before the store was taken over by the city, Grant and I made several trips there to add to our coffers. Do we still have our supplies? Or did the murderers raid our apartment and find our stash of goods? Maybe the only things they were looking for were the women and children. I give an involuntary shudder. We could have been there.

"Do you want to use my bathroom? I have a camp shower set up with plenty of water," she says.

"Thank you," Kirstin gushes. "I'd love to if you wouldn't mind. Shelby? Want to come with me? We'll take the boys and clean them up too."

I look to Grant, who gives me a slight nod. "Go ahead. I'll stay with our stuff."

Annette's one-bedroom walkup apartment is spotless. Like, we could eat off the floor.

"I warmed up some water before I left. It should be enough for the boys. I'll start more for you and Shelby," she tells Kirstin. Inside her immaculate apartment, her voice seems stronger and I don't have to strain to hear her. Maybe she's just shy.

Instead of using the shower, we put both boys in the tub and they have a shallow water bath. Annette gives Mason a rubber duck and a toy boat to play with. I love watching as they laugh and splash.

When there's more water ready, Kirstin takes them out, dressing them in the final clean outfits in their bags, while I shower. Using a camping shower takes some getting used to. Making sure not to overuse the water before being able to rinse is the key. I make sure there's enough water to wash my hair, but I don't bother with conditioning since I have a small travel-size container of leave-in conditioner in my duffle bag. I put my sundress back on, then fix my makeup and watch the children while Kirstin showers.

"Thank you so much," Kirstin says after she's finished. "I almost feel like a new woman."

"Amazing what a shower can do," Annette says, her smile lighting up her face. When we were in the shelter, I thought of her as plain, homely even. But now, I can see she has a natural beauty about her. She does little to play it up, wearing her hair pulled back and no makeup. Her clothes are what I can only describe as frumpy. But that smile.

"You're so right," I agree.

"I'll walk you back. Maybe your husband will want to shower?" Annette asks.

"He might, but my guess is he's already found some water and cleaned up at our camp. He's pretty resourceful."

"I can tell he is. It was obvious while we were sheltering that he's aware of things and knows what's going on."

I smile at the compliment. I can't think of any person better equipped to get us through—whatever it is we'll be going through—than Grant. Even knowing this, I still have a knot in my stomach thinking of the days ahead. The murders at our building, is this a sample of what might be in store for us? Will they come back after we move back in? Can I protect myself? Can Kirstin protect herself and the boys? I shake my head to try and dislodge the worry.

When we return to camp, Grant has damp hair and a fresh smell. He gives me a big smile, then turns to Annette. "Thank you for that. I know Shelby appreciated it."

"It's what neighbors do," Annette says—at least I think that is what she said. Once again, she's quiet and hard to hear.

"I'm going to see if Lucy wants to use my place. I'll talk with you later," she says with a wave goodbye.

A little while later, a dinner of stew and bread is served. It's nothing short of amazing.

After dinner, Harry says, "Folks, we know this has been a terrible day. Chief Daniels and Sheriff Spieth will get you back in your building sometime tomorrow. We'll also have a burial service for those we lost. For those interested, we're going to hold a short prayer and song time this evening. Several of us did that in our lockdown room and really enjoyed it. So, anyway, we'll move over to City Hall Park for any that are interested. Let's start in about fifteen minutes."

"I don't have a watch," someone yells, which results in several quiet chuckles.

"That's okay," Harry says. "You'll be able to see when we're ready to start."

"Are you going?" Kirstin asks me while she starts to stand.

"No thanks. I'm going to relax here."

"You sure, Shelby?" Grant asks.

"Why? You want to go?"

He shrugs. "I thought I might."

"Go right ahead. No one's stopping you."

"I can stay with you, no biggie." Grant relaxes back on the grass.

"Keep an eye on my stuff for me?" Kirstin asks.

"Absolutely," I say, making sure I use a calm, even tone followed with a small smile.

The meeting starts and, even though Grant stayed with me, it's obvious he wishes he had gone. His eyes rarely leave the group, and he appears to be straining to hear.

"Why didn't you just go?" I ask.

"I'd rather sit here with my beautiful wife, that's why." He picks up my hand and kisses my fingers.

"What's going on with you? Are you getting religious again?"

His eyes go back to the group. I watch as he works his jaw. It's several seconds before he quietly says, "I might be."

I let out a loud sigh. "And what will that mean for us? You know what it was like for me growing up, with my dad being a holy roller and my mom understanding reality. Is that what you want for our child?"

"I was kind of hoping you might be interested in exploring things with me."

"Religion? No."

"Not religion. God, Jesus, learning more. You made a point of telling me you aren't an atheist or an agnostic, remember? I thought that might mean you were at least open to the idea."

"And you made a point of telling me, many times in fact, that you left here because you were expected to be someone you weren't. And your dad's religion was a big part of that, remember?"

"That's true, but— " He takes a deep breath and slowly releases it. "But something has changed. It started when we found out about the baby, but it's become much stronger since the attacks. Shelby, I've felt . . . something different. A need for something more."

"Something more than me? More than us?"

"No, not that. Not more than you or us. It's hard for me to explain. I just feel like something's missing. You and I are great, but we could be even better. And I think the thing that's missing is—you're not going to like hearing this."

"Then maybe you shouldn't continue," I snap. "I think we're fine just the way we are."

We sit in uncomfortable silence for many minutes. While he tries not to, I often find Grant's gaze returning to the Bible study group. I make a pointed effort to not look in that direction. But I can't help but look over when a voice rings out strong and clear, singing acapella and sounding amazing. The song is about a crown of thorns being placed on someone's head—Jesus' head, I guess. The tune is familiar, but the words aren't the way I remember. And the words mean little to me. The fact it is quiet Annette singing—that surprises me. While I'd heard her voice combined with others when we were sheltering, the way she sings alone almost brings tears to my eyes.

"I don't believe it," Grant says. "I can barely hear her when she speaks, but listen to her sing. Wow!"

Now I'm unable to keep my eyes off the group. She continues to sing, without once faltering or fading. As she sings, I realize tears are running down my face. The words, brought to life by her voice, tell a story. A story of sadness and brutality as the song tells how Jesus was killed. But in the final verse, there is hope and triumph. I hear the change in her voice as she sings about a stone being moved and Jesus rising from the dead.

During the final hallelujahs, she has the same amazing smile on her face that I saw in her apartment. In those words, she transforms to beautiful—angelic, almost.

For several seconds, a complete hush fills the air. Then it's broken by applauses, hoots, and more.

I look to Grant as he wipes his eyes.

"What was that?" I whisper. "Not the same song as in the movie *Shrek* or that the one group sang on their Christmas album."

He shakes his head. "No. The tune is the same, but the words are different—very different. This is the story of Jesus."

"You've heard it before?"

Grant nods. "The last Easter service I went to with my folks. The choir sang it."

"It's an Easter song? Why sing it in June?"

"It's a song about hope. It's perfect anytime."

Chapter 15

It's been a week since the EMP. We've been back in our apartment for two days after sleeping outside for two nights. Six women and fourteen children are still missing, with zero clues as to where they were taken. The bodies of two women were found in an empty building a few blocks away. Jesus's wife, Babbie, was one of those found. There's a suspicion that a single man who lived in our building, and can't be located, might have been involved.

Our apartment was ransacked. We lost the few supplies we didn't have stashed away, but the things Grant put in the walls were not found. He'd also taken out a section in each closet and then replaced the sheetrock. Even though the repair job wasn't great, those areas are also intact.

Kirstin, who was already low on food, lost almost everything. Taking Grant's advice, she had hidden a few things using the underneath of her box springs. Thankfully, those items remain, but it's not much. The rest of the building residents are in the same boat. And our building isn't the only place that's had troubles. While there weren't any other massacres, there were break-ins at shops and a couple of homes. All houses were unoccupied, the homes of people who were traveling when the attacks started.

Chief Daniels and his officers are now going door to door. They're taking a census to find out who's in Prospect and who isn't. They're also checking to make sure there weren't any more deaths. While so far there haven't been any mass killings, they've found several people who died of unexplained causes, a few apparent suicides, and even a couple murder-suicides. So much for the song Annette sang about hope.

As I look at people now, there's little hope in anyone's face. Even so, the prayer service and singing continues. Each night there's a group gathering at the park. Annette sings a song, with the rest of the group joining on the chorus. She hasn't repeated the song from the first night. Part of me wishes she'd sing it again, but part of me is glad she hasn't. As it is, I can't get the tune out of my head.

Since the EMP took everything out, music has been something I've greatly missed. Even when the cyberattacks happened, I could at least play the few songs I had saved to my phone. Now, there's nothing. My neighbor Lucy Fleming said she had a CD player that ran on batteries, but it was stolen when the murderers broke in. I've thought about asking Harry if he might know where I can find something like that. I really miss music.

Kirstin and Milena are trying to get the mayor's tabletop printing press working. It has all its parts, but there's a problem with the plates or letters or something, so it's still a work in progress.

All the large whole-house generators that many people and businesses were using after the cyberattack were ruined by the EMP. As expected, our cars didn't start. Even though I knew mine wouldn't, I still cried. So did Kirstin. I don't think Kirstin was crying about her car as much as she was crying about the greatly diminished chances of her husband ever making it home.

"What do you think?" Grant gestures to the marker outline on the wall.

"I think we're never going to get our deposit back."

He gives me a look halfway between a smile and a grimace. "I think that's a safe assumption."

"You're sure it'll match up on Kirstin's side?"

"I'm sure."

"And you don't think we're being a little bit ridiculous?"

"We need options."

Yesterday, when Grant told me he thought we should go furniture shopping, I thought he might be losing his mind. We have plenty of furniture. Then he said, "Not just for us, but for Kirstin too." That's when he explained his idea of connecting our apartments. That way, if someone was breaking into one apartment, we could get out through the other one. Hopefully via the front door, but at the very least off the balcony. Unfortunately, our second-floor apartments won't make that easy.

We have the fire escape ladder Pamela bought us. The day after we discovered the massacre, Grant asked Kirstin if she had a ladder. When she said she didn't, he disappeared for a while. When he returned, he had a homemade version constructed from rope and two by fours. But even with the ladder, there's no way she'd be able to get both boys down safely.

Grant traded some camping supplies for a doored media cabinet. It's not very big, less than four feet tall and only two feet wide. He built a platform to lift it up a little higher, removed the shelves, and opened the back. Kirstin already had a cheap armoire in her bedroom for storing the boys' clothes. At over five feet tall and three feet wide, with two drawers on the bottom and double doors above, it's considerably larger and better suited for our plans. The doored section has a hanging rod, which Grant left in place, then he opened the back up the same as he did on our cabinet.

The next step is cutting out the wall of each apartment, then the two pieces will go into place. Before we go through the trouble of cutting a hole between the apartment walls, we test each cabinet to make sure we can get inside the front and out the hole on the back.

I wish we had a bigger cabinet; ours is close to not working as it should! Grant's smaller frame makes it easier for him than it is for me. And if my belly gets much bigger, I'm really going to struggle. Kirstin is even smaller than Grant, so it's a breeze for her.

While our new media cabinet will be nothing more than a hidden doorway into Kirstin's apartment, her armoire can still be used. The clothes hanging above the open back will even help keep its actual purpose a secret. Grant is planning to add a hook and eye latch on each cabinet to secure the door from the inside in hopes of giving us additional seconds to make our escape. I'm not sure what to think of this. I can see the wisdom, especially after what happened while we were in lockdown. But, really? Something like that couldn't happen again. Not with all of us living here and the town trying to survive.

"We'd best get ready to go," Grant says. "I'll work on this when we get back."

I grab my new purse: a small backpack with items Grant has deemed essential. He has a similar pack he carries each time he leaves the apartment. The large duffle bags are still at the ready in case we need to evacuate again.

We're going to the park for a city-wide meeting. The mayor and his helpers started going around town yesterday to let everyone know about it. While we're not exactly sure what is on Mayor Stringer's agenda, we have a good idea based on the rumors floating around.

Even though it's not quite meeting time, there's already a large crowd gathering around the amphitheater. Kirstin walked down with us. She sees Annette in the group and encourages us to stand with her.

While Annette is nice, she makes me uncomfortable. Grant knows this, but he walks us toward her anyway.

"Thanks, honey," I mutter under my breath.

He gives me a wink and a smile. "You're very welcome, my darling."

Annette and Kirstin carry on like they haven't seen each other in weeks, when I know for a fact they were together at last night's church service. Annette even went to Kirstin's apartment afterward.

"Well, hello there, young lady," a man's voice says.

We all turn to look. With a tight smile, Kirstin says, "Hello, Mr. Majors."

"Please, Kirstin. Haven't I asked you to call me Richard?"

Ah, so this is the owner of the Prospect Record. From the stories I've heard, I expected him to be more dashing. Instead, the only word I can think of to describe him is *oily*. His hair, his skin, the way he dresses—oh, his clothes are clean; he's just . . . oily. Even his voice and the creepy way he talks to Kirstin is oily.

"Who's your friend?" Richard Majors asks, working his oily gaze up and down me. I narrow my eyes.

"Grant Cameron, Mr. Majors." Grant thrusts his hand out. "Paul Cameron is my grandpa."

Richard Majors sneers. "Oh, that's right. You're the one from the car wreck. I heard you were back in town."

Grant stiffens. "Yes, since last fall. This is my wife, Shelby."

"Do you have a bun in the oven?" He reaches a hand toward my stomach.

Grant lifts his hand, interrupting the connection.

"Whoa there, buddy. No harm intended, just offering my congratulations is all."

I start to tell him what he can do with his congratulations, when Grant smiles and says, "Thank you." Putting his arm around me, he turns me away from Richard Majors. I hear a slight snicker out of either Kirstin or Annette, I'm not sure which.

In a loud voice, Richard says, "So your dad is still disowning you?" I feel several eyes turn and look at us.

Without turning back in the oily man's direction, Grant says, "Goodbye, Mr. Majors."

The oily man humphs and mutters under his breath as he makes his way through the crowd. There are comments from a few other people

75

nearby, wondering what was going on. Grant squeezes me a little tighter before whispering, "That guy's always been a jerk. My grandpa can't stand him, and you know he likes pretty much everyone."

In a slightly louder voice than usual, Annette says, "That was impressive."

Kirstin and Annette both laugh.

"What does he mean about the car wreck?" Kirstin asks.

Grant drops his head slightly, as I say, "It's not something we talk about."

"No, no. It's okay." Grant meets Kirstin's eyes. "It happened eight years ago, when I was seventeen. I was taking my Aunt Marian and my cousin— " his voice catches " —my little cousin Melody to Thermopolis. My brothers, Dax and Bryce, were also with us. We were going swimming for the day. I wrecked the car. Marian and Melody were killed."

"Oh, I'm so sorry," Kirstin says.

"I remember that," Annette whispers. "I didn't realize . . . I'm sorry, Grant. I didn't know it was you."

"Yeah, it was me."

"Your brothers were okay? You were okay?" Kirstin asks.

"I broke my arm, Bryce broke his leg, and Dax hit his head."

"And what did he mean about your dad?"

Grant shakes his head. Before he can answer, the mayor walks up on the stage, followed by Chief Daniels and Sheriff Spieth. Over the bullhorn, the mayor says it's time to get started.

He gives the crowd about a minute to settle before he says, "Thank you all for showing up tonight. I'll trust those of you who are here to share this information with anyone who didn't show up. We'll also be posting this new information on a bulletin board that will be set up shortly after we're finished."

There's a rumble through the crowd.

"So, you'll all be happy to know, beginning tomorrow, we'll have two community meals available each day."

Cheering erupts. Kirstin and Annette hug each other. I look to Grant; he's biting his top lip. "That's good, right?"

"Wait for it," he whispers.

"Wait for what?"

"The rest."

76

Mayor Stringer smiles brightly, letting the crowd enjoy the news. After it starts to calm, he says, "We'll be using the food so graciously donated by the grocery stores."

Donated? That's an interesting version of what really happened.

"In order to ensure those who are in the most need are best served, we'll have specific guidelines for the meals."

"What's that mean?" a voice cries out.

"How will you know who really needs it?" someone else yells, with several variations of the same question coming from different parts of the mass of people.

"All good questions," the mayor says. "Quiet down and I'll tell you how it'll work."

He allows several seconds only, even though there is still plenty of rumbling, before he says, "When you show up for the first meal, we'll record your information. You won't be turned away that day. You'll be fed. Within the next eighteen hours, we'll perform a home visit. At that visit we'll determine your need."

"What's that supposed to mean?" several ask.

"Exactly how it sounds."

"So you're going to check my house?" a lady yells.

"Yes, ma'am. We'll do an inventory. Any usable food items will be added to the town pantry. Then you'll be free to eat the town meals."

"This is America! You have no right!"

At that point, the mayor loses control of the crowd. He lets it go for several moments.

Grant taps my arm. "We need to go. Kirstin, Annette, let's move out of here."

He bends over and picks up Mason. As he moves us through the pressing crowd, the mayor begins to regain control. We keep moving as the mayor continues, "Okay, folks. I understand some of you may not like this. But this is how it must be. This is the only way we can be sure people get what they need."

A guy we're squeezing past yells, "Sounds fair! Keeps those hoarders from getting extra."

"Keep moving," Grant tells us, as another guy yells, "You shut your mouth, you don't know anything."

"Go, keep going," Grant says. "Don't look back."

Against Grant's suggestion, I turn to see what's happening as the two men get face to face. Others yell for them to knock it off, while some physically separate them.

"That's enough!" the mayor yells. "Beginning at this moment, any violence will be met with consequences. Keep those two separated, or Chief Daniels and Sheriff Spieth will step in." The mayor makes a motion with his hand, and several deputies and police officers appear along the edge of the crowd.

We're near the back of the crowd on the side of the park closest to our apartment building. As soon as we reach the far edge, Grant says, "Let's put several feet between us and them."

"What's going on?" Kirstin asks. "Did the mayor just declare something like martial law?"

"I don't think so. At least, not yet."

"All right. Now let's settle down," the mayor bellows. "We have a few more things to get through. Again, you'll be able to read the new guidelines after we're done."

He motions to where Harry and another guy are dragging a large rolling bulletin board across the lawn, stopping at the edge of the amphitheater.

"Okay. So, while we have food for now, we also need to start raising food. We're going to need to start planting. We've got two and a half to three months until our first frost. It's not a lot of time for growing what we need for winter, but it'll get us *some* food. We're also using the greenhouses at Harmony Gardens. They have some plants ready to go, but they'll need help getting things started. Starting tomorrow, we'll have a signup sheet to help at the greenhouse. In addition, every house will need to plan on growing space. You've heard the phrase *grow food not lawns*? That's going to be our motto."

Another murmur goes through the crowd. Several people shout out questions, and a few raise their hands.

The mayor lifts the megaphone. "We'll give you more information over the next several days, but we're all going to need to work together to get through this. These are unprecedented times. None of us have experienced anything like this. It's going to be rough, and there will be times we hate it, but we will keep going. We will work hard these next several months so we're ready for winter."

He lowers the megaphone and looks out over the crowd.

"We're also removing all rules on livestock within city limits. Thanks to several of our nearby farmers and ranchers, we've got a small start on livestock. We've had donations of chickens, goats, dairy cattle, and meat cattle. We're going to spend several days putting housing in place and figuring out the details of animal feed. That will be an additional volunteer position. We'll begin the gardens and livestock plans tomorrow. When you sign up for your meals, you'll be given the opportunity to sign up on one of the volunteer sheets. For now, all positions will be Monday through Saturday, with Sunday off."

He takes another pause while the restless crowd digests this newest information. I'm encouraged. It sounds like a plan is in place to get our town through this time. While we are okay on food for now, there will come a time when we won't be. At least there's hope we'll get through this.

"While the food needs are important, there will be other volunteer opportunities added over the next several days. It's going to take all of us to make this work."

"Are you really only looking for volunteers?" someone yells out.

The sheriff leans in and says something to Mayor Stringer.

With a grim look and a nod, he turns back to the crowd. "There will be volunteer opportunities for many positions. All adults and children over the age of fourteen will be expected to put their name on at least one list."

"That's not volunteering!" a voice yells out, with many more echoing the same sentiment.

Someone else yells, "So we have to work for the food?"

The mayor searches the crowd, trying to find the owner of the voice. Over the bullhorn, he booms, "Did you have to work to buy your food before?"

A hush falls over the group.

"Is it really such a foreign concept that you might have to contribute? At the last census, Prospect had a population of 9,814. We know that's fallen slightly, and we estimate around 9,500 now. How do you propose we feed that many people without everyone working together?"

He gives a hard look around. "There's no more trucks bringing us food and goods. We don't have a clue what's happening in the rest of Prospector County. Sheriff Spieth sent a deputy to check on the town of Wesley. He hasn't returned yet. We're in a bubble, folks. Cody,

Casper, Cheyenne . . . we don't know. Washington, DC, might as well be on another planet. We're on our own, and we'll do what we need to survive."

A small smattering of applause starts, which soon gathers momentum. Annette joins in. Kirstin, holding Caleb, smiles brightly. I look at Grant. His clenched jaw and tightened fists tell me he won't be joining the ovation.

The mayor smiles and raises his hand, making a downward motion. "Thank you. I knew I could count on all of you. We'll meet again in three days, at the same time, when we'll catch up on what is happening. Now, if you are staying for the church service, it'll start in a few minutes. The rest of you are free to go. Be back here at ten tomorrow morning for the first community meal, and we'll get going. Prospect strong!" He pumps his fist in the air.

Almost everyone repeats the phrase and the gesture as the mayor hands the megaphone to the sheriff and walks quickly away from the crowd. A few people try to stop him, but he shakes his head and keeps going.

"Are you going to the service?" Kirstin asks.

I'm shaking my head no when I hear my name followed by Grant's name. "Hey, I'm glad I found you!" Grant's brother Bryce hollers.

"Hey, Bryce," I say, embracing him in a hug.

"Are you guys okay?" Grant asks, clapping him on the shoulder. "We thought you'd be in town before now."

"Yeah, been busy. Mom and Grandpa sent me to find you. C'mon over and see them."

"I'll take Mason," Annette says, reaching for him. "There's too many people here for him to walk around."

"So maybe we'll see you at the service," Kirstin persists.

I smile. "Probably not. Let us know when you get home so we can— " I raise my eyebrows at her to remind her about the hole we plan to put in our apartment walls this evening.

"Sure," she says.

"Ready?" Bryce asks.

"Is Dad here?" Grant asks.

"Does it matter? Can't you just ignore him or something? Mom really wants to see you."

With a shake of his head, Grant says, "Lead the way."

Chapter 16

When we reach the family, Grant's dad is conspicuously absent. Pamela opens her arms to me, embracing me in a crushing hug. She turns to Grant next. "We've been so worried. Paul had to put that old truck of his back together before we could get into town."

"What was wrong with the truck, Grandpa?" Grant asks.

"Remember me telling you about that carburetor flooding? Thought it just needed a good cleaning. I was wrong. 'Course, we were holed up in the root cellar until yesterday. Thought we were being bombed or something. I finally convinced your dad and PJ it was safe to come out."

Grant's uncle PJ gives a slight shrug. "It's not like Dusty and I didn't go out to take care of the livestock, Dad. We just wanted to make sure you, Pamela, and the boys were safe." PJ turns to Grant. "It was all I could do to keep your dad from heading into town to look for you."

The shocked look on Grant's face causes PJ to smile. "He loves you, Grant. He's stubborn as all get out, but that doesn't change his love for you. I think a little yielding from you would go a long way."

"I . . . I'll try."

"No. Try not," PJ says in a creepy voice. "Do or do not. There is no try."

"Jeez, Uncle PJ." Bryce laughs. "Your Yoda needs some serious work."

"Yeah, well. Seriously, Grant. You can do this. You and Shelby need to be at the ranch with us. After that speech . . . " PJ sighs. "It might work for a short time, but things will go bad soon enough. And your apartment is way too close to the action."

"Come home with us tonight," Pamela says. The men all nod their agreement.

"We're okay," Grant says. "People want to work together. When we were in the shelter, we heard more of the mayor's plans than he just shared. He's smart and will help Prospect. I want to help too."

"You can help from the ranch," Paul says. "You heard him. We're going to donate livestock and help the town. Your mom's incubating eggs so they'll have chickens and ducks. Bryce is working on live trapping some of the wild rabbits. Figure we can raise them up for eating. Give some to the town to raise up too. We could use your help."

"We'll see, Grandpa. So you got the truck running? Anything else still working?"

"All of the dirt bikes and quads," Bryce says. "Grandpa thinks his Jeep would run if it would have been running before this happened."

"Pshaw," Paul says. "I'll get it working. Just you wait and see."

"We have the horses," Dax says with a wink. "You think you can still ride, Surfer Boy?"

"You know it."

"I'll get the Jeep running," Paul says, ignoring Dax and Grant as they rib each other. "I'm sure it'll work. The truck wasn't affected by the pulse thing. Drove in here just fine. Just the same old same old with that bucket of bolts." Even though the words indicate the truck is nothing but trouble, the tone belies his love for the thing. It's an old dump truck from the 1950s. With its rusted hood and faded paint, it's not much to look at. A few months ago, he drove it into town to take a load of cow manure to a friend outside of Prospect. He stopped by for a short visit and proudly told us, "*This old GMC still cruises right along at forty-five miles an hour. If you're not in a hurry, she'll get you where you're going.*"

"Do you have the parts you need?" Grant asks.

With a shrug, Paul says, "Yup. Think I do. You gonna help me work on it, just like you used to?"

Grant smiles and again says, "We'll see."

"Water?" I ask. "Do you have running water?"

"Somewhat." Paul shrugs. "Our big generators were fried by that pulse thing, but we've got a couple of small ones. Figured out a way to have cold running water into my place, but not the other ones yet. PJ and Dusty are working on an idea for piping water directly from the creek into those water storage tanks we have, all gravity fed. That'd be best for the long term."

"Straight out of the creek?" I ask.

"Yep. We can purify it in the tanks before it goes into the house."

"Or we can set up a charcoal and sand system to purify it," PJ says.

"Enough of the details," Pamela says, pulling me close. "You two are really doing okay?"

I nod, while Grant says, "We're okay, Mom. We're helping the lady next door, and I want to do my part, to help thank the city for housing us during the bomb scare. We're needed here right now."

"Okay," Pamela sighs. "But promise— "

"Mom."

Pamela nods. "Are you two going to the church service? It looks like it's about to start."

"Are you staying for it?" I ask.

"We are. Come on, Shelby. We brought chairs. They're in the back of the truck, parked over by Hank Owen's place. Bryce, Dax, hurry and grab them."

"No need," Dusty Cameron, Grant's dad, says, walking toward us with several camp chairs in each hand.

My stomach tightens as I try to give him a smile. I wish he liked me.

Grant averts his eyes to the ground.

"Shelby," Dusty says, "the red chair is for you. It's the most comfortable."

I think that's the first time he's ever said my name. And that's the kindest thing he's ever said to me. Tears sting my eyes as I mumble my thanks.

"Shall we stay, Shelb?" Grant asks.

We stay for the service. While I pay little attention during most of it, I'm again drawn to the singing, especially Annette's amazing voice. Not only her voice, though. The words to the song draw me in, as she sings about being a flower quickly fading and a wave tossed on the ocean.

Pamela and Bryce loudly sing the chorus, along with most of the group. Even Grant's dad is singing, though not as robustly as Pamela. As usual, I love the tune, but the words leave me with questions. *But because of who you are?* Are they talking about God? Because I'm quite sure, if He does exist, God doesn't care anymore about them than He does me. I'll never understand how people who seem intelligent buy into the myth. How can anyone believe in some invisible being? Even to the point they think they are condemned for eternity if they aren't zealous in their fake belief.

At least Mom and Grams made sure I knew the truth. I won't fall for this. Besides, Grandma was one of the kindest people I've ever known, and she says her mom and dad were both kind and generous, genuinely good people. According to Christianity, they've all been condemned to hell. I don't think I want any part of a God who wouldn't let my wonderful Grams into His heaven.

After the service is finished, Pamela says, "Sure wish we could take you out for an ice cream cone. Wouldn't that be wonderful?"

"A piece of pie from Mildred's Diner is what I'd want," Paul says.

Restaurants are something I miss. Being able to go and sit, talking and enjoying each other while the drinks and food magically appear.

"We don't have pie, but we do have those cream filled cookies in individual wrappers," I say. "Want to go to our apartment for dessert? We could even make coffee."

Pamela hugs me. "That would be— "

"We should get home," Dusty interrupts.

"I think we have time for a cookie and a cup of coffee," Paul says.

With a shake of his head, Dusty snorts, "Fine."

Inside the apartment, Grant gets the coffee going while Pamela and I pull out not only the filled oatmeal cookies but also nutty wafer bars.

"Hey," Bryce says, grabbing a wafer bar, "those are my favorite."

Dusty passes on coffee and treats.

"So when you guys were hiding in the basement of City Hall," Paul says, "did you happen to go into the tunnels?"

"I thought that was just a rumor," Pamela says.

"Nah. I've told you. It's a fact. The tunnel connects the new City Hall with old City Hall. Of course, after the new City Hall was built, the old one was called the Annex Building. They shut that down a dozen years ago— "

"Longer than that, Dad," PJ says, while Dusty nods. "At least twenty years."

"Okay, sure," Paul says. "They had a church in there for a while and now, you know, they do that winter market thing there."

"Right," Pamela says. "I love going to that. Shelby and I went several times this past winter." She pats me on the leg, and I can't help but smile.

"Anyway, there's a tunnel between the two buildings."

"You've been in it?" I ask.

"Nope. But it's there. There's even a second tunnel between the old Prospector Hotel and the Annex Building."

"Now, Dad . . . "

"Swear." Paul lifts his hand in the air. "That's where they got the idea to put the tunnel between the two city halls."

"Why?" Bryce asks. "Why put in tunnels in the first place?"

"Because of the mayor—the first one, Emerson Bunn. He owned the hotel and lived on the entire top floor. He didn't want to have to walk outside in the winter. When they built the original City Hall, he paid for the tunnel. He liked the tunnel so much he talked about adding a second one between his hotel and the carriage house. That one didn't happen, though, as far as I know."

I shake my head. "That seems like a strange story. How long was he mayor?"

"Hmm. A long time. He died in office. Thirty years at least."

"So this tunnel is legit?"

"Legit?"

"Is it real or a rumor?" Grant asks.

"Real, of course. Why do you think I'm telling you about it?"

Pamela and I share a look.

"Okay, okay." Paul raises his hands. "I haven't seen it with my own eyes, but my pop told me about it. He said they used to go down there and smoke cigarettes. But it's boarded up now. With the hotel being so close to the creek, there was a water issue. Good thing he didn't put the tunnel in between the hotel and carriage house since it's even closer to the creek. That would've been a mess for sure."

"Where's the carriage house?" I ask.

"Do you know that big building behind the hotel? Just across the alley?"

I shrug. "I don't think so."

"It looks like a smaller version of the hotel. They hold weddings and other events there now, but it used to be where Bunn and the hotel guests kept their horses. The barn was right next to it. They tore that down a few years ago and put those little cottages in so they could have more lodging space."

"Well, it's an interesting story," Pamela says. "As much as I hate to, we'd best get going."

"When will you be back in town?" I ask.

"Not anytime soon," PJ says.

"Weren't you worried about leaving the ranch unattended?" Grant asks.

A small smile plays at his dad's lips as he nods. "We were. That's why Angelo and his daughter are there."

"Tricia? I thought she moved away," Grant says.

"She moved back after her husband died," Paul says.

Grant turns to me. "Tricia used to babysit us."

"And if I remember correctly," PJ says with a huge smile, "she was Grant's first crush."

I watch as crimson creeps up his neck, across his face, and even tinges his ears.

"Really?" I say with a laugh.

Grant rolls his eyes. "I was eleven. So, they're staying with you?"

"Yep. We needed help keeping watch, and they felt safer at the ranch. You'd be safer there too."

Grant's eyes glance toward his dad who returns his gaze with a slight nod.

"Thanks, Grandpa. We'll probably take you up on that, just not quite yet."

After they leave, I am almost giddy. The eye contact and slight nod from Dusty were so much more than he's given since we moved here. There were no apologies or conversation other than a slight nod when the goodbyes were said. I turn to Grant and ask, "Well?"

"Well, what?" He has a slight grin on his face.

"Well, your dad, of course!"

He nods. "It wasn't too bad."

"I thought it was great." I give him a kiss. "So . . . do you want to tell me more about Tricia?"

With a laugh, Grant says, "Not really."

"Are you working on the wall?"

"It's too late now. We'll do it tomorrow."

Chapter 17

The new opening between the apartments ends up better than I expect. While both are very rough and not properly finished, Grant makes sure everything is braced and safe so the ceiling doesn't fall in on us. Once the furniture pieces are in place, we test going from our apartment into Kirstin's and vice versa. We hurried to complete the project while Kirstin was in the food line. Since she'll have to consent to an inspection, we had to change our plans slightly in order to better hide the hole from her side. The original plan was to leave the back open, having only the hanging clothes as camouflage. We decided there was too much chance the city inspection would include moving things around. Grant is now using the piece he cut out of the back to fill in the armoire hole, while still allowing it to easily slide out of the way.

A short while ago, Kirstin returned from her meal, and now we're testing everything. Not only did we crawl through the furniture pieces into the other apartment, but we tried the fire escape ladders too. I'm okay getting into our media cabinet and out of Kirstin's armoire, but the ladder was a no-go. With my enlarged girth, I'm clumsy. And with the children, it's extremely dangerous, especially when using the homemade ladder from Kirstin's balcony. I was so nervous even trying to get on the ladder that my asthma started acting up.

"Let me see if I can come up with something else," Grant says. "What we really need is another adult, someone to hold the ladder while Kirstin carries the baby and I carry Mason."

"If I can get down, I could hold the ladder," I say.

"That same someone needs to hold it for you. I think if it didn't move so much, you wouldn't be so scared."

Very softly and sadly, Kirstin says, "If Ethan was here . . . "

I put my arm around her shoulder, and she briefly rests her head on my arm.

Straightening, she says, "Annette and I were talking yesterday. She's nervous about living on her own. I might ask her to move in with me."

Grant nods. "That's probably a good idea. Not just for the ladder issue, but so she isn't alone. I'm not sure any female should live alone right now."

I give him a look and start to object. "Shelby," he says with a tinge of exasperation in his voice, "you know what I mean. Did you forget about the women who were taken?"

"I haven't forgotten. Did you forget they weren't women living alone? And several men were killed?"

"Believe me, I remember. I'm just saying, if Annette moving in with Kirstin can provide a measure of safety for Annette, and help Kirstin out too, it's smart. This has little to do with women and men being unequal."

Kirstin gives me a small smile. "It is true, though. Men and women are different. There are certainly things my husband can do that I can't do. And if he was home, we wouldn't have the issue with climbing down the ladder."

"Well, I for one happen to believe in women's rights. If Annette wants to move in with you, that's one thing. But she shouldn't feel forced to move in with you because she can't defend herself."

"Would you want to live alone right now?" Grant asks me.

"That's . . . that's . . . " I sigh. "No. No, I wouldn't."

Grant nods. "If she decides to move in with you, we'll try it again. Otherwise, I think we need to figure on the escape hatch being useful only to get to the other apartment and hopefully out the hall and away before we're discovered."

"The escape hatch?" Kirstin asks with a smile. "I like it. It's brilliant, Grant. Part of me wishes I could tell others about it because it's so ingenious."

Grant gets a panicked look.

"Don't worry." Kirstin gives a waving motion with her hands. "I know we can't tell anyone."

"Right. If anyone knows, we risk it not working as it should."

"Do you think just having the one option is enough?" I ask.

"What do you mean? We have a couple of options: the regular door, the balcony—especially if we have Annette here—and the escape hatch to go between the apartments."

"I was just thinking, what if we had another option. You know, like the apartment next to us."

Grant tilts his head as a small smile makes its way across his face. "That's a pretty good idea."

"You mean, knock that wall out too?" Kirstin asks, a slight look of shock on her face.

I shrug. "The apartment is empty. The family that was living there was gone when the attacks started."

"I like the idea. I'll check the apartment out tomorrow, see if we can make it work."

"Too bad we're on the second floor," Kirstin says. "Even though we can go linear, it still doesn't help us get out."

"True, but it does give us another option. Speaking of options, there's something else we wanted to talk to you about. Shelby, you want to go ahead?"

"Yes, sure. But let's sit down. All this crawling around . . . " We move to Kirstin's couch. Once we're settled, I say, "You know how Grant's mom wants us to go to their ranch?"

"Oh." Kirstin's face falls. "Of course. I thought you didn't want to go? Are you going to?"

I raise my hand in a stop motion. "Not now. But it's an option. They're concerned that people might not remain as cordial as they were at last night's meeting."

"Everything was fine at the brunch. People were happy to be there. Happy, like us, for the food."

"Right. For now. But what about those people who don't want the inspection? They could revolt."

"Maybe." She scrunches up her face. "I'd like to think they wouldn't, but I guess it's possible."

"So, since they were all here, we asked them if you and the boys could go with us. You know, if it was something we needed to do."

I expected a thankful reaction from Kirstin, so I'm shocked when she says, "I could never leave here."

"Why's that?" I ask, while Grant nods and says, "I can understand why you feel that way."

I give Grant a questioning look.

Kirstin smiles. "What if Ethan comes home? How would he find me?"

"I've been thinking about that. Is there a clue you could leave in the apartment? Something he would understand but would be meaningless to anyone else?"

"I don't know. What are you thinking?"

"Maybe you leave a note on the wall that says something like *our anniversary picnic*."

She scrunches up her face. "I don't understand."

Patiently, Grant says, "If there was something special you did somewhere, like you went on a special date at a different location in Prospect, we could leave a clue here to lead him there. And then there could be another clue there—something only Ethan would know— that would lead to another spot. After a few of those clues, we could leave a more detailed note for him."

"You think that would work?"

"Maybe. If the clues were right for Ethan to decipher but vague enough no one else would understand. The final note would be a risk since it would tell where to find you. So we'd really have to be sure only Ethan could find it."

She shakes her head. "I can't really think of anything."

"That's okay. You don't have to right now."

"You think I should go with you? I don't want to impose." Her final word is cut off by a loud wail from Caleb. Kirstin takes a minute to grab him from his crib.

When she returns, I say, "We'd hate to leave you. We'd feel so much better having you and the boys with us."

"What about Annette?"

"Her too," Grant says. "We didn't know about her moving in with you when we talked with my family. But Shelby asked about her anyway."

Kirstin nods. "Let me think about the clues you suggested. It would be like a scavenger hunt, right? Ethan likes those kinds of things, so he'd do well at it. He used to do that geocaching thing too."

"Yeah, something like that. But vague and stuff only you and he would know. Special places in and around Prospect."

"Okay. I'll think about it. I'm going to go talk to Annette. See what she's decided about moving in here."

"Might be a good idea for you to put some things together," Grant says.

"Meaning?"

"Clothes and supplies. Kind of like we did for your bags. That way, if we had to leave from someplace else and couldn't get back here for the bags, you'd have things you need. It would be at least an overnight walk to get to the ranch."

She closes her eyes and takes a breath. "I guess that would be smart."

Chapter 18

The last few days have been busy. Annette moved in with Kirstin, and Grant made a stash of goods for all of them near our stash. Just in case, he added a few more of our items there too. I think we now have more stuff buried in remote places in Prospector County than we have in our apartment! Harry was the one who did the cursory inspection of Kirstin's apartment. He didn't even give the armoire in the living room a second glance.

Even though she knew it was only supposed to be an inspection for food, Kirstin was concerned they'd take her handguns. She told me a few days ago that she carries all the time. I was shocked; I had no idea and told her so. She gave me a wink and said, "That's how it's supposed to be." Her husband also has a handgun, which he did not take with him on his trip. Harry saw the gun safe in her room but made no mention of it.

With Annette, we can use the ladders to exit each apartment from the balcony. It's still rather precarious, but it's doable. She had absolutely zero problem climbing on the ladder and nimbly making her way down. And holding it for me to go down was also no problem. Even though we're able to do it, I hope we never have the need.

Grant took out a section of wall between our bedroom and the apartment next door. He was able to borrow a piece of furniture from another empty apartment in the building—where one of the murdered men lived—to cover the hole in our room. The next-door apartment had a world map poster hung up in the bedroom. The thing is crazy big, over four feet wide and three feet tall. Grant hung it over the opening. We'll just break through it if we need to use that escape hatch. He made another ladder, like the one for Kirstin's apartment, for exiting the next-door apartment via the balcony.

Kirstin and the boys continue to get their two meals a day, along with the bulk of Prospect. Because Caleb is so young, she was given a pass for working at the greenhouse, but she is on a list to provide daycare for other children while their parents work. The setup for that is in process and is expected to begin within the next couple of days.

The beautiful green space at our apartment is being dug up for a vegetable garden, just like the rest of the lawns in Prospect. Right now, the only lawns not being removed are at the city parks. Those will follow at some point, but Mayor Stringer wants to focus on backyard gardens right now. His theory is those will be easier to tend since they will be right where people live.

Moving the livestock into town is still a work in progress. It sounds like the plan now is to use a place on the very edge of Prospect as the town's farm instead of moving them into the city limits—less work setting things up.

We're getting ready to go to another meeting at the park. It's scheduled to start at seven o'clock, as soon as the food line is completed. And, of course, there will be another church service afterward. Every night, if it's not raining too hard, there's a service. We haven't gone since the time with Grant's family. But with our windows open, we're so close we still hear the preaching and carrying on. And the singing. I'm so desperate for music, I almost enjoy the singing. Yesterday, I caught myself humming one of the songs! It was the one Annette sang when Grant's family was here. I really need to find something to play real music.

"Are you ready?" Grant asks, walking into the bedroom. "Wow! You look amazing."

"I do? My makeup isn't right. I'm so low on my eyebrow powder I had to do it differently."

"I love it. You look amazing."

"I've put on more weight. At least right here." I motion to my stomach. "It's really bumped out."

Grant steps toward me, pulling me into a hug. "You are beautiful."

"You haven't mentioned my shoes lately."

He steps back slightly, looking in my eyes. "Are you still upset about that?"

"No. Not exactly. I realized you were right. I guess I'm a little disappointed you haven't noticed the shoes I've been wearing."

"Oh, I've noticed!"

I raise my barely made-up eyebrows at him. "And?"

"And I approve. Out of self-preservation, I chose not to say anything."

"Hey!" I give him a slight tap on the shoulder but can't help smiling. "So, you think these are okay for making a quick getaway if needed?" I lift my sneaker-clad foot, twisting it to show all sides.

"Sure. Those are great. Though, the hiking boots you were wearing when we were putting in the garden are my favorite."

"Yeah, well, the sneakers look better with this dress. And I don't know how much longer I'll be able to wear those shorts I had on with the boots. They were a little snug."

"So wear the hiking boots with a dress. Who cares?"

I give him a look. Though not the ideal look, my vintage knee-length clam digger shorts don't look terrible with the boots, especially when I add a button-up shirt over a tank top and tie the overshirt right above my belly. Maybe I can loop a rubber band through the button on the shorts. That should give me a little more growing room.

Grant reaches for my hand. "So, you ready to go?"

We hold hands as we walk over to the meeting. While I love Grant more than I ever thought I could love anyone, these days since the attacks have been rough. In some ways, we're closer than ever, but in other ways, we've grown apart. We both have our own things going on in our heads to contend with. Some days I think he's being totally over the top with the plans he's made. Other times, I think we haven't done enough. The uncertainty gets to me. There's been no new word on the hospital that is being set up. Maybe the mayor will update us on that this evening.

The crowd is even larger than the last city-wide meeting. This time, Grant keeps us on the edge. Kirstin's newspaper friend Milena Maynard joins us. While she still looks good, she isn't quite as fresh looking as the day we ended the shelter in place in the basement of City Hall. She has dark circles under her eyes and a pallor to her complexion.

Kirstin must also notice because she asks, "Are you feeling okay?"

With a small smile, Milena says, "Lots to do. I was up most of the night trying to get things sorted out on the printing machine. And that was after working in the greenhouse most of the day."

Annette says something, which none of us catch, so Milena asks her to repeat it.

"I didn't think you were taking the meals," she says.

"No, I'm not. But I still wanted to help. And I will be taking the meals soon. I'm almost out of food. How about you, Annette?"

"I brought the food I had with me when I moved in with Kirstin. I've been making my own meals when they go for theirs. Like you, it won't be much longer until I'm out. I always thought I kept a well-stocked pantry. Guess not."

"It's getting ready to start," Grant says, motioning to the mayor and Chief Daniels as they step up on the podium.

I notice Milena seems to stiffen. She has her notebook at the ready. I glance at the paper, which already has several things written on it. Her handwriting is terrible, and I can barely make it out. What I do think I read causes me to also stiffen.

"Thank you all for coming tonight." Mayor Stringer's usual confident delivery seems strained. And his usual pulled together appearance is anything but. He's rumpled instead of fresh pressed, wearing jeans with dirt on one knee and dull, old cowboy boots. "Some of you may have heard the rumors . . . " He pauses and looks toward the sky. I tense. "The rumors that we've been having an increase in violence and theft. Last night, there was an incident at the Smith ranch. As you may know, this is where we've been setting things up to house the city livestock. Mr. Smith was hit over the head."

There's a huge rumble from the crowd, and Mayor Stringer raises his hand. "He'll be fine, but the perpetrator is still at large. And this isn't the only incident. We've had an increase in home break-ins and there have been other attacks. Because of these issues, in cooperation with Chief of Police Daniels, I'm issuing a dusk-to-dawn curfew."

This causes more than a rumble from the crowd. This is also the part of Milena's note I was able to make out. I'm not surprised. Grant and I have talked about this, as we've heard more activity at nighttime than we think we should be hearing. A couple of nights ago, we were even awakened by what sounded like breaking glass. We found out the next day someone had busted out the windows of a car.

"The details are simple," Mayor Stringer bellows. "From the time the sun sets until it rises, stay in your home. We'll put it in writing and add it to the bulletin board. Chief Daniels is going to be adding officers to his department. He has a list of people he's chosen and will be talking with them in the next several days."

"What about Sheriff Spieth?" someone, possibly the oily Richard Majors from the sound of his voice, yells out.

"The sheriff has his team in place," Mayor Stringer answers.

"That's not what I mean, and you well know it. Rumor is he's against this curfew and that's why he's not with you tonight." Yep, the oily guy.

"Sheriff Spieth has his hands full with the county. He's completely dedicated to allowing Chief Daniels to continue to monitor the city, just as it's always been."

"Answer the question!" someone else yells.

"I believe I just did," the mayor returns.

"Is this martial law?" someone else asks.

"Not even close," the mayor says, while Chief Daniels shakes his head. "The curfew is for everyone's safety. With the increase in violence, it's necessary to help keep everyone safe."

He loses control of the crowd again. Personally, I don't know what the big deal is. It's dark and people should be home anyway. I do hear many people yelling about their rights being violated and the Constitution being trampled.

"Is that true?" I whisper to Grant.

He shrugs. "I don't know. Maybe. Probably. But one thing I learned during the time I was on my own, when you're trying to survive each day, you don't think much about the Constitution. That wasn't a conversation any of the other guys and I had."

"You and the other homeless?" I blurt out, a little too loudly, based on the look I receive from Annette.

Grant gives me a grim nod. "Right."

"All right, people," Mayor Stringer shouts through his bullhorn, "let's calm down. We have a few more things to share." He gives a few moments for the crowd to calm. It does, barely. "That's better. Harmony Gardens reports they are well staffed. Thank you all for volunteering."

"Volunteering!" someone shouts. "Ha! Like we had a choice?"

Mayor Stringer eyeballs the shouter. "Starting tomorrow, if you volunteered for the Harmony Gardens or for caring for the livestock and have not been contacted about either position, you'll need to sign up on one of the new sheets we'll have available."

There are groans through the crowd, but he doesn't really lose control this time. "We'll have groups available for other needed things, including salvaging, kitchen work, cleaning crews, and more. So again, if you haven't already been contacted and were either working or scheduled to work at the nursery or livestock, you must sign up on a new workforce. For now, we'll continue with a Monday through Saturday schedule, except for kitchen work. We'll need Sunday people in the kitchens, but you'll have a day off during the week."

The meeting continues along this vein for a few more minutes before the mayor ends it with, "We'll meet again in three days."

As the crowd begins to disperse, a guy near us says, "Three days. Great. Wonder what he'll spring on us then."

His friend says, "Man, this apocalypse sucks. I thought there'd at least be zombies."

"Yeah," the first guy says, "and as much food as we could steal."

"And all the women we'd want," guy number two says, as both give a creepy laugh and walk away. I blanch at their conversation.

"Those two, they're mostly just talk," Milena says. "Except, I did hear they ended up in county jail the night of the cyberattacks. Tried to rob Bill Vanderberg—do you know him? He owns Prospect Pawn and Gun?"

I shrug. I know where the building is, but I haven't been there.

"Anyway," Milena continues, "a couple of guys were there and stopped it. I heard Glen was so scared when the guys fought back, he wet his pants."

I can't help but laugh. "Which one's Glen?"

"The stinky one," Milena says with a laugh.

Chapter 19

"What do you think he'll spring on us tonight?" I ask from my position on the couch, stretched out and relaxing from my day.

"I don't think there will be anything too big. Maybe a few more volunteer positions."

"Volunteer?"

"Yeah. Probably should have done some air quotes, huh?"

Our busy days blend. It's now the end of August, and we've been working at this survival thing for two months. Things have changed in these weeks. Even though we only recently signed up for the community food—just so we wouldn't put a target on our backs as being people who still had our own supplies—we both joined different volunteer crews weeks ago. I'm a backup at the daycare center held in City Hall, plus I'm the main worker in the garden at our apartment.

We're eating fresh lettuce and radishes, which are a huge treat. I didn't even like radishes before this, but now I almost crave them. There's tomatoes, squash, and pumpkins growing too. They're still ridiculously small but will hopefully be usable before it freezes. One of the garden experts says he has some ideas to help extend the season and give them time to grow. We also have several root crops that he thinks will be ready to harvest before the ground freezes. My garden isn't large, but when combined with the others in town, it'll really help.

Grant is on the salvage crew, a perfectly fitting job for him. They are assigned the task of going through any empty houses to find usable items. At first, when they said empty, I thought they meant unoccupied. They did—houses for sale or rent and not being lived in, where the owners do not live locally, are on the list. As are the many vacation rentals with faraway owners. But also on the list are homes where the owners have died and they don't have relatives around.

The first day he was on salvage duty, Grant came home that night and said, "We need to rethink our food. One of the houses we went through had been targeted by thieves."

"Okay?"

"Yeah. They put holes in the sheetrock."

"Why?"

He shrugged. "Guess they thought the people might have hidden things in the walls."

"Who would think that? I mean, besides you?"

"Keep in mind, I learned it from someone too. I guess it's not a big secret."

That night, he broke curfew and made several trips to his out-of-town caches.

"Are you sure about this?" I asked.

"I think it's necessary. I know we can get community food, but I'm concerned— "

"I mean, you're going to break curfew to take these things out to the country. What if you get caught?"

"I'll be fine. You know that guy that worked at my grandpa's station sometimes?"

I gave him a blank look.

"He's a couple years older than me. Gramps gives him extra work when he has trouble making ends meet."

"The one with the ears?"

"Yeah." Grant nodded. "Him. He's sort of been deputized. He said he'd look the other way for me. He also said they aren't really doing anything about people that break curfew unless they cause trouble."

"It's safe for you to go? You won't be arrested?"

"I should be fine."

"*Should be.* I'll be a nervous wreck until you get back."

To store things in the wall behind my picture, Grant had used PVC pipe, laying it horizontally and connecting with a string he could fish up. He loaded the pipes up in a backpack and took those on his first trip. He hadn't had enough PVC pipe to use the same method in the bedroom, behind the posters. For those, he'd used a variety of shallow boxes, taping them shut, and the same string method so they could easily be retrieved from the wall cavity. I watched as he pulled the boxes out of the hole my Rosie the Riveter poster was hiding.

"Won't those be a problem to stash?"

"Yeah. The cardboard's a rodent magnet. I'm going to hang them. Mind if I use those dark green pillowcases?"

"The scratchy ones? Sure, that's fine. Hang them like a bear bag?"

"Right. They won't be hidden, but it's better than doing nothing, I guess."

The next day he brought home buckets and an ammo box.

"Where'd you get those?" I asked.

"Traded for them."

"For your cache?"

"For *our* cache." Two more trips to his hiding spot that night, and he declared us finished. The small amount of food in our kitchen and in one section of the closet wall were, in Grant's opinion, reasonable to keep on hand. When we finished the food in the kitchen, we had our inspection and started taking community meals. Part of me feels a little bad about eating the community food when we have hidden food. Grant says we should think of it as our rainy-day fund. Even with the gardens and the food the city commandeered, there will be shortages. He doesn't want to risk me not having enough food for our baby.

Milena and Kirstin have their paper going. It's not much more than a single sheet of information put out one time per week. Both say maybe someday they can have a real newspaper again, but at least now they feel like they're helping keep the town in the know.

A few weeks ago, Grant said many more houses have been added to their list of places to clear out. The number of deaths has increased considerably: elderly who couldn't get the medicines they needed to survive, plus more suicides and murder-suicides. The crew no one wanted to be on, the burial crew, is the one the city leaders are working hardest to fill. We have little doubt there will be more deaths. Medicines are a concern for many. I'm still okay with my inhalers, and since we were in the basement of City Hall, I haven't had anything close to a real asthma attack. Still, like every other commercial medication, I can't just go to the pharmacy and pick up a new one. The city did end up with some medications when they took things over, and inhalers are one of those items. Mainly, I am focused on trying to keep my symptoms under control. And I hope, after my baby is born, I'll go back to not having asthma.

I'm very glad I have the garden to keep me busy. I can't imagine what things would be like if all I could do was sit at home. That night in June when the planes crashed, which now seems so long ago, Grant and I were glued to our phones, searching social media and news channels for more information.

While I miss the instant facts that used to be at my fingertips—and I very much miss electricity, turning on a faucet and having water, and being able to listen to music—there's a peacefulness without the constant information overload. I spend more time outside than I have since I was a child.

Working in the garden, I'm careful not to overdo it. My incredibly large belly gets in the way, and sometimes my breathing is an issue. Many days I'm the only one in the garden, so working at my own pace is no problem. Like so many others, I'm tired.

I've had two prenatal appointments since the new hospital was set up. *Hospital* may be a generous term. It's slapped together and lacking in many critical items. My OB/GYN, one of the many doctors presumed lost in the fire, was great. The new person who is taking care of me doesn't seem nearly as caring or knowledgeable. Grant reminds me that she still knows how to deliver a baby and that is the most important thing.

I'm impressed with Mayor Stringer's organization. In addition to the hospital and putting all the crews together, he's set up several daycare centers in various places around town. Since we're mostly on foot, things must be within walking distance. Even though food is only cooked on this side of town, it's hauled to two additional locations for distribution. I know one of the mayor's plans is to set up a second cooking facility. Maybe that will be announced tonight. Unfortunately, they still have the sewer stink on that end of town, with no remedy for it. The mayor did have a team go house to house and help close off the bathrooms. I hear that helped make living in the homes bearable, but there are still issues overall.

"I think I'll skip the town meeting. I'd rather just stay right here."

"Probably a good idea," Grant says, kissing me on the forehead. "Kirstin said she's not going. Caleb seems fussy, and she's worried he's coming down with something."

"He's okay?"

Grant shrugs.

"What about Annette?"

"She's going. At least, I think she said she is. You know it's a struggle sometimes . . . "

I smile my agreement. Letting out a sigh, I heft my large self off the couch. "Just in case he says something important, I think I'll join you."

"You sure? There's no harm in you staying home and resting."

"I'm sure."

"Don't forget this." Grant hands me my inhaler off the side table, and I tuck it in the pocket of my overshirt. I've taken to wearing a uniform of sorts: either the denim clam digger shorts with a rubber band at the button or an elastic-waisted jersey skirt along with a tank top and a button-up shirt for my garden work. Oh, and the hiking boots. It seems like I live in hiking boots. Sometimes I look longingly at my other shoes, the cute platform pumps, spectator pumps, mules, and assorted heeled sandals. But with the garden work—and my size—I don't wear them. They're all shoved at the back of the closet now, gathering dust and occasionally mocking me.

"No one seems very upset about the curfew now, even though they made such a big deal about it when it was announced," I say, as Grant locks the door to our apartment.

"Right. We're all too tired to do anything at night anyway. Plus, what's there to do? It's not like there's bars or restaurants to go to."

"Or movie theaters. I miss movies. It'd be nice if that were still an option."

"Stop a minute," Grant says. Turning me to face him, he whispers, "We might be able to do that. A few of us were talking about trying to figure out a movie night."

"What? How?"

"There are still generators that work and at least one family who had an alternative-powered home. One of the guys on the crew said they're talking about figuring something out. It's not a high priority, of course, but it's in the works."

"Wouldn't that be wonderful!" I gush. "It would feel so normal."

Grant starts walking again. "It's nothing official. But maybe someday soon."

I'm all smiles as we approach the crowd. Tonight's group seems slightly less than the last meeting, but there are still several people in line for the evening meal. As is our norm, we stay on the edge, standing next to Annette and Milena. As I look around, the people there seem to wish they were elsewhere. Maybe at home, stretched out on their couch? None of us are used to the physical labor needed to grow our own food. Or, as in Grant's case, spending the day trying to find usable goods. They walk from home to home as they do their search. Our mostly sedentary society is having a huge awakening. People are already losing weight as their calorie needs increase due to the increase in physical activity.

There's little fanfare or response when Mayor Stringer and Chief Daniels take to the stage. Since the first town meeting, the sheriff hasn't joined them on the stage nor do we see much of him, but he does have several deputies along the edge—the same way Chief Daniels has several officers. Mayor Stringer is looking much more his old self this evening, still slightly rumpled but not to the degree he did at the past meetings.

"Good evening, neighbors," the mayor says. "I want to start with commending you all for the excellent job you are doing with your Victory Gardens. I know many of you haven't spent much time growing your own food and this is all new. But through your hard work, it won't be long until we're all enjoying fresh greens in our diet. I never thought I could love a salad the way I do these days."

There's a small unenthusiastic spattering of courtesy laughter and minor applause.

Mayor Stringer responds with a large smile and his awkward clapping while holding the bullhorn in one hand.

"I know this has been a long time coming, but beginning tomorrow, those of you on the east side of Prospect will be able to enjoy your meals at Jim Bridger Park. Everything is set up for cooking and serving."

This garners considerably more enthusiastic applause and plenty of hooting and hollering. The mayor basks in it for a moment before raising his hand. With one hand in the air, his entire body falls backward after one loud bang and then a second. I watch in disbelief as Chief Daniels reaches for his sidearm. Another loud bang and he's on the ground.

"Get down, Shelby!" Grant yells, pulling me to the ground.

"What's happening?" Milena screams. "Did someone just shoot the mayor?"

I'm on my hands and knees with my arm over my head, pulling my body as tight around my stomach as possible. Grant is up against me, covering my body as best he can. Around us, people are screaming and running. There's more shooting and then a loud explosion shakes the ground. A second one follows.

"What's going on?" Annette, huddled next to me, asks in a whisper.

A voice bellows over the crowd, "Stop moving. Stop moving and we'll stop shooting."

I hazard a look. The oily newspaper owner, Richard Majors, is standing next to a slumped over Chief Daniels. A shot rings out. He doesn't even flinch as he puts the bullhorn to his mouth. "Stop. Moving. Now."

"Get down. Get down now," Grant yells out to people around us. He even reaches out and grabs one lady by the leg pulling her down next to us. He's not the only one. Others start screaming for people to get on the ground.

"Good. Good way to help your neighbors. You're saving lives out there," Richard says in a calm, condescending tone. "Now let's all settle down."

A few seconds later, another shot rings out followed by a woman screaming. A shot ends her screaming.

"My people have a commanding view and are excellent snipers," Richard Majors says. "When I said stop moving, that is what I meant! Anyone trying to leave will be shot. Got it?"

He puts the bullhorn down and leans in to talk to another guy on the stage. "Who is that?" I whisper, in a ragged breath.

Grant squints his eyes slightly. "I don't know him. Wait—maybe . . . isn't that the guy from our building? The one they said was missing after the massacre?"

"Is it? I thought . . . he had . . . a . . . ponytail?"

"Maybe he got a haircut. I don't know for sure, but it might be him. Use your inhaler. Can you do it bent over like that?"

"N-no. Need . . . to be . . . upright." My breathing sounds like a freight train as I struggle to control it. I'm coughing and my chest hurts.

"Breathe with me, Shelb," Grant whispers, as he takes a loud breath and slowly lets it out. *What does he think this is? A cheesy movie?* I ask myself as my throat tightens. I squeeze his leg to let him know I hear him and I'm trying.

"Okay," Majors says. "Now that you all seem to understand what is happening here, I want you to sit up. Just sit up and look at me. Don't move from your spot, but all eyes need to be on me."

"Shelby," Grant whispers, "don't look around. Just look at him."

I nod, as I try to move from my curled position. My chest feels like there's an elephant sitting on it, making everything difficult.

"Annette? Milena?" Grant asks, helping me reposition.

"Okay, Grant," Milena says. Annette makes a whimpering sound.

I keep my eyes to the ground as I move to my bottom. Grant reaches in my shirt pocket, pulling out my inhaler. He uncaps it and gives it a shake, holding it up to my mouth. I move my face toward it, taking in a deep breath. I nod and he dispenses the bronchodilator. I go through my process of taking in the medicine, feeling somewhat better as I hold my breath, then slowly let it out.

"Again?" he asks.

I hold up a finger to indicate we need to wait a minute. I focus on my breathing as I count. As the tightness in my chest lessens, I hear the cries around me.

"Yes, yes. It's so sad. Boo-hoo," Majors says. "Let this be a lesson to you all. I mean what I say and say what I mean. Those who do not obey are dealt with promptly."

I start to raise my eyes. "Really, Shelby. You don't need to look. You don't want to see this."

With a nod, I squeeze my eyes shut. I reach for the inhaler. I'm recovered enough I can handle this on my own.

"Now, residents of Prospect, you may have guessed there's a new mayor in town. Mayor Majors. It has a nice ring, don't you think? For most of you, things won't change much. You'll still have your little jobs, but the difference with your new mayor and old mayor is I won't be blowing smoke and making you think you're volunteering for your work. Everyone works. And everyone gets community meals only. You will turn in your food for community use. You have two days to make this happen, because on day three my team is going door to door. Anyone found with food in their home will be swiftly dealt with. And you've already had a demonstration on how that works."

I feel Grant shudder next to me as I take another dose from the inhaler.

"In addition to turning in your food, you will also turn in your firearms. If you're wearing a firearm, you will leave it here tonight. Any firearms in your home will be turned in with your food. Unless you are an appointed member of my team, you are not allowed to own a weapon."

Several gasps run through the crowd.

"Do you have your pistol?" I whisper.

Grant shakes his head.

"We're going to be adding a new crew starting right now," Majors continues. "A cleanup crew. I want every male between the ages of fourteen and seventy to move up here by the stage. You'll be putting this park back in order. Women and children, you may leave. You will go directly to your home—but those of you women who have a gun will deposit them in one of the garbage cans." He points to a garbage can with an armed man standing next to it.

"There's one on each side of the park. Everyone is expected to show up tomorrow for their regular work crew. You may receive new instructions at that time. If you do not have a designated work crew, arrive right here at seven in the morning. Bring your food and guns with you whether going to your crew or the park." Majors looks around at the shell-shocked crowd. "Did I not make it clear what I expect to happen?"

"Get up," Grant says, standing then helping me. "Annette, Milena, can you stand?"

Annette quickly gets to her feet as Richard Majors yells out, "Let's move, people."

I do my best to not glance around, to not take in the carnage. Grant leans in, tickling my ear, and says, "Go home quickly. Tell Kirstin to be ready to leave."

I meet his eyes, giving a slight nod. "Annette, can you help Shelby?"

Grant rubs his hand along my arm, then turns toward the stage. I avert my eyes to the ground; I don't want to see what is between here and there.

Chapter 20

While not an all-out run, we move faster than I should, considering I've just had an attack. We haven't gone far when I begin to wheeze. "I have to slow down."

"We have to get you home," Milena says, dragging me by the arm.

"I can't. I'll— "

"I'll help her," Annette says. "You should go to your place, Milena."

"You're sure?"

Saving my breath for breathing, I give a single nod.

"I'm sure," Annette says. "Shelby, do you think— "

I nod again.

"You're sure?" Annette asks.

"Yes!" I say in a croak.

Annette leans in toward Milena. I can barely make out her words. "Be ready to leave. We have a plan."

Milena's eyes go wide. She nods, then turns and starts running in the direction of her apartment.

We're moving again, slower but still at a decent clip. "When do you think we'll go?" Annette asks.

"Grant . . . said . . . "

"Oh! Don't say anything. We can talk when we get there."

When we reach the main door to the building, Annette unlocks it and helps me up the steps. I have to stop halfway up to catch my breath, then again at the top. We finally get to my apartment. I'm shaking so hard I can't get the key out of my daypack.

"Let me get it," Annette says. Once we're inside, she helps me to the couch. "What can I do?"

"Just . . . give me a . . . minute."

She nods. "I'm going to get Kirstin, make sure she knows what's happening."

I give her a look. How could Kirstin not know? She had to hear everything.

Annette nods. "I'll be right back. I'm taking your key with me, okay?"

I lift one shoulder in response as she runs out the door. I reposition slightly, putting both feet flat on the floor, then lean forward and rest my elbows on my knees. I consciously lower my shoulders and attempt to relax my neck and shoulder muscles. I breathe in slowly through my nose—one Mississippi, two Mississippi. I pucker my lips and fully exhale through my mouth—one, two, three, four. I repeat the breathing process four additional times before there's a light tap on the door and the knob jiggles. Annette pops her head in. "It's us."

"Hurry!" Kirstin says. "Get inside."

Annette and Mason come in with Kirstin right behind them, holding Caleb. She shuts the door and sets the locks.

"Oh my gosh, Shelby. Are you okay?" She rushes over to me. "Are you breathing okay now?"

"I'm okay."

"Did you do pursed lip breathing? That always helps my brother."

I raise a hand and nod. Even though I'm better, I'm not up to having a full conversation.

"I can't believe what happened," Kirstin says with a sniff. "I'm just—it's so terrible. How was he even able to do that? Mason and I just stayed on the ground until the shooting and explosions stopped. Then we heard that awful Richard Majors. I . . . I went out on the balcony to try and see. I wish I wouldn't have."

"After I got into Kirstin's apartment, I looked over to the park also," Annette says, talking much louder and faster than I've ever heard her. "It's bad. So bad. I wanted to see how long until they'd be finished and Grant would be here. I think it'll go quickly. I'll go back and start packing things up. Okay?"

"We should be ready," Kirstin says. "We have the backpacks and diaper bags."

"I want to make sure we get all of the hidden food," Annette answers. "There's not much, but . . . " She shrugs.

"Good idea. I'll stay and make sure Shelby is okay." She gives me a wobbly smile as a gunshot rings out. I drop my head in my hands. Annette pulls Mason to the floor while Kirstin wraps herself around Caleb. We stay in our protective positions for several minutes, waiting for additional shooting. There's nothing more, just the single gunshot. I can't help but fear the worst. The one shot, could it have been used on Grant?

Kirstin sits up slightly and looks me directly in the eyes. "Do not worry. Grant will be back shortly." She reaches her hand out, motioning toward Annette, who scoots over by us. Each of them takes one of my hands. Kirstin bows her head and begins to fervently pray. While her tone washes over me, the words blend together. At her amen, I found myself repeating it. She gives my hand a squeeze.

"I'm going to go get the food packed," Annette says.

It's not long before Annette returns. It's past dark before there's a soft knock on the door. We added a hasp to the inside of the door and nestle a chair under the knob when I'm alone or we're both home. Annette jumps up and goes to the door.

"It's me," Grant says softly from the other side.

Once he's in the apartment, I'm shocked at his appearance. Blood and dirt cover clothes and bare skin. "Let me clean up," he says, walking toward the bathroom.

Annette, Kirstin, and I are completely silent while he's gone. Caleb and Mason, lying on a blanket on the floor, are playing with each other. Mason makes noises and Caleb tries to mimic.

After a few minutes, Grant returns clean and in fresh clothing. He sits on the easy chair, rubbing his hands over his face.

"How was Majors able to do this?" Kirstin asks. "I mean, how didn't we know?"

Grant shakes his head. "There were a few people asking this, too, while we were— " He clears his throat. "Someone said they'd seen a string of people in and out of Majors newspaper office but didn't think anything of it."

"I guess they wouldn't," Kirstin agrees with a nod. "I mean, who would've thought? Anyway, are we leaving? We should go."

"It was terrible." Grant shakes his head. "I've never . . . I can't believe they . . . "

"How many?" Annette asks softly.

"No way to really know. A hundred? Maybe more. The explosions" —he shakes his head again— "they were along the edge where the police and sheriff deputies were stationed. The ones who weren't killed in the explosion were shot. I didn't see any of them. I don't think any of our police force survived."

"What about the sheriff?" I ask. "He wasn't there, right?"

"I don't know where he is. I didn't see him before we started, but the explosions . . . " His voice trails off.

"So, we're leaving?" Kirstin asks again.

Grant leans back in the chair and stares up at the ceiling. I'm about to repeat Kirstin's question, when he says, "I don't think so. They're going to be extra alert tonight, waiting for people to sneak out."

"How many people are helping him?" Kirstin asks.

"Lots. I didn't see them all, but he had at least a hundred men watching us as we cleaned up the park. That Ellis from the basement shelter was one of them."

"Ellis?" Kirstin says, shock evident in her voice. "He's a—he said he's a Christian."

I smirk. "Figures."

"What's that supposed to mean?" Kirstin turns on me, voice full of venom.

I lift my hands slightly in a surrender manner. "Never mind."

She narrows her eyes at me, then abruptly turns her head.

"Did you see Harry? Harry English?" Annette asks, in a voice I interpret as she doesn't really want to know the answer.

"He wouldn't have joined Richard's group!" Kirstin cries out.

"That's not what I meant," Annette looks at the ground while answering.

"Oh," Kirstin whispers.

"He wasn't with us while we were—I didn't see him."

"What about— "

"I don't know. He wasn't one of the people—the bodies—I moved."

"We heard a shot," Kirstin says.

"Yeah. We all had to disarm, throw our weapons in the garbage cans just like the women did before leaving. Then we were frisked. One guy had a pocket pistol. They shot him right there."

"Who was it?" Kirstin asked.

With a combination shake and shrug, Grant looks at the ground.

"What will they do with the bodies?" I ask.

Grant bites his lip. "Burn them. They wanted to do it tonight, but they decided to wait until tomorrow. We took them to the hospital rubble. Several were told to go back tomorrow to take care of it."

"You?"

"Not me. So, let's do our best to get some sleep tonight. Go to your regular workplaces tomorrow. We'll see how things look to leave tomorrow night. Shelby, you should probably go to the daycare you've been assigned to as a backup. They'll be checking where everyone is and reassigning as they see fit. They made sure we knew that before we left. And I wouldn't be a bit surprised if they started the door-to-door searches tomorrow. I think he lied about waiting forty-eight hours."

"Will they have the food lines tomorrow?" Kirstin asks.

"He said they would. Show up like usual."

"They usually bring food to the daycare."

"I don't know. He made it sound like that wouldn't change tomorrow. Food line at ten in the morning and five in the evening."

"I always knew there was something off about Richard Majors," Kirstin says. "But this surprises me."

"Not me," Annette says. "He hated Mayor Stringer. You know that the election before last he ran against him, right?"

We all shake our heads.

Annette nods. "Yeah. The previous mayor retired, so there wasn't an incumbent. Richard thought he was a shoo in. He was wrong. Mayor Stringer won by a landslide. Richard thought he cheated. He couldn't accept the fact he isn't very well liked."

"That makes sense," I say.

"Really?" Kirstin snaps. "You think it makes sense that losing an election would result in a massacre?"

"Okay, we've had enough for tonight," Grant says calmly. "We're all distraught over this. Let's meet tomorrow night, and we'll decide what we're going to do."

"Oh," Annette says, even softer than she's been speaking, "I told Milena we had a plan and that we'd let her know."

Grant nods. "That's fine. Have her come here tomorrow night also. Let's say around seven o'clock."

"You think they'll let her?" I ask. "Will they allow us free movement?"

Annette and Kirstin both have a new, terrified look on their face. "They can't prevent that," Kirstin says.

I raise my eyebrows in response.

"Use your locks and the chair," Grant says to them while standing up. "If anyone tries to get in, use the escape hatch."

As soon as they're gone, Grant pulls me into a hug. "Your asthma is okay now?"

"I'm good. It was pretty bad for a while, but . . . " I shrug.

"How full is the inhaler?"

"Less than half. The one in the nightstand is almost full."

"Okay. And you have one in the duffle bag that hasn't been used at all. Will that be enough to last until the baby is born?"

Will it? And after he's born, will the asthma go away? I don't know. "It'll be fine. You don't think your parents heard the shooting and drove into town, do you? Or tomorrow when they start the— " I swallow hard. "When they burn the bodies."

"I've wondered. I don't think they'll just come driving into town. They'll be smart about it."

"So, they'll be safe?"

"Yeah. They'll be safe." Grant stands up. "I need to take care of something. I'll be right back."

"Where are you going? You can't leave. They'll— "

"I won't leave the building. You know the empty apartment down the hall?"

"The one where they found one of the murdered men?"

He nods. "I'm going to put some of our things in there."

"Why?"

"Because I don't trust those goons not to start their door-to-door search before they say they will. And I don't want them finding us with the shotgun and duffle bags." He starts rummaging through my duffle bag, taking out my inhaler and a few other items.

Goons. That seems like a very fitting name. "But they could go to the empty place too."

"They could. But they wouldn't know the stuff is ours." He holds up the inhaler, showing me my name on it. "Put it in your daypack."

"What about the handgun?"

"I think it's pretty well hidden. They'd really have to tear the bedroom apart to find it, and at that point . . . " His voice trails off. I get his meaning. At that point, we wouldn't be around when they did find it. We'd be dead.

Chapter 21

With our heads down, Kirstin, the boys, and I trudge to the daycare center. The slaughter led by Richard Majors left Grant and I awake until well after midnight. When I finally fell asleep, it was riddled with bad dreams. Kirstin said she barely slept too. She was so scared for her children, worried something might happen in the middle of the night.

Everyone in Prospect, of course, knows what happened last night. Tear-streaked faces pinched with fear—and sometimes anger—greet us. There's little chitchat as parents drop off their children, holding them close and whispering they'll be right back, giving an extra kiss and nuzzle before reluctantly releasing them and hustling off to their assignment. More than one gives a backward, longing glance with tear-filled eyes. No one needs a reminder of what will happen if they don't do what is expected of them or arrive late at their assignment. There are a few hurried comments of, "I always knew that Richard Majors was no good." But I also hear, "I had no idea. He was always such a nice man."

Kirstin says there are several children missing this morning. Did they go to a different daycare instead of this one nearest their home? Or were they casualties from last night? Grant didn't say anything about children dying.

This daycare center was set up in a room at City Hall. Not one of the basement rooms we sheltered in, but a main-floor room. It's close to the hospital where they're burning the bodies, causing several of the children to get sick. Many are babies and toddlers unable to tell us they aren't feeling well, so we can't even get them to the bathroom in time. Surrounded by the smell of the sickness and the atrocious smoke smell, I make many runs to the bathroom myself. I'm so thankful the toilets still flush.

At a quarter until ten, Kirstin says, "I'm going to see if people are lining up for food."

I swallow hard. "No way I can eat. And I'd be surprised if many of the children can."

"I know, but we need to try. We're not getting enough food as it is."

113

She's right. In the time since the EMP, I've noticed she's lost weight. Even though she only had a baby a few months ago, she's already lost most of the baby weight. A couple of days ago she mentioned she thought her milk supply was decreasing. Kirstin steps out of the room, returning several minutes later.

"Looks like it's fine. The line has started, and the table is being set up. So now we'll just have to wait and see if they bring our food over."

"What time has it been arriving?" I ask.

One of the other workers says, "Not long after ten. They have delivery people bring it to us, the other daycares, and some of the workers who can't get away. But for everyone else, they'll serve until one o'clock so people can take turns arriving."

"At least that's how it usually goes," Kirstin says.

Grant and I started getting meals a few weeks ago, so I've stood in line for brunch many times. I usually wait until the very end so I don't have to stand in line too long. By keeping some of my food from the day before, like bread or rolls, I can have something resembling breakfast.

In the evening, they start serving at five and finish around six thirty. It goes quicker since people aren't trying to stagger the meal around work. And I think less people eat in the evening. Grant said many of the parents have only been going to one meal most days, out of fear the food will run out and their kids will go hungry. There always seems to be fewer people there in the evening, except on town meeting nights. Last night they were still serving when the shooting started.

It's close to eleven before someone arrives with the daycare food. "What happened?" Kirstin asks one of the ladies carrying a soup pot. She has a black eye and a swollen nose.

"It's nothing." Her tone indicates she won't be continuing the conversation.

One of the other delivery people, an older teen, says, "Her husband hit her."

The bruised woman shoots a look at the girl.

"Well, he did," the girl says.

The group sets the food on a waiting table and then leaves the room. On her way out, the girl stops and says, "He shouldn't hit her. He's been doing it since the EMP, but today she looks worse than ever. He's going to— " She shakes her head. Her voice drops to a whisper. "She says it's just because he's stressed, and after last night he's

114

even more stressed, but I'm scared for her." She quickly leaves, closing the door behind her.

When the long day is finally nearing the end, two fully armed men wearing bandannas as masks arrive at the daycare. Kirstin and the other two workers visibly pale; I'm sure I do also. I focus on my breathing. What's with the masks? Are they hiding their identity or trying to look the part of a bandit?

"I want everyone's name, current address, and former occupation," the taller of the two says. "We'll start with you." He points at Kirstin.

After they get our information, the other man asks, "What about the kids? Should we get their info too?"

The tall one looks at him and says, "You think they know their addresses?"

"Oh. Good point. I guess not."

The tall one turns back to us. "There's a town meeting tonight. All citizens are expected to attend. The only exception is if you are a single parent and have children under the age of twelve, then you are excused."

"What's the meeting about?" one of the other ladies asks.

"What do you think it's about?" he sneers. "Did you happen to miss the announcement that things are going to be different around here?"

I arrive home about fifteen minutes before Grant. He stops by the apartment, then dashes out to take care of water for us and Kirstin. He was cautioned that there is a new limit of only five gallons at a time. With the limit, he returns quickly, giving us about an hour before the town meeting. The smell of the burning bodies has lessened slightly— either that or I've become accustomed to it. "Are we going to turn in our hidden food? Our guns?" I ask.

"I have no intention of turning in either. The handgun is still hidden, and I was able to move the larger duffle and the shotgun to a new cache."

"When did you do that?"

"During my lunch break. We were emptying a place near the Prospector Hotel. You know, that big house with the windows you like?"

I nod as Grant continues, "That one. The owners were both—you know—last night. One of the goons showed up this morning with a list of new places based on last night's murders. Anyway, I was near here and took the chance, but I didn't have time to move your duffle bag."

"Why would you take that chance? What if— "

"I know. It was probably dumb."

"Probably?" I can barely control my anger. "What were you thinking, Grant? You could have— "

"Yes, I'm sorry. I just want to make sure we have what we need to make our escape."

I bite my lip, trying to control my anger, my hurt. I take a deep breath and then slowly exhale. In a semi-normal voice, I say, "When do you think we'll leave?"

"I'm hoping we can leave tonight. We'll take what we can. Whatever's left, they can have when they get around to emptying our apartment."

"My duffle bag has a few snacks in it. Will we get in trouble?"

"They won't know it's ours, since it's still in the empty apartment."

"How will we know if we can leave tonight?"

"By how the meeting goes. I'm hoping we can get a good view of Richard Majors's— "

"Goons?"

"Yeah, I was thinking thugs, but goons fit."

"Do you know what the meeting will be about? Will they be killing people again?" I hear my voice cracking as I talk. I don't want to go to this meeting. I'm afraid. Afraid if the shooting starts again—if there are explosions—Grant will be killed. I will be killed. Our baby . . . I hold back a sob. Grant pulls me into his arms, holding me as I cry.

Finally, he says, "It's time to go. We'll have a few minutes to eat before the meeting starts."

Kirstin will be staying home with her boys. I feel a wave of envy that she can stay behind. She and Annette took turns going down to get their supper, both sharing their portion with the boys. Kirstin doesn't want them anywhere near Majors's people. Annette walks over to the park with us. On the way, she says she talked with Milena today. We'll meet her at the park, then form a plan for our getaway.

The meal service is just finishing up when we arrive. We're able to get in at the end of the line. The thin soup, ladled into bowls we brought, and bread hold little appeal. The crowd, usually talking and even occasionally laughing, is completely silent, the look of distraught and disbelief evident. Lucy, from our building, is in line ahead of us. I attempt a small smile, but she immediately drops her eyes.

Richard Majors's goon crew is standing along the edge of the crowd, not only men but a half dozen women also. Like the ones who visited the daycare today, all are wearing a bandanna, many are covering their faces but some are using it as a kerchief or headband.

I guess the bandanna is to differentiate them as being with Richard. Because without it—other than the fact they are the only ones armed now—they'd look just like the rest of us. They're dressed in a standard casual Wyoming look. All are wearing blue jeans, mainly Wranglers. Several are in button-up western shirts topped with a cowboy hat. Others wear ball caps and T-shirts. One is even sporting a shirt with a picture of a bison on it that says, *Do Not Pet the Cuddly Cows.* The shirt makes me think I may know that guy, someone who shopped regularly at SuperMart. Likely, if I'd lived here longer, I'd know more of these people. Grant probably does, but he hasn't said anything about it.

Last night, I asked him who all was with Richard Majors. He just shook his head and whispered there were too many. He did make a point of saying he didn't see Majors's wife last night. Is she part of the town takeover?

I'm able to eat about half of my soup; Grant finishes it for me. I stash my bread for breakfast.

"We'll be okay," Grant whispers, squeezing my hand.

Tears sting my eyes. I don't want to die. I don't want Grant to die, and I don't want our baby to die. These crazy men, they don't care about any of us. How does someone who was supposed to be a pillar of the community, a respected businessman, resort to this?

"Where's Milena?" Annette asks, looking around.

"I don't see her," Grant says. "Maybe she got held up?"

"She wouldn't be late. The guys who came around made it clear we had to show up on time. She said he spoke to her directly, by name."

"Why?" I ask.

Annette gives a slight lift of her shoulder, eyes darting, searching the crowd. She bites her lip and shakes her head. "I just know she wouldn't be late. I still haven't seen Harry English either. Do you see him anywhere?"

Grant positions us on the edge of the park, closest to our building. Where he'd usually put space between us and those nearby, this time he moves us in closer. We're still on the edge but not separate, as we usually are. None of us see Harry or Milena in the crowd.

"Can we stand back a little more?" I ask.

"Let's not. I'd rather we be more of the crowd than separate, in case . . . " He lifts a shoulder instead of finishing his thought.

I nod, understanding. In case they start shooting again, we won't be as easy to pick off.

The crowd is mainly silent. Occasionally a low whisper will carry across the breeze, but it's far different from the previous gatherings. Even the whispers stop when Richard Majors takes the stage.

As quiet as it is, I doubt he even needs the bullhorn. He uses it anyway. "Thank you all for coming tonight," Richard says with a smirk. "Tonight, we will begin the process of building a new, stronger town. The previous leadership, if you can even call it that, had us believing with a little hard work we'd be fine come winter. He lied to you. Today I found his pie charts, notes, and graphs showing more than half of you would die before spring." Majors pauses as the crowd reacts.

"Don't believe him," Grant whispers. "He's trying to scare everyone. Scared people are easier to control."

"It's working," I whisper, feeling the fear enveloping me. Not just my fear, the fear in those surrounding us.

Except Annette. She stands tall and strong. She takes my hand, her strength rushing into me. I stare at my hand, then look up to Annette. Eyes filled with tears, she attempts a small smile. She squeezes my hand, sending a rush of strength through my body.

"Now, friends," Richard says, "I'm not okay with that. I'm not okay with losing any of the fine citizens of Prospect. I've come up with a new, better plan to ensure our survival. Not just our survival but our ability to thrive. Come spring, instead of half of you being worm food, we'll be the beacon of the area. We'll be the place for everyone to congregate and seek refuge."

There's a light rumble through the crowd.

"He wants to bring in more people?" I ask in a whisper.

"Wait for it," Grant answers.

"For what?"

He lifts his chin toward Richard. "You'll see."

"I know, I know," Richard says. "Right now, that seems unwise. But the plans I have will allow us to use this calamity to our advantage. Through my leadership, I will keep you safe. I will not only keep you alive, I will allow you to prosper. In the next several days, there will be many changes—changes former mayor Stringer was too weak, too indecisive to make."

He looks around the crowd before saying again, "I will keep you safe."

There's a small smattering of applause. They're applauding the man who last night assassinated our mayor and murdered many more. I'm suddenly sick to my stomach. Grant wraps his arm around me. Annette, still holding my hand, gives it another squeeze.

While not overly enthusiastic, there's enough applause for Richard Majors to bask in it, smiling from the podium, allowing the ovation to continue until it dies off naturally.

"Thank you. Thank you. Tomorrow, we'll begin forming new working groups. We'll continue many of the things started, but we'll refocus to other areas. The dusk-to-dawn curfew remains in effect, with the additional caveat that you must be in your home unless you are on a designated work crew or approved assignment."

A collective gasp passes through the crowd, but Majors ignores it. "Tomorrow, show up at your regular workstation. At that time, you may be reassigned. Within the next few days, you'll be given new identification, which you'll be required to keep on you at all times. You will need to bring your state-issued driver's license with you. The new identification will be based off the old ID."

"What if we don't have a driver's license?" someone near the front asks.

"Then bring your state-issued ID, work badge, or student card. You need to bring something with a photo. Everyone ages twelve and over will receive a new identification card. If you do not have anything that will work, you need to bring a current photograph."

"Twelve and over?" a lady near us mutters.

"Now," Majors continues, "it brings me no pleasure to tell you that my good friend Sheriff Spieth was caught sneaking out of Prospect last night. It seems he heard the commotion, and instead of coming to the aid of *you*, those who entrusted him to provide for their safety, he tried to run away like a coward."

"I don't believe it," Grant whispers, his mouth right next to my ear.

I shake my head in response.

"Thankfully, my men apprehended him," Majors says with a smile. "He is currently awaiting a speedy trial in his own jail, along with several others who are known instigators."

Annette leans into me and repeats, "Instigators?"

Grant leans across me. "You know, people who he deems troublemakers. Those who might disagree with him would be my guess."

"Milena," Annette says, tears filling her eyes. "She'd fit that criteria."

My eyes tear up as well, as I give a slight nod. While I haven't seen her interact with Richard Majors, I know there's bad blood between them.

"The trial for our shamed sheriff will be held tomorrow evening," Majors says. "Once the verdict is decided, justice will be swift."

"A jury trial?" someone bravely asks.

"Trial by judge. And I'm the judge."

A murmur runs through the crowd as Majors runs his eyes across the group, making direct contact with as many as possible.

"Creepy," the lady near us who was concerned about the kids needing ID cards says. She must have been a little too loud because one of the goons is instantly on her. She screams as he yanks her arm and starts dragging her to the edge of the crowd. A second bad guy is there immediately, grabbing her by the other arm. "No! No!" she cries out. "I didn't mean anything. Please!"

I look back to Richard Majors as he says, "Ah, I guess we need to have another lesson."

"Get on your knees," one of the goons says.

I look back toward the lady.

Grant grabs me and pulls me into him. "Don't look, Shelby."

She screams, "No! No!" Then a shot reverberates through the park. I feel my chest tightening. They shot her. They shot her for commenting.

"Okay, folks," Majors says calmly over the bullhorn. "I really thought we had enough examples last night. And that's too bad. I think that was Mandi. Shame. She went to school with my daughter. Boys, you make sure to treat her right, now. When you take her to the fire, carry her gently. Be respectful."

"Yes, boss," one of them responds.

"Well, friends, I guess that's enough for tonight. Show up on time to your workstations tomorrow, bring your identification, and be prepared for your new work assignments. We'll meet again tomorrow night. Same time, same rules of required attendance."

The three of us don't speak as we quickly leave the park. When we reach our building, Grant holds the door open for several others, motioning us to wait. Once they are in, he whispers, "Go to Kirstin's place. I'll be there shortly."

Annette and I practically run up the stairs, then hurriedly knock on Kirstin's door. Even though Annette has a key, with a chair under the knob, we need to be let in. There are a few moments of rustling, then a hesitant, "Annette?"

"Shelby too," I say. "Grant's on his way."

"I heard a shot," Kirstin says as she opens the door.

I take a quick look for Grant. Not seeing him, I close the door and Annette fixes the locks and puts the chair back into place.

"The shot?" Kirstin asks.

I drop my head and give a small shake.

"I went to school with her," Annette says.

"Her?"

"Mandi . . . I can't remember her last name," I say. "She muttered under her breath a few times. I guess they heard her. Richard Majors said to make an example out of her."

"Not an example," Annette says. "A lesson."

"Is there a difference?" I ask in a less-than-kind tone.

Annette glances toward the balcony. She screws up her face, starts to speak, gives a shrug, then says, "I'm not sure. But it feels like there is. Like he's trying to teach us, not just show us. I'm not sure I can explain it."

I shrug. "Okay, I guess I can see that."

Annette reaches for Kirstin's hand. "Milena wasn't there tonight."

"She wasn't? I thought it was mandatory?"

"It was. One of Richard Majors's people— "

"Goons," I interrupt.

Annette nods. "Okay. One of them made sure to tell her she had to be there tonight."

"Right. You told me earlier how they made a point of that. So why wasn't she there?"

"Majors said they arrested the sheriff trying to leave town and are holding other people they deem a threat."

"What? They can't do that."

"They did," I say. "And there's going to be a trial tomorrow night. With Majors as judge and jury."

Kirstin closes her eyes. Annette gives Kirstin a few more details of the meeting.

When there's a lull in the conversation, I ask, "Are both boys in bed? Are you guys ready to leave?"

"Are we going?" she asks with an excited lilt to her voice. Or maybe it's a scared tone. It's hard to tell. "We shouldn't leave without Milena."

Before I can answer, there's a slight scratching at the door and Grant's very low voice. "It's me."

I start to move to let him in, when Annette says, "Let me."

He's barely in when Kirstin asks, "What's the plan?"

"I don't think we should go tonight. They're still too hyped up. Too vigilant. Maybe tomorrow, or in a few days, they'll start to let their guard down."

Kirstin drops her head. "We need to find Milena before we go. We need to take her with us."

Grant nods, his mouth in a grim line.

"I think they got her," Annette says. "Don't you think?"

"Seems likely," Grant says.

"What can we do?" Annette asks.

Grant shakes his head. "I don't know. If they have her at the county jail, it'll be hard to get her out."

"Why are so many people helping him?" Annette asks. "I saw people I know wearing those masks—not just Ellis tonight, but others. Even a lady who was a friend of my sister's was part of Majors's goon group."

"My guess is it won't be long until Majors has most of the town behind him. He used some interesting phrases tonight. Last night, too, but I didn't catch those as much."

"What do you mean?"

Grant shakes his head. "He just reminded me of a guy I used to know. A former professor who was always going on about things. He especially spent a lot of time talking about Hitler, Stalin, and more. Some of the things Majors said reminds me of the phrases the professor used. And Stalin did these 'Show Trials' to prove he was treating the accused properly. Of course, I think most—if not all—the people on trial were found guilty and then executed. I'll be honest, I didn't pay a lot of attention to his ramblings at the time. Kind of wish I would have now."

"Well, you can bet Richard Majors has a plan," Annette says in a much stronger voice than she usually uses. "He's always scheming something. My parents never liked him."

"And your grandpa doesn't like him either," I say to Grant.

"Right."

"So . . ." I pause a moment while I think about what I want to ask. Grant raises his eyebrows at me. I shrug and say, "I'm just wondering, do you think Majors knows your grandpa doesn't like him?"

"I have no doubt," Grant scoffs. "They have a long and sordid history. Why?"

"I guess I was just wondering, if he did grab Milena— "

"I'm sure he did," Annette interjects.

I nod. "I agree. So if he's grabbing people he doesn't like— "

"Will he go after my grandpa?" Grant asks, eyes widening.

I tilt my head in response.

"Not yet," Annette says. "He'll be too busy with the town. He'll get Prospect set up the way he wants it first. Then he'll work his way out."

"I agree," says Kirstin. "I think what you guys said about him making us a hub or whatever is very telling of his intentions. But he'll need the manpower to back him up. He'll win over Prospect first, then start taking over the ranches and surrounding communities. We've all heard the town of Wesley has had some troubles with that apartment complex being taken over and the sheriff's deputy executed. My guess is they'd welcome Richard Majors with open arms."

Grant nods. "I think Kirstin's right. Mayor Stringer was doing fine. But his way of leading was not as— "

"Murderous?" I say.

"Yeah, that. Plus, he wanted everyone to *want* to help. He wanted them to feel a part of the team. And Majors . . . " He pauses a moment.

123

"I don't know. It was just so odd how people cheered him tonight. He's offering safety, I guess."

"He's offering the illusion of safety," Annette says. "And you know how he said to treat the woman he'd just had executed with respect? That was calculated."

"Absolutely," Grant says. "So, let's see what tomorrow brings. Kirstin, it sounds like you're still excused. Maybe we'll be able to tell if they're starting to get comfortable. If they are, we'll leave tomorrow night."

Chapter 22

After a second night of little sleep, getting out of bed is a challenge. As I sit up, I'm lightheaded and dizzy. It didn't help that a thunderstorm came up in the middle of the night. With the wind howling and the thunder cracking, along with worrying about everything going on, I barely slept.

I'm running so late by the time I finally drag myself out that I barely have time to do my makeup. As I'm in the middle of it, I wonder why I'm even bothering. I've seen very few others wearing any cosmetics. Few take any time with their appearance at all, many not even using a hairbrush. Several of the daycare children have the beginnings of dreadlocks.

Maybe I should take a wide-tooth comb and a pair of scissors with me today? I'll even talk to Kirstin about the possibility of bathing some of the children.

Even with the added work of hauling water, Grant and I still take a daily sponge bath. Now that Majors has instituted a five gallon a day limit, I'm not sure we'll be able to continue doing this each day, but we'll do our best. Many people have given up on personal hygiene. I'm concerned about what this could mean in the coming days. Will we be more susceptible to illness?

When Grant and I first met, and he told me about his interesting living situation, we had a big talk about cleanliness. While it's widely believed all transients are nothing more than dirty bums, Grant said that's not entirely true. Sure, there are many who don't put cleanliness at the top of their list because of mental health issues and their living situation. And they are, unfortunately, highly likely to contract and spread communicable diseases.

While Grant would have been considered homeless by the strictest standards, he wasn't living in the homeless camps. He was a subset of homelessness by choice, allowing him the freedom to pursue his passions. He spent time surfing, hiking, rock climbing, and more. He traveled across the country, picking up odd jobs and doing temp work to fund his next move. While he made a point of continuing with regular bathing and such, he also came to believe an overly sanitized environment could be dangerous.

"A healthy immune system needs bacteria," he once told me when I pulled a small bottle of hand sanitizer out of my purse. "Germs are important for your immune system."

Maybe so. But filth is taking it a little too far. Of course, does it really matter? With Richard Majors in charge of the town, we're all at his mercy. He's proven he has no problem with executing those who offer any resistance. The lady last night was only making comments.

Kirstin looks about as bad as I do, but her boys are their usual jubilant selves. She's done well at protecting them from the horror of our lives. It was bad enough after the attacks and the EMP, but we were starting to get things together. We had a chance with Mayor Stringer. What about my baby? When he's born, will he have a chance? Will Richard Majors keep the hospital running?

"What are they doing?" Kirstin asks, pointing to a couple of Majors's goons.

"Looks like they are going to build something," I say. "Right now, they're just stacking the lumber . . . maybe something on the stage? To make Majors higher?"

"Higher? Oh, like elevate him?"

I shrug. "Maybe?"

"Why? The stage is already elevated fine. Nah. This is something else."

"I don't know. And I'm not really sure I want to find out." I drop my voice to a whisper. "I don't think he has our best interests at heart."

"No kidding."

Shortly after all our children arrive, Majors's goons show up to tell us we're all permanently assigned to the daycare and the work schedule has now changed to seven days a week. And beginning tomorrow, we'll start at six am and end at six pm. Also starting tomorrow, we'll have the ten am and six pm meal service with an eight pm daily update meeting. Kirstin, along with other single parents of very young children, is still excused. A wave of jealousy shoots through me. I'd love to be excused from the meetings.

Throughout the morning, I manage to work the knots out of the hair of several little girls. Midafternoon, I ask Kirstin what she thinks about me trying to figure out a way to clean the children up better.

"I'm not sure. The parents would need to be okay with it. I know it's just a water issue. It's hard for me to keep Mason and Caleb clean too. If it wasn't for Annette helping and Grant getting water for me so often . . . " She shrugs. "If you can figure something out, we could ask. Or maybe we just use the bathroom here? Get a little tub and call it good."

"That's not a bad idea. Grant and I have plastic dish tubs we use for dishes. But if we could have a bathtub or shower, it would make things easier. Maybe Annette would let us use her camp shower? I'm going to check the building. Maybe there's a full bath, like in a private office or something."

"Where will you get the water? We only have enough delivered for drinking. Even before Majors took over."

"Good point. I'll figure something out. Be back in a few," I say, taking my flashlight keychain out of my purse.

"Shelby."

"Yeah?"

"Be careful. They made a point of saying we had to be at our workstations."

"I'll be okay," I say with a small smile, even though she does have a point. Maybe I should just stay here, not worry about this.

Kirstin raises her eyebrows at me. "Okay, if you're sure."

I straighten my shoulders. "Yep. Be right back."

The soles of my hiking boots echo through the hallway. I start with the room next door, the Prospector County Clerk's office. Grant and I got our marriage license here. The lock on the door has been broken, and the inside is in complete disarray. A quick look around tells me there aren't any private offices with a bathroom. Just down the hall, the men's and women's public restrooms are as expected. Toilets and sinks, but no shower. I check each office on the main floor before making my way upstairs.

While there's a couple of larger offices, such as the county planning and zoning office, most are smaller individual ones, including Mayor Stringer's office. He had a reception area and then his private space. No bathroom. He must have used the second-floor public bathroom. After determining the upstairs is a bust, I go back to the main level and find one of the staircases to the basement—the same one we used when sheltering.

At the staircase, I flip on my small flashlight. I wish I would've thought of this when I was home, then I could've grabbed a more substantial light. Even though it only puts out a thin beam of light, at least it's bright. The smell of the basement still holds the sweaty stench from those of us who sheltered here in those few days after the EMP.

The first room looks identical to the one Grant and I stayed in, except the bathroom—a sink and toilet only—is on the opposite side. Three more rooms yield the same results. I don't bother checking the room we stayed in; I'm way too familiar with it to know it doesn't have what I'm looking for.

At the very back of the L-shaped basement is a locked door. I try to remember if anyone was staying in this room when we were sheltering. I don't think so, and I have no idea what this room might be like. I bet if Grant were here, he'd be able to get this door open. Oh well. What are the chances there'd be a shower in the one room I can't access? Slim. There's a skinny door on the opposite wall. I try it—also locked. Based on the size of the door, it's probably a closet or storage room anyway.

Even though the closet door is obviously locked, I give the handle a rattle.

"Okay, Shelby, I guess that's it," I say aloud. I can't help but giggle over the fact I'm talking to myself. "Good one." Does talking out loud mean I'm losing it? "Only if you start answering yourself," I mutter, then giggle again.

I freeze mid-giggle when I hear a rustling from the other side of the door. I take off running. When I'm almost to the corner, I hear, "Shelby, stop! Wait a minute."

Looking back, I skid into the corner. I lose my footing and slide to the ground, landing on my hip. *Oomph.* I can feel my chest start to constrict as I struggle to get my feet underneath me.

"Shelby! Are you okay?"

From my hands and knees, I give a hurried look. "Harry English?"

"Are you okay?" he asks again, rushing toward me. "Did you hurt yourself? Your baby?"

"I—I'm fine. I think." I move to my knees. Feeling my throat tighten, I readjust so I'm on my bottom. "Give—just give me a minute."

He waits expectedly as I work on regaining my breath.

"What can I do?" he asks.

I shake my head and hold up a finger as I continue with my pursed lip breathing. I left my daypack behind; it's hanging off a hook in the daycare room. Not smart. My face is starting to tingle, and I consider asking if he could go for my inhaler. He puts his hand on my shoulder.

"Father, God, touch this child. Fill her with Your healing breath. Take the pain and fright away, allowing her to breathe easily, to breathe in Your blessings. Fill her with comfort. I bring Shelby before You to ask for Your healing touch and to keep her baby safe. I pray these things in Your powerful name, amen."

I stare at him, eyes wide, as I feel my chest loosen. The heaviness lifts.

Harry gives me a smile and a nod. "Better?"

"Better," I whisper. "What—why? I don't understand."

"The power of prayer, Shelby. And the power of God. Ask and ye shall receive."

"You know that I don't— "

"Don't believe all that mumbo jumbo? Sure. But I do, and I prayed for your healing. Looks like it might have worked," he says with a wink.

"Y—yes, I think it did."

"Do you have any pain from your fall?"

"No . . . mmm." I move slightly, feeling a twinge. "My hip, but it's okay. I'm okay. What are you doing here, Harry? You scared the life out of me!"

A look of grief passes his face, followed quickly by embarrassment. "Hiding." He shrugs. "Here, let me help you up."

"We thought you might be among the dead," I say once I'm on my feet.

"You sure you're okay?"

I answer with a nod.

"I should be dead," he says. "I was working on a spreadsheet up in my office instead of attending the meeting. I heard the shots and then the explosion. I could see the craziness from my office. I saw Mayor Stringer laying there. I should've tried to help, but instead I've been hiding."

"Didn't they look for you? They said they were rounding up people."

"They did, that first night. I was in the tunnel."

"The tunnel to the Annex Building?

"You know about that?"

"Not really. Grant's grandpa told us. So, you're just staying down here? Hiding out?"

He shrugs. "I wasn't planning that. I thought maybe we could get a resistance together." He raises his fist in the air and says, "Wolverines!"

I blink my eyes and shake my head. "I don't know what that means."

"Oh? Yeah, I guess you're too young. You didn't even see the remake?"

I lift my hands in a questioning motion.

"Never mind." He shakes his head. "What are you doing down here, anyway?"

"Looking for a shower."

"A shower? In an office building?"

"I thought maybe there was an executive office."

"Um, no. We're not that kind of town."

"I'm helping with the daycare. Some of the children need a bath. And I don't know about your resistance or Wolverine group. Last night— "

"I saw. I was watching from my second-floor office. He started the brainwashing. There won't be many people that don't go along with him, but I did see a few who didn't look convinced."

I nod. "It was so crazy when they applauded. After he'd killed so many the night before . . . "

"He offered them the idea of a better life, one in which they do not have to toil to survive."

"But he killed our mayor! And at least a hundred other people."

"Right. He instilled fear. Which makes people do crazy things." Harry shakes his head. "Then he gave them hope. They can't look at it logically. Plus, critical thinking has gone out the window. We've been spoon fed information for so long that people have forgotten how to think on their own. Our leaders at every level and the so-called celebrities are our brains now."

"Um, okay. I'd better get back. Do you need anything?"

"Resistance fighters."

I give a sad chuckle. "Can I talk to Grant? He might know if there are others like you."

"Aren't you like me? I think you are, Shelby. I can tell you aren't going along with Richard Majors. I knew from the day we met you have a mind of your own."

"No. Not me." I shake my head, but he gives me a look. I rush on, "I'm not a fighter. I'm going to have a baby."

"Exactly."

"No," I say, raising my hand like a stop sign. "I'll talk to Grant. I'll come back tomorrow if I can and tell you what he says. But we're leaving. We're going someplace safe."

"To his family ranch? It won't be safe. Not for long, anyway. You heard Richard talking about making Prospect a hub. He's planning on taking over the entire region. He'll take your family farm."

I can feel the blood drain from my face.

Harry's face softens. "I know Richard Majors. I know the kind of— " he hesitates a moment, then spits out "—*man* he is, if you can call him that. And he picked some of the biggest lowlifes around to help him. A few of them would sell their own mothers."

"We can't help you," I say, much firmer than I intended.

"I understand. If you can bring me news, that will help."

"We might leave tonight. If we don't, I'll come back. Should I knock on the closet door?"

"The closet door?"

"The little door you came out of."

"Oh, I guess it does look like a closet. I'll hear you when you come down one of the main staircases. Just say your name. I'll come out. Or you can use the outside basement entrance. It's locked, but I hid a key."

"You hid a key?"

"Yes, in the birdbath. Under the rock in the center."

"In the little garden? Near the front door?"

"Yes."

"That's not even near the basement entrance."

"It's not, but the key works for all the doors. As far as I know, none of the others are locked."

"Don't you think Majors might find it suspicious the basement door is locked but none of the others are."

"Yes, he might. That's okay. I half hope he'll send someone down here to investigate."

"Why?"

131

He shrugs.

"Okay." I turn to leave.

"Shelby?"

"Yes?" I ask, turning to face him.

"I'm praying for you. For all of us."

I nod. "Do you think that will help?"

"I know it will. You've experienced the power of prayer." He turns and starts walking down the hallway.

Chapter 23

"You could stay home tonight," Grant says, rubbing his hand up my arm.

"What if they notice I'm not there?"

"I can't imagine they would."

"What do you think happened today? With Harry? I mean, it's crazy to think . . . "

"What do *you* think happened?"

"Well . . . " I chew on my lip, trying to come up with something. "I think it's probably what my doctor said could happen. He said the asthma could leave again, that it's common to not have symptoms in the second trimester."

"Even when you were feeling an attack come on?"

"C'mon, Grant! You can't honestly think—you don't really believe *prayer* can stop an asthma attack?"

He lifts one shoulder. "Did I tell you about Vegas? About the guy we called The Preacher?"

"I suppose he healed people with prayer too?" I snark.

Grant shrugs. "If you don't want to hear about him, I don't have to tell you. I'm completely okay with you rationalizing what happened today any way you want to." He drops a light kiss on my forehead. "I need to go."

"Fine," I huff. "He healed me with prayer, are you happy now?"

He shakes his head. "See you soon."

"No. Wait. I'm coming with you," I say, hefting myself off the couch.

"You're feeling okay? Your hip doesn't hurt too much?"

I paste on a smile. He can think what he wants, but prayer . . . really? "Just a little. I was surprised to see the giant bruise."

"I'm surprised you didn't have a full-blown asthma attack from him scaring you like that."

"I was having one, at least it seemed like it was starting. But he stopped it."

"Well, good thing he did since you didn't have your inhaler on you. You need to— "

"I know, Grant. I shouldn't have left my daypack behind. I'll do better."

"You need— "

"Grant, enough. Honestly, I'm a total mess right now and don't need you reminding me of the things I've done wrong."

A look of hurt clouds his face. "I'm sorry, Shelb. I didn't mean to scold."

"Fine, then don't. Let's just go."

Even though we often walk over with Annette, tonight she's meeting us at the park. She wants to find Milena before the meeting. We step out of our building and look toward the park. I stop abruptly.

"Grant," I gasp. "The building project they were working on, is it— "

"I think it is," he whispers.

"What do you call that?"

"Gallows."

"For the sheriff?"

He gives a combination shrug and nod. "You sure you don't want to stay here?"

I'm reconsidering attending when I notice one of the goons staring in our direction. "I'd better not." I motion toward the goon with my chin. "Let's just go. He said there would be a trial, right? Maybe he'll be found not guilty."

"I'd be surprised."

Tears sting my eyes as we start walking. I should've stayed in the apartment. Watching them hang the sheriff is not something I want to witness. When we reach the growing crowd, it's obvious our concern over the gallows is well shared.

Annette lifts a hand in acknowledgment, her red-rimmed eyes meeting mine.

"You found her?" I ask.

"He has her," she answers in a hiss.

"Majors?"

"Who else? He's putting her on trial too. But the rumor I hear is he's holding the trials in private. Those found guilty . . . " She motions to the newly constructed gallows.

We wait only a few minutes before Majors arrives on the stage.

Annette sucks in a deep breath when she sees Sheriff Spieth, Milena, and half a dozen others—one of them another woman—all bound with their hands in front of them, being led to the stage.

"Oh no," I whisper.

"Shh," Grant cautions.

"Good to see all of you fine citizens tonight," Majors says, wearing a very large and totally inappropriate smile. "We've made some excellent changes today. While several of you will remain in your previous assignments, we've managed to lighten overstaffed areas."

I glance at Grant. Like me, he's still in his previous job. His group of salvagers has been deemed important, an essential position. So much so, people from less important groups were added. The garden and nursery group is one area decreased, apparently finding food is more important than growing food.

"You should give yourselves a round of applause," Majors says, clapping his hands with the bullhorn clanking awkwardly.

An unenthusiastic ovation follows. To keep up appearances, and avoid being singled out as rabble-rousers, the three of us clap cautiously.

"Okay, then," Majors says. "Let's get to the main event."

The crowd lets out a collective gasp as one of the prisoners struggles against his captor.

"Well, it seems we have a perfect place to start. Let's bring Mr. Peter Garvey up here. And how about Bill Vanderberg too."

Peter Garvey continues to struggle as he's pulled to the stage. Bill Vanderberg, on the other hand, doesn't fight or resist. When his captor puts a hand on his shoulder, he shrugs it off. Even from a distance, it's obvious he's been beaten. He has a black eye and red bulbous nose. My eyes dart to Milena. Unlike Bill, her face looks fine. She stands tall and straight, eyes forward, with a small smile and an almost serene look on her face.

"For those of you who don't know," Majors says, "Peter and Bill are both known agitators. In fact, every person up here has a history of causing trouble. Except for your former sheriff, but I'm getting ahead of myself." He pauses a moment as one of his masked goons walks over and whispers something to him.

Majors nods. "You know, my associate just suggested we do this a little bit differently. He's right. Let's get down to brass tacks." He visibly straightens. With a smirk he says, "I, Richard Majors, as the

135

current mayor of Prospect, have held a fair trial for these eight persons. As such, I am now ready to pronounce judgment. Peter Garvey, you have been found guilty. Bill Vanderberg, guilty— "

"You can't do this!" a man yells out from the middle of the crowd. "You can't just decide they're guilty without due process."

"Ah . . . is that you, Jude Poppe? I half wondered if we'd be hearing from the esteemed counselor. You see, Jude, and everyone else in the crowd who may have a similar thought of *due process*" — he makes those annoying air quotes— "the town of Prospect is now outside of the Constitution. When the former mayor decided killing off half of you was acceptable and allowed, based on his interpretation of Constitutional rights, I stepped in. I knew your lives were not expendable. The Constitution says you should have equal protection, not only protection for the chosen few, those the mayor deemed worthy. But the truth is, Jude, the Constitution has no bearing on our life today. It was written in a different time."

A slight rumble goes through the crowd and Majors raises his voice, "And, as such, it's been thoroughly watered-down over the years to resemble something substantially different than intended. Due process stopped mattering when your fear found you applauding the Patriot Act and other similar things. So yes, Jude. Yes, I can pass judgment on them."

He pauses and bores his eyes directly into the center of the crowd, probably searching out Jude Poppe to stare him down.

After several beats, Majors continues, "In the next few days, I will be presenting new documents specifically for our town and region to get us through this time. This charter will outline the steps necessary for us to survive this time of hardship. With my leadership, I will take you all through this and out the other side. We will be strong. We will be resilient. Prospect will no longer be the ugly stepsister to Cody. We'll be the trading center and hub of our region."

He pauses, expecting applause. When none is forthcoming, the goon on stage begins to clap. A few in the crowd join in as the goon makes motions with his arms in encouragement.

Grant gives a lackluster response. "Clap, ladies," he says out the side of his mouth. Soon the applause goes through the crowd like a wave.

"Thank you, thank you. Now, let's get back to business." Majors's gaze travels over Peter, then Bill, and on to the rest of the prisoners— appearing to rest on Milena. He gives a nod. "With the power vested in me, I have found these eight before me guilty of crimes against not only the City of Prospect but also its fine citizens. Their form of insubordination will not be tolerated. We're all in this together and must act as one. As such, these eight are sentenced to death by hanging."

"No. Please, God, no," Annette whispers, as Peter Garvey and the other lady in the group scream and thrash. Milena seems to stand even taller. She throws back her shoulders and sings out, "*My country 'tis of thee, sweet land of liberty . . .* "

Bill Vanderberg, Sheriff Spieth, and a couple of the other prisoners join in.

"Oh, now, isn't that sweet," Majors says, speaking over their singing. "Could someone shut them up?"

Bill's jailer punches him in the face. Milena and the others sing louder, as several people from the crowd join in. Annette raises her voice above them all, garnering a look from a nearby female goon. I make eye contact with the goon; she quickly looks to the ground. Even with her mask-covered face and a baseball cap pulled low, I'm almost positive it's Lucy from my building that sheltered with us in the City Hall basement. She goes back to staring at the ruckus on the stage as the crowd erupts, singing loud and strong.

I open my mouth to join in as Richard Majors unholsters his sidearm. He takes a loose aim then shoots Bill Vanderberg. A few people in the crowd scream and move away, while the bulk of the crowd presses forward, singing even louder. Majors adjusts his aim. I watch as his arm lifts slightly from the recoil and the goon holding Milena falls to the ground. I stifle a scream as she also falls. Simultaneously, Sheriff Spieth slams into his jailer, knocking him over. Then everything falls apart.

Once again, I'm on the ground with Grant protecting me. Annette scoots against me from the other side, the two of them pressing against me and my baby. My throat tightens and my chest starts to constrict. *No. Please, not now. Please, God, please help me.*

The singing is now silenced, but the shooting and screaming continues. I put my lips together, working on my breathing. *Please, please.* A feeling of warmth washes over me. My throat and chest begin to relax. I take an unlabored breath. The asthma attack is gone as quickly as it started.

Through the bullhorn, Majors yells, "*Stop moving!* If you move, you will be shot. And stop the screaming, you bunch of ninnies."

The screaming dies down, replaced with sobbing and sniffles.

"Now, I'm disappointed that we had to have another lesson this evening. I thought we had an agreement. I thought you all realized following the rules would keep you safe. Disobedience has consequences. Look around. When you do not obey, the result is death. It's a hard lesson, but in this new world, it's necessary." He pauses a moment, then turns to one of his goons. "There's one over by you writhing on the ground. We won't be wasting resources on him."

A single shot rings out as the goon ends the injured man's life. I lift my head, hazarding a glance toward Majors and his bullhorn.

"And your sheriff has once again proven his lack of concern for you. In the melee, he once again turned tail and ran. Not to worry. We'll find him and bring him to justice. Let me make it abundantly clear, the former sheriff is a fugitive. So are the three criminals he took with him. Anyone found harboring a fugitive will be immediately dealt with."

"Milena?" Annette whispers. "Do you think she got away?"

I shake my head. "I don't know. Maybe."

"I'm sure she did. Praise the Lord," Annette replies.

"If you're on the salvage crew, you will stay and clean up this mess. The rest of you, get to your homes. We'll round up the fugitives and complete this process tomorrow night."

Chapter 24

Annette paces from the windows to the balcony in Kirstin's apartment. "She might be okay, right? They won't find her."

"Maybe," Kirstin says. "I pray so. But Richard Majors doesn't give up easily."

I know Annette thinks Milena was one of the prisoners who got away, but I'm not sure. I saw her fall. Did she fall because she was shot? We've only been back at Kirstin's place for twenty minutes or so when Grant knocks on the door. Once he's inside and has relocked the door—including putting a chair under the handle—he says, "We're leaving tonight."

"Let's go," I say, standing up from the couch. Annette nods her agreement.

"Wait," Kirstin says. "Is it safe?"

"It's no longer safe to stay here," Grant says. "They're completely unhinged. And I think now is the time with them looking for the sheriff and Milena."

"She got away?" Annette asks, tears filling her eyes.

"Oh yeah, and they're furious."

Annette smiles. "Wouldn't leaving tonight be dangerous? If they're looking for them?"

"It would, except I overheard their plans."

"Really?" I exclaim.

"Majors is having the bulk of his crew— "

"Goons," I interrupt.

He raises his eyebrows at me. "They're going to the sheriff's place on the east edge of town. They seem to think he'll go there for supplies. Several goons are also going to Milena's and the other escapees' homes. He's leaving a skeleton crew to patrol and monitor the rest of us. One of his guys, the one that was on the stage with him— "

"It's his son," Annette says.

"What?"

"His son, Scott. I'm almost positive he was the one on stage with him."

"Is his daughter part of the goon squad too?" I ask.

"Uh, no. She died a few years ago. Why are you asking about her?"

"I didn't know she died," I say. "But when they executed the lady— "

"Oh, right! He said she went to school with his daughter. Yes, Mandi and his daughter Shelly were a few years behind me. Scott is my age. Did you know them, Grant?

"No, I don't think so."

"I guess you wouldn't. You were probably still in middle school the year Shelly graduated. Anyway. Scott. I'm sure it was his son, Scott. What I'm not sure of is where Richard's wife is? I've looked for her at the last two meetings, but she wasn't there."

"Probably told her to stay home where it's safe," Kirstin huffs.

"Maybe," Annette says.

"That would make sense," Grant agrees. "And I think you're right about it being his son. He—Scott—said after the last few nights, and all of the killing, that people would be too scared to cause any trouble."

"What about the singing?" I ask.

"Scott was concerned about that at first, but Majors thinks it was only a few that got everyone else riled up. They both say once the sheriff is dead there won't be any issues. Tonight is the night. We need to go."

"I'm going to stay here," Annette says, barely audible.

"You can't," Kirstin answers. "It's not safe."

"Milena— "

"She's going to be fine," Grant says. "The sheriff won't get caught this time. And if she's with him . . . " He ends with a shrug.

"What about— " I raise my eyebrows at Grant, encouraging him to read my mind.

"Yeah. I've been thinking about that."

"What?" Kirstin asks. "What's going on?"

"There's, uh— "

"There's talk of a resistance," Grant interrupts, touching my hand lightly.

"Good. I want in," Annette says with more strength and fervor in her voice than ever before. "You guys go on to the ranch. I'm going to stay and fight."

"I've got a better idea," Grant says. "Let's go to my folks' place." Annette starts to say something, but Grant slightly raises his hand.

"We'll regroup, make sure Shelby and the boys are safe, and then come up with a plan to help."

Annette shakes her head.

"I think it's a good idea," Kirstin says. "Besides, Annette, I'll need your help getting the boys there. I don't think we can do it without you."

"Who's in the resistance?" Annette asks.

Grant shakes his head. "As far as we know, it's one person with an idea."

Annette's face falls. "One person."

"Right."

"Can we talk to him . . . or her?"

"Can we, Grant?" I ask.

"Well, we might. But let's get ready to go. It'll be dark soon, and I want to leave just before the sun sets. I think that will give us the best cover, and Majors ordered his people to not even think about heading back until it was too dark for them to see."

"So, we'll leave while it's still twilight?" Kirstin asks. "Won't they see us?"

"Maybe. But people are sometimes still out then, hustling back to their homes. We might not be noticed, or at least not be considered out of the ordinary."

"But if we're carrying our bags— "

"Take only your daypacks. Kirstin, you can take the diaper bag too. We need to look . . . normal. You guys get ready. I need to run an errand. I'll be right back."

"Where are you going?" I ask, a feeling of panic washing over me.

"I want to check something," he says with a small smile. "It's fine. C'mon. I'll take you to our apartment so you can be sure you have what you need in your pack." He turns to Kirstin and Annette. "We'll be back in twenty minutes. Lock up tight behind us."

Grant leaves me at the apartment with a kiss and a reminder for me to secure the door. My daypack isn't very big and doesn't hold much, but I check to make sure it has what I need. I refill my water container, plus a second one for Grant and me. He also has a container in his daypack that we'll fill before leaving.

I look around. Several days ago, I put a couple photos I don't want to lose in my pack: one of my parents and me when I was a baby, one with my grandparents, our wedding picture, and a couple others.

There are also a few in my duffle bag and Grant's duffle bag. Sadly, most of the recent pictures I had were on my phone or on digital frames—all of those were lost with the EMP. Do pictures even matter anymore? When people are dying when speaking out, is memorabilia important? Is Richard Majors right? Was the Constitution already useless?

I hate to admit it, but I've never even read the Constitution. I can't even really think of any of the Amendments. I know there's freedom of speech, which we don't seem to have now unless you want to end up like that Mandi lady. And there's a right to have a gun—another thing we don't have. I shake my head. I can't get wrapped up in worrying about this. Getting to the ranch, to safety, is what's important right now.

There's a soft knock at the door, followed by, "It's me."

After I undo the door and let him in, Grant says, "It's almost time. Are you ready?"

"Did you get what you needed?"

He shows me a key. "From the bird bath, right where you said it'd be."

"For City Hall?"

"Leaving town is going to be dangerous. I thought this might help. We'll take the tunnel between City Hall and the Annex Building."

"We might see Harry. Maybe take him with us?"

"If he'll go, yes. That's what I was thinking."

"After the Annex Building?"

"We stay hidden in the shadows and make our way to the creek. Ready to go?"

"I have a few things put out for you." I motion to the countertop.

"Perfect."

"How's the water in your pack? Does it need filled?"

"Good idea." He pulls it out, and I motion for the bottle, taking it to fill while he shoves the snacks and water bottle from the counter into his small backpack. "You have everything?"

I nod. "I'm ready."

He puts his pack back on, and I follow suit, then we head toward the door. My hand is on the chair, ready to move it out of the way, when Grant says, "Wait a minute, Shelb."

"Yes?"

He gently pulls me into a hug and kiss. After a long minute, he says, "If there was any way to avoid this, I would. If we could be safe here, just hide out— "

"We can't."

"No. And even at the ranch, it might not be safe. What Annette said the other night is true. Eventually—maybe not even before much longer—Majors will try to take over the entire area. The way he talks, he has big plans. We'll need to stop him. We'll need to form a resistance. But I want to find someplace safe for you and our baby first."

"I'll fight with you."

He gives me a sad smile, then kisses me again.

Grant has us leave the apartment building in pairs. Annette and Mason are first. Kirstin argues that she should be with both boys, but she finally gives in, understanding Annette and Mason together would seem completely innocent and they'd be able to move quickly. Even so, she hugs him and plasters kisses all over him, not wanting to let him go. Before leaving the apartment, Annette has us join in a circle—a prayer circle—holding hands as she sends up petitions for our safety. I surprise myself when I join the "amen." Grant gives my hand a squeeze, saying, "Thy will be done."

I give a slight nod. *Okay, God. If You really are there, help us get out of Prospect. Help us reach the ranch safely.*

My eyes fill with tears as Annette holds up the key Grant retrieved and says, "See you in the basement."

As hoped, there are still several people out, making their way home or wherever. Grant watches from the balcony, handgun at the ready. He says it'd be unlikely he could do anything more than make a distraction from this distance, but it might offer Annette and Mason enough time to escape. He'll be able to keep eyes on them until they reach the edge of the building. Then he'll listen for any sound of distress. Annette assured us if she's caught or there's a sentry there, she'll scream to the heavens so we know not to follow.

Kirstin has Caleb secured in some kind of baby carrier, kissing the top of his head. She has a second carrier for Mason in the diaper bag. They decided, at his age and size, it would be best for him to walk alongside Annette. It may be a little less obvious that they're on their way out of town. She gives a small shudder and leans against the escape hatch furniture.

Grant instructed us to wait and be ready—should he need to start shooting, he doesn't want us in this room. If things go bad, we'll be ready to leave immediately by using the escape hatch between our apartments. From my apartment, we'll go through the wall into the empty apartment. Grant promises he'll be right behind us and we'll figure a way out of the building from there, whether via the homemade fire escape ladder or some other way.

Ideally, the goons would go to Kirstin's place—since that's where the shooting came from—and we'll be able to simply slip out the hallway, down the stairs, and into the empty first-floor apartment we've been stashing our gear. From there, we can use the place's patio—on the opposite side of the building from our balconies—to make a beeline for the deep ditch Grant and I walked. We've made plans with Annette. If things go bad, she'll meet us where the ditch connects to the creek. And if needed, she'll take the creek all the way to the ranch. Of course, we hope none of that will happen and we can go with our original plan and not our worst-case-scenario plan.

It's many minutes before Grant says, "They're around the building."

"They made it?" Kirstin asks with a smile.

"As far as I can see. They disappeared at the corner. It's, what, another ten yards to the steps? I waited to make sure I didn't hear her cry out. Time for you to go, Kirstin. You'll go straight to City Hall. Don't take the path through the park like Annette did."

"Yes, I got it."

"You have your gun?"

"Of course." Kirstin gives a small smile. We know that if she's stopped and caught with the gun it won't go well for her—another reason Grant is keeping watch. Her husband's handgun was cached several days ago. With Majors's restrictions on movement, Grant stashed it in a nearby location where he could leave it without being obvious. Unfortunately, it's unlikely we'll be able to sneak back in and retrieve it, but it's also unlikely anyone else will find it.

Kirstin's husband's gun is a larger caliber and, according to both her and Grant, could do more damage. They discussed her keeping that one, but she's more comfortable with the tiny little gun she carries.

She offered Ethan's gun to Annette, but she declined, saying she hadn't shot enough to feel comfortable. Right after saying that, she pulled out a pocketknife and popped it open with a flick of her wrist.

144

"Now this, though, I'm okay carrying." It struck me as funny and I laughed like a crazy woman.

Tears fill my eyes as I give Kirstin a quick hug. "See you soon."

"See you soon," she parrots. At the door, she turns back, giving us a small wave.

"Just a few more minutes," Grant says, putting the chair back in place under the doorknob, then returning to the balcony.

I wait by the escape hatch. After a few minutes, Grant quietly says, "Something's happening."

"What?" I ask, starting to walk toward him.

"Someone stopped her. Stay at the hatch!"

I stop but stay where I am, halfway between the balcony and the escape hatch. With my heart suddenly pounding in my ears, I'm struggling to focus.

"I don't think it's one of Majors's people. No mask. Be ready to leave just in case."

After what feels like an eternity but is likely only several seconds, Grant says, "I think it's okay. She's moving again. Yeah, she just gave a thumbs up sign."

"Who was it?"

"I'm not sure. A woman, I think, but I don't know."

"But everything is okay?"

"She's almost to the edge of the building and the lady went the other way. I think it's fine."

"You're sure?"

"As sure as I can be. Kirstin is out of sight now. We'll give it a few more minutes and then we'll go. It's getting close to dark. We need to hurry."

"I'm ready."

A few minutes later, hand in hand, we step out of the building. "Try and look natural," Grant says, pulling his shirt down slightly to make sure it covers his holstered sidearm. Like Kirstin, we know what will happen if we're stopped and caught with the gun. And like Annette, we're both also carrying a knife. Mine is only a kitchen knife that Grant fashioned a sheath for out of cardboard and duct tape. I hope I don't have to use it.

"Mm–hmm. I'm trying."

We head toward the hospital rubble, the opposite direction from City Hall. Our plan is to walk around the block and enter from the other side. Hopefully, anyone watching won't notice that all of us went to the same spot. Walking quickly, just like the few people still out and trying to get inside before curfew, we make our way to the next block and then around. When we get to the sidewalk of the main entrance of City Hall, we bypass it and go around to the basement entrance. I'm a couple steps behind Grant when the door opens. Annette motions us inside.

"You made it," she says with a smile. "We all made it."

"Let's keep moving," Grant says. "Shelby, where's the tunnel?"

I lead the way to the small door Harry came out of the other day. As soon as we're near it, I say, "It's Shelby."

After a moment, a muffled, "Who's with you," is returned.

"Grant, Annette, and Kirstin, plus her boys."

"Were you followed? Anyone see you come in here?"

"N-no. I don't think so."

I glance at the others, who all shake their head. Grant quietly asks Kirstin, "Who were you talking to?"

She tilts her head in question.

"On the way over here," Grant clarifies.

"Oh! Lucy. You know, from our building."

"Lucy?" I exclaim. "She's one of them."

"What? No. Lucy." She says her name slowly. "We sheltered with her."

"I know. Harry, let us in. We need to keep moving."

Chapter 25

Harry opens the door, stepping aside as I say, "Lucy was at the park last night. She was masked. She's one of them. I'm sure it was her. She looked directly at us when Annette started singing."

We're in a storage room with old desks, printers, and other office stuff. "I thought this was the tunnel?" I say to Harry.

"Where are you going?" he asks.

"Using the tunnel to get closer to the creek," Grant says. "Where is it?"

Harry pauses, looking Grant up and down. "You have room for a few more?"

"At the ranch?" I ask.

He gives a single nod in response.

"Who is it?" Annette asks.

"I think you know." Harry gives Annette a small smile.

"Milena?"

He nods. "Plus the sheriff and the other escapees."

"They can come with us," Grant says. "You too, if you want."

"Yep. I think it would be best, at least for now. But temporarily only. I'm going to—never mind. Let's get moving." He takes us to the back of the room, to another skinny door.

"How'd you know we were down here?" I ask when we reach the second door.

"There's a spot within the tunnel where I can hear anyone on the stairs or in the basement hallway. I've set up camp there."

"And Milena?" Annette asks.

"No. But we'll get to them shortly."

He ushers us inside the tunnel, locking the door behind us with not just the doorknob but also a hasp lock secured with a padlock. Then he moves a desk in front of the door. The tunnel is a hallway very similar to the basement hall, with tile floor and cement walls and ceiling. "I thought it was in disrepair," I say.

"The tunnel? No. It's fine, as you can see."

We go only about thirty yards before finding his sleeping bag and other gear. "Give me just a minute to pack up."

Other than Caleb babbling slightly, we're completely silent while he puts everything together and then shoves it in a garbage bag.

"Do they know about this place?" I ask.

"Majors? He probably knows the rumors as well as anyone. We've never kept the tunnel a secret. And when the Annex was used for city business, the tunnel was well traveled. That's how I know about the acoustics—from going back and forth between the two."

"I thought it was falling apart?" I say, remembering what Grant's grandpa Paul had said.

"Nope. Not this tunnel. But the hotel tunnel, it's a mess. Here we are," Harry says, as we reach another door and he unlocks the knob and hasp lock. "Let's keep quiet as best we can. The door from upstairs is locked, and we should hear anyone trying to get down here, but . . . " He shrugs. Kirstin looks worried for a minute, until Harry says, "We'll only be here a short time. I'm sure the boys will be fine."

Once we're out of the tunnel, we're in another large storage room. Harry puts his finger to his lips and motions us to the right, down a hallway and around a corner. I'm starting to feel like a mouse in a maze. We finally reach another door. He gives a soft knock, pauses, and then knocks again. "It's Harry."

There's a rustling at the door before it opens a crack. A blackened eye greets us.

"Who are your friends?" a rough voice asks.

"Grant, Shelby, Annette, Kirstin, and her boys. Grant and Shelby are the ones I told you about. Milena knows them all."

He nods and opens the door. "Better keep the kids quiet."

"I'll try," Kirstin says in a snappy tone.

"Ready to move?" Harry asks.

Milena lifts her head and gives us a small smile. "Shelby, Harry said he talked to you yesterday. He thought maybe your ranch would be safe for us. Your folks won't mind?"

Grant shrugs. "Let's just go and worry about the details later."

Milena gives him a strange look.

"It's possible one of Majors's— "

"Goons," I say quickly. Grant puts a hand on my shoulder. "Well, they are," I mutter.

"It's possible one of his guys saw them go into the building," Harry continues.

The rough-voiced guy says several harsh words before saying, "And you led them to us?"

"So we can get out of here," Grant says. "What needs to happen?"

Rough Voice shakes his head. "Help me with the sheriff. Harry, can you and one of the girls get Jerry moving? He's better than he was, but he's still not great. Great thinking bringing children and a pregnant one to help get us out of here."

"Enough, Donnie," Sheriff Spieth says in a haggard voice. "Just get me on my feet. Milena will help steady me. You can help your brother, Donnie. He needs you more than I do."

While I have never met Sheriff Jason Spieth, or even seen him up close until the attacks started, I had known of him from a few women I worked with at the SuperMart. In his late-forties and never married, he was often discussed as Prospect's most eligible bachelor. I'll admit, he's handsome for an older guy. He's tall and very well built, and even in his injured condition I can see the bulge of his muscles under his slightly too tight T-shirt.

He was a police officer somewhere else and moved here for the slower pace a few years ago. He worked as a deputy, then he was assigned to finish out the previous sheriff's term when he retired early. After that, he ran for his own term.

As Milena helps him up, the extent of his injuries causes me to cringe. His bright blue eyes are bloodshot and blackened. His nose is crooked, and he has several cuts across his cheeks and forehead. I avert my eyes so I don't notice his pain with movement.

Within a few minutes, everyone is up and ready. I carry Harry's garbage bag of goods so he can help move Donnie's brother, Jerry. Donnie grabs a shotgun that was leaning against the wall. "Any of you numbskulls think about showing up armed?"

Grant lifts the tail of his shirt up slightly, while Kirstin says, "You're a jerk."

"Hey, I'm just saying we have a weapon shortage and it'd be nice to be able to defend ourselves. Sheriff Spieth, are you well enough to handle this six-shooter?" he asks, motioning to a handgun on a table.

The sheriff extends his hand in response.

"Okay, folks," Harry says, "I know we're all stressed and tensions are high. Try and take it down a notch, Donnie. These people are not the enemy."

"Sure, Harry, whatever you say."

After a reminder from Harry to keep it down, we move into the hallway. He motions us to go the opposite direction from our arrival to the room. As we make our way through the labyrinth, he quietly says, "It might be a little wet."

"What might be a little wet?" I ask.

"The tunnel."

"The old tunnel?"

"Yeah. We'll take it from here to the hotel. I checked it a few days ago, and it wasn't too bad. But we did have a little rain last night, so . . . " He shrugs.

The old tunnel is very different from the one that connected City Hall with the Annex Building. This one is more like an old miners' tunnel, complete with rotting beams and a dirt floor. We dodge the wet spots as we move through it.

"Can we stop a minute?" Annette asks. "I think Jerry needs a break."

"We're almost out," Harry says. "Can you keep going? We'll rest soon."

I can't make out Jerry's response, but we don't stop moving until we reach the end of the tunnel and we're once again in some sort of storage room. This time, instead of office equipment, there are old lamps, bed frames, and kitchen supplies.

"Where to?" Grant asks.

"Well," Harry says in a whisper. "Here's where it's going to get interesting. When I checked the tunnel the other day, I also went through the hotel. There are a few people living here, probably ones who were on vacation when the attacks started. We need to get out of the hotel without being seen. I'll go up and check it out while Jerry and Jason catch their breath. Donnie, are you doing okay?"

I glance over at the gruff man. He's pale and trembling. He waves Harry off in response.

Harry nods. "Okay, I'll only be a few minutes. If I'm not back in ten, something's gone wrong. Go back to the tunnel and wait for a new opportunity."

I can feel my chest constrict at the thought. If we can't get out of here tonight, what do we do? Hide out underground until they find us? Thankfully, I don't have to fret for long. Harry returns after only a couple of minutes, giving a smile and double thumbs up.

"Annette, how about I take this big guy." Harry indicates toward a droopy eyed Mason. Caleb, secure and comfortable in his baby carrier, fell asleep before we exited the tunnel, which helps since quiet is now a necessity.

"Everything is okay?" I ask.

"There wasn't anyone in the lobby or the hall to the courtyard. We'll go straight there to the back gate. Then I think it's best to go in pairs to the creek line—might be less visible than our whole group. No talking once we leave the basement, not until we're well away from Prospect."

"Jerry will need to rest," Milena says. "Sheriff too."

"I'm fine," Sheriff Spieth says, waving her off.

"You can have a brief rest at the gate," Harry says. "We'll need a place to hole up tonight."

"I know somewhere," Grant says. "It's close to the creek. I'll watch for everyone."

"Once we get there, we'll take a few minutes and then Grant and Jerry will go first."

Grant looks at me and starts to shake his head.

"I'll make sure Shelby is okay," Harry says. "She'll be with me and Mason, bringing up the rear. We need you to lead us to your hidey-hole."

Pursing his lips, Grant says, "Fine."

Harry pairs up the rest of the group, which isn't easy with the injuries. Milena will help the sheriff. Annette is with Donnie. Kirstin, carrying Caleb, is going alone right after Grant.

"Once you're out of the courtyard, cross the alleyway and head down the side of the hotel's old carriage house. At the end of the building, it's only a few yards to the tree line. Get in the cottonwoods and make your way upstream. They've had people watching the bridge, but you should be able to stay hidden. If someone sees you . . . do what you must do. If you could do it quietly, that would be best."

Harry makes eye contact with each person in the group. There are stoic nods of agreement.

Everything goes as planned to the gate. It's slightly cloudy, giving us enough of the moon and stars to keep from stumbling but hopefully to not be seen. As soon as we're at the fence and ready to exit the courtyard, I worry the gate will squeak and give us away. I breathe a

151

sigh of relief as it opens silently. Grant gives me a smile and a quick kiss. Tears fill my eyes as I nod a goodbye.

Grant and Jerry quietly leave. I want to watch them go, but the eight-foot-high privacy fence prevents me from seeing beyond the courtyard. Harry pulls the gate shut without relatching it. After several minutes, he motions for Kirstin to go. It's at least twenty minutes after Grant left before Harry, Mason, and I are the only ones remaining. I'm sitting on one of the garden benches. Harry is standing with Mason snuggled up against his shoulder, sleeping soundly. I can only imagine how heavy he must be. Once we meet up with the group, he should go in the carrier to make the rest of tonight's trek easier.

I close my eyes and take several deep breaths. When I open my eyes, Harry motions to me. *Time to go.* With a nod, I rise to join him. We slip out the gate, and he quietly closes it behind us.

I'm slightly awkward carrying Harry's garbage bag of supplies. He's slightly awkward carrying Mason. It's less than the length of a football field to the tree line edging the creek. We move quickly and carefully, staying along the side of the building.

We're well over halfway when Harry grabs my elbow, forcing me to stop.

Barely audible, he says, "There's movement just past the building."

I suck in a breath.

He motions me to go back. Once we've returned to the start of the building, we walk in front of it, almost hugging the wall to stay in the shadows. When we reach the corner, he motions me to wait. Stooping down, he peeks around the corner. I notice his pistol in his hand. I have no idea when he took it out of his belt, or how he can hold Mason with one arm and the gun with the other.

He moves back toward me and motions for me to put the bag on the ground. Once I do, he hands me a sleeping Mason.

"I'll cover you while you go to the next building." He motions to the first of the string of rental cottages. I nod. He peeks around the corner again, then motions me to go.

Once I'm at the next building, he picks up the bag and follows me. We repeat the process, allowing me little time to rest. We cross three more cottages before he motions toward the creek. At this point, we don't have many more options—two more buildings and then the alley ends and we would need to cross a road. A road with a bridge crossing over the creek that's guarded by the goon squad. There are lots of trees and we're well hidden, so likely this is the best spot to choose.

When we finally make it to the creek, I'm shaking from exertion and fear. Harry finds me a hidden stump in the brush to rest on. After a few minutes, he whispers, "We shouldn't stop until we're well beyond the bridge. Make sure you're rested enough, then we'll go."

Moving along the creek while carrying Mason will be a challenge. I consider asking Harry for the bag back, but after the scare we had, I know he needs to be able to use the gun. With the bag under his arm, it doesn't hinder him like Mason would.

We make our way silently beyond the bridge. I don't see or hear anyone and wonder if Majors even has anyone on patrol. We carefully pick our way through the trees and thick brush, going another hundred yards before he finds us a spot to rest. I don't know how far Grant walked with Jerry before deciding it was a safe spot to wait for everyone else. Would he go all the way to the abandoned cabin near where he stashed some of our stuff? We did talk about that being a place we'd meet if we were ever separated, so it makes sense. Even though our pace isn't overly swift, it's still quicker than is prudent with me carrying Mason; my balance isn't great, and I almost slip.

We're well out of Prospect when Harry says, "Let's rest again. We should be safe now."

I nod my agreement as he leads me to a fallen log. "Where do you think they are?"

"You don't know? When Grant said he knew of a place, I figured you knew it too."

I shrug. "Maybe this old cabin along the creek. He took me there before."

"The Kirby cabin?"

"He didn't tell me what it's called, but it's missing half its roof and one wall."

"Yep. That's it. That'd make sense. There's good vantage points from there, so he'd be able to see anyone coming, whether up the creek or up the road."

"Yes, we could see the road from there, but it's not close by the road."

"Right, just a view of it."

After a few minutes, he reaches for Mason. "Swap ya."

"You sure?"

"I don't think we're being followed, and it's unlikely Richard would have his people this far from town. Not without a good reason, anyway."

We walk on, stopping once more, before Harry says, "I think we're close to the cabin."

I have no idea. In the dark, everything is confusing. It feels like we've walked considerably farther than Grant and I did on our hiking day.

We take about twenty more steps when I hear, "Shelby."

"Grant?"

A few seconds later, he's giving me an awkward hug with the garbage bag squashed between us.

Chapter 26

We stayed the night at the old cabin, with Grant, Milena, Kirstin, and Harry taking turns on watch. I offered to help but was told I needed the rest. Not that I was able to rest. Grant had a few camping supplies stashed for us, including a hammock for each of us. Grant put Jerry in his. I offered mine to the sheriff, but he quickly declined, saying he was already set up on one of the camping pads with Donnie sacked out on the other.

Grant added the hammocks to our supplies because of their small size. I wasn't convinced they were a good idea, thinking they'd be too much trouble and we might have an issue finding trees sturdy enough to tie to. Grant and I even laughed about being inside the hammock as a bear burrito. Would a bear come waltzing by in the middle of the night and think someone hung a human burrito for him to snack on? Even though I was apprehensive, this hammock is amazing, especially with little Mason snuggled in next to me.

The sun is just beginning to lighten the sky when Grant wakes me. "You ready to get up?"

"No. I could still sleep for several hours."

"As soon as we get to the ranch, we'll get you in a proper bed for a proper sleep."

"How's everyone doing?"

"Jerry's about the same. Sheriff Spieth seems better. Donnie . . . " Grant shrugs. "He's grumpy."

"Do you think that's his usual demeanor?"

"Could be. Or maybe it's just been a rough few days—you know, with almost being executed and all, both him and his brother."

"I guess, but he could be a little nicer."

Kirstin puts Mason in the fabric carrier she stashed in the diaper bag. It's a long stretch of material that she wraps around Milena several times, forming something like a backpack she tucks Mason into.

"How far is it from here?" I ask Grant shortly after we begin our trek.

"About five miles."

"All uphill?"

He gives me a small smile and a nod in response. I stifle a groan. With the injuries, and carrying the children, we're moving very slowly. We stay near the coolness of the creek. The large plains cottonwoods, quaking aspen, and thick willows provide a decent amount of shade, and the rapidly moving creek seems to add to the cooling effect. Grumpy Donnie is pale but insists he's fine. Jerry doesn't even pretend to be okay, letting Grant and Harry take turns helping him. Annette helps the sheriff when he needs it, which isn't very often. I wonder if he's really doing as well as he seems to be or if it's all an act.

Grant has Annette carry a backpack from our cache while he carries his duffle bag and his daypack. We have more items cached nearby, but he doesn't mention those. He also doesn't mention grabbing any of Kirstin's stashed items. When I quietly ask about them, he says, "Later."

It's early afternoon when Grant has us stop.

"We're almost there. Why don't you all stay here and relax for a while. I'm going to go ahead. My guess is they'll have someone on watch, so it's probably best if I go alone."

"You want me to go with you?" I ask.

"You might as well stay and relax. I can make good time and come back for you." He gives me a quick kiss goodbye and takes off up the creek. We've had little to eat today. Harry had a few snacks in his supplies, and we shared the granola bars and things we have, but we haven't taken the time to make a real meal. I'm so looking forward to getting to the ranch, relaxing, and eating. Everyone gets comfortable and does their best to rest. Harry and Donnie keep watch, while Jerry and the sheriff sleep. A while later, we hear the rumble of a small engine.

"Okay, folks, let's move," Harry says. "Get into a hidden spot, just in case these aren't our friends."

I can feel my heart start to race as my breath catches in my chest. Kirstin reaches for my hand. "All will be well. Trust in the Lord."

I give a slight nod. I want to give a better answer. I want to say that I want to trust, that I want God to open my heart. Even in my fear, a song Annette sang at one of the evening services runs through my head. While I can hear the tune in my mind, I can't quite remember the words . . . something about asking God to open the eyes of my heart so I can see Him.

I haven't thought about music since the night of the massacre, when Richard Majors killed the mayor, the chief of police, and over a hundred other people. Music had left my heart. But now, while hiding in the trees, hoping and—dare I say—praying the noise we hear isn't one of Majors's goons, music is trying to get back into my life. Not the best timing by any means.

As the engine stops, I try to make myself small. I have Mason and Caleb with me, and Kirstin is about ten feet away with her little gun out, ready to protect us.

"It's me. I'm back," Grant hollers out. "I have my brother with me. We're coming in. Holster your weapons. We are coming in."

"Understood," Harry responds. "Okay, guys, stand down."

Grant not only has his brother Dax but also two quads, each pulling a small trailer. We load Jerry into one trailer, and I ride in the second one with Mason and Caleb. The sheriff admits his exhaustion and rides double with Dax. Harry drives the second quad with Donnie as the passenger. Of course, Donnie insisted he was well enough to walk, but the sheriff overrode him.

It's nice to ride, but it's not much faster than walking, considering Grant and the others are able to keep up with us on foot.

As soon as we're close enough to the ranch and I can catch a glimpse of Pamela, with Dusty at her side, I raise both hands in an enthusiastic wave. Pamela blows me a kiss and appears to be jumping up and down. Dusty lifts his hand in a reserved wave, but a smile spreads across his face. My eyes fill with tears. Even though I know my parents and grandparents loved me, I don't think I ever saw them express it so effusively. The quad isn't even stopped before Pamela's reaching for me and pulling me into a hug.

"I'm so glad you're here. I've been so worried," Pamela says, as Dusty lifts the boys out of the trailer and then offers me his hand. Kirstin and Annette take the boys while Pamela holds on to me.

"You've heard what happened in town? We were afraid you'd come into Prospect and— " I hold back a cry.

"Oh, Shelby, we heard. We know all about it. The night Richard Majors took over, Chaplain Rick showed up here along with Toby James, the boy who's been staying with him."

"Chaplain Rick? Why?" I ask.

"You know, after the hospital fire, we all thought he was dead. It was a miracle."

"Right, I remember." I nod in agreement. "But why'd he come here?"

"Oh, yes. Of course you do. He went to school with PJ and Dusty. They've been friends forever. I guess he just thought it was safe. They were late to the meeting and saw the shooting begin. Rick's first instinct was to shoot back— "

"Isn't he a preacher?"

"Sort of, yes."

"But he was going to use his gun and kill people?"

"To save others, yes. But then he realized how many there were, and with the explosions, there wasn't anything he could do."

While I don't fully understand how someone who claims to be a preacher—a Christian—can be okay with killing others, I decide to let it go for now. "So they're here?" I ask, glancing around. "It looks like there's several other people here too."

"Come on, Shelby, walk with me. Let's get you into the house and comfortable. I can answer your questions there."

"I should help get everybody situated."

"Mom's right," Grant says, walking up to us. "You need to go into the house and rest. I'll help figure out where everyone's staying."

I nod my agreement, realizing just how tired I am.

"You look beautiful," Pamela says. "I can see our baby has grown quite a bit since I last saw you."

"I'm huge."

"Let's get you off your feet."

A few minutes later, I'm stretched out on the sofa with my hiking boots off. It only takes me a couple of minutes to realize those boots were on my feet way too long. "I'm so sorry about, you know . . . " I motion toward my feet.

"Oh, don't you worry, Shelby. You can take a bath in a bit, but let's get you rested first."

I settle back into the sofa. "So, Pamela, all these people?"

"Escapees." She shrugs.

"From Prospect?"

"Yep. You know that Angelo, his daughter, and grandchildren have been here since after the EMP?"

I nod, remembering them teasing Grant about Angelo's daughter being his first crush. I must admit, I've wondered what she looks like.

"The rest came after Richard and his— "

"Goons."

"What?" She gives me a funny look.

"Oh, nothing, we just call them goons. You know, the guys and gals helping Richard Majors. It doesn't matter. You were saying?"

"Rick and Toby showed up that first night. Then a few more the next day."

"Do you know all these people?"

"Of course we do," she says with a smile. "Do you think we just let anybody stay with us?"

"Well, maybe."

Pamela throws her head back and laughs. "Oh, Shelby. You are such a gem. We do know everyone here. I've been praying and praying that you and Grant were safe, that you'd be able to get here. When I opened my eyes this morning, I just knew today was the day. I knew you'd make it here safely today. And it is such a blessing you were able to bring Jason Spieth and Harry English with you. They'll be an asset for sure. I'm glad your friends are here too. Grant told us about— " She pauses and visibly swallows. "I just can't believe Richard was going to hang our sheriff. And Milena, that sweet girl. That just makes no sense at all. Of course, I couldn't believe he killed our mayor and the chief of police either. I never liked Richard Majors, but I never realized just how . . . how incredibly— "

"Evil," I insert.

"Yes, evil is the correct term. Crazy may also work."

"Where's everyone else?" I ask. "Kirstin?"

"We're going to put Kirstin and her boys, along with Milena and Annette, in the trailer—you know, the one we use for the guides we hire on each season?"

I shrug. I know of it. I've only been to the ranch one time before this, when Dusty was out of town at some convention thing. Grant and I weren't exactly welcome when Dusty was around.

"Yes, so they'll be staying there along with Milena and Annette. There are already two single gals—sisters—in there, a couple of Dax's friends from school."

"A girlfriend?" I ask, raising my eyebrows.

Pamela shrugs. "Not that I can tell. The one is the same age as Dax. The other is a year younger. I've met them when they were all in FFA together, but both went off to school and were back for the summer. Their parents were killed in the explosion Majors set off."

159

"Oh, that's terrible."

"It is. They're having a rough time. But I'm confident they'll be fine. I know they're both leaning on the Lord."

We visit for a few minutes more as she shares with me the details of the people staying here. I admit, without knowing any of them, I'm confused. At least the ranch has space for everyone. With it being a hunting lodge, they have several small cabins for people to stay in before and after they hunt.

"We've made an arrangement with the other ranches too," Pamela says. "The Vasquezes and the Smalls closer to Prospect, along with the McCracken family just up the road from us. We're all keeping watch and have set up a way to communicate with each other."

"How are you communicating?"

"Handheld radios."

"Like walkie-talkies?"

"Yes. We had a few for hunting, and each of the ranches have a few. Up here, cell phones don't always work, so they're helpful for communicating when working about the ranches. We use a very brief word or two—a code—to communicate."

"That's smart," I say.

"It's necessary."

When I finally decide I've rested enough, Pamela helps me to the bathroom so I can clean up. Since we've talked to them that day in Prospect, PJ and Dusty were able to set up a gravity-fed system to bring water into the house. It's cold creek water they're purifying with bleach, but it works okay. Pamela heats a generous amount so I can take an almost luxurious bath.

"When you're finished, we'll see who else wants to use your water. I bet at least the little boys will need a bath."

As I lie back in the warm water, I catch a glimpse of my left hand. The spot where my wedding ring should be is bare. The small diamond engagement ring and simple band are in a pocket of my daypack. I've lost weight in my hands, and the rings no longer fit. I examine my fingernails; they're uneven and the cuticles are thick and jagged. In the early days after the EMP, when I first started taking care of the garden at the apartment, I spent time each evening tending my hands and feet. One day, I stopped. I can't even remember when I last took the time to work on my hands or feet. I lift my right foot up in the air, the polish is faded from all but one spot on my big toe.

And shaving—that's a thing of days' past also. Not that I can even bend properly to see my legs to remove the hair. Besides, we ran out of razors weeks ago. Grant isn't even shaving anymore. Thinking of his scruffy beard makes me smile. I noted his dad and the rest of the men here are all clean shaven; maybe they'll have a razor to loan him. Maybe Pamela has one for me and some nail polish. I can get a manicure and pedicure and feel like a proper lady again.

While I'm lounging in the tub, thinking of the pampering I'm going to do, my thoughts drift to Richard Majors and his reign of terror. What's the use of pretty nails when there's someone like him around? His goons could show up on our doorstep any day. With the sheriff, Milena, and the other fugitives, we'd all be hauled away. A shiver runs through my body.

Chapter 27

"Okay, so Annette will go in first. She'll leave the sack in the garbage can. Then, fifteen minutes later, Bryce repeats the process with his sack." Sheriff Spieth looks around the room.

I glance at Pamela; a pinched look paints her face. She—most of us—are against Bryce going into town. Even though he's the logical choice, it just doesn't seem right. But he's likely able to go in without being noticed. Annette has lived in Prospect her entire life and is more of a risk, but she'll be wearing a disguise—an old wig belonging to Grant's grandmother. Seems she had an affection for altering her hairstyle to fit her mood.

I only met Grant's grandma Katherine once. She passed a few days after we arrived in Prospect last fall. In fact, she was the reason we came here, so Grant could say goodbye. We only planned on staying a short while, not moving here. But two weeks later, his great-grandfather, Paul's dad, passed at the age of ninety-nine, four days before he turned one hundred.

I know Grant feels some guilt about being gone those few years. During the time he was away, he called his great-grandpa John every Sunday. Like the rest of the Cameron family, he lived on the family ranch. His house was the original dwelling built when he and his bride first moved here. John's wife died before Grant was born. Even though Grant stayed in contact by phone, he feels he missed out on John's final years.

Even at the age of ninety-nine, John was fully independent to the end, passing sometime during the night. Grant, his brothers, Paul, and John had gone fishing that day. The hope had been to lessen some of Paul's grief over losing his wife. I know Grant cherishes the memory of the day.

After John's funeral, we talked about leaving; we both had a desire to be in the Northeast part of the country to watch the fall colors, something neither of us have ever seen. But we just kept putting it off. And then we decided to get married, and it just seemed right to stay in Prospect. Now, with the way the world has changed, it's likely we'll never have an opportunity to visit anyplace else.

"Okay," Sheriff Spieth says. "It should take twenty minutes for the package Annette leaves to ignite. The theory is Majors's people will come running to investigate. Then you'll pick off as many as you can. Remember, do not shoot unless you are completely sure it's one of Majors's people. We know from our time in town, and from the observing we've been doing this last week, they're still wearing bandannas to distinguish themselves as belonging to Majors, not always covering their face, though."

"Yeah," Harry says. "I think they finally realized wearing a bandanna all day wasn't too smart."

I shudder at the memory of Harry sharing how he watched through the spotting scope as one of the goons was sweating profusely while on watch. Even though it's now September, it's still warm during the day. He'd wipe his hand across his forehead and occasionally sip from water underneath the bandanna, but he wouldn't remove it.

Pretty soon, he fell out of the tree stand he was using as a perch. The fifteen-foot fall didn't even wake him up. It was an hour later before another goon came around and used a radio to call for help.

Harry has no idea if the guy survived the overheating and the subsequent fall. But after that, they started tying the bandannas around their arms or forehead instead of over their face.

"Once you've confirmed your target, take your shot. Remember, only two shots before you move to your secondary location." The sheriff looks up, making eye contact with PJ, Dusty, and Dax.

Each of them will be positioned with long range rifles to take out the goons. Today is our first assault, using what Paul is calling guerrilla warfare. While the small group is picking off their targets, the bulk of us will be at the ranch in a defensive position in case they realize who is behind the attack.

"When the second detonation occurs," the sheriff continues, "the hope is there will be more confusion. Take advantage of this confusion, but don't stay in one spot for too long. Each of you is confident that you do not need a spotter?"

"Yep," PJ says. "A second person will just slow us down."

PJ looks to Dusty, who nods, and then to Dax. I sense a slight hesitation before Dax says, "Right."

"Okay." Sheriff gives a single nod.

"And we're sure about this?" Dax asks hesitantly. "We're sure we shouldn't just take out Richard Majors and be done with it?"

"While I like the idea," Sheriff Spieth says, "I'm not sure we'd really be done with it. Absolutely, if you have a shot at Majors—Richard or Scott—take it. But depleting their force is also important. Don't just wait for Richard to show up."

Dax gives a single nod.

"Right, Dax?" Paul asks. "You understand?"

"Yep, Grandpa. I've got it."

"Okay, then," the sheriff says. "Annette and Bryce will return here immediately after leaving their packages. In and out. Annette, you'll wait for Bryce?"

"Yes. Then straight back to where we hid the quads and then to the ranch."

"Right. But you three" —he motions to our snipers— "will scatter and find a place to hole up overnight. Make sure you're not followed, then make your way back here tomorrow. After that, we regroup and plan for our next assault."

"Don't stay so long trying to take out the bad guys that you're discovered," Paul says. "If each of you can get four, that'd be a good start."

"You think they'll know it was us?" Pamela asks.

The sheriff and Paul share a look.

"Probably not this time," Paul says. "But eventually, yes. That's why we've been working extra diligently on our defenses."

"And why we have a plan of escape," Harry adds.

The night we arrived here, after our own escape from Prospect, the plans began for these attacks and our eventual escape. There was much discussion about where we would go after it was discovered we were the ones picking off the goons. Sheriff Spieth wanted to head over the mountain, eventually ending up in Cody. He feels that is the best chance for finding help to take out Richard Majors.

While we all agree with that, the route would be too difficult for the children, me, and a few others. We wouldn't be able to move over the first mountain range fast enough. Instead, after taking time to fully recover, brothers Donnie and Jerry headed off toward Cody.

Grant was right about Donnie. After we got to the ranch, he started to mellow out, even helping on the ranch in addition to taking watch. He was still a little uptight but not nearly the jerk he was at first. I guess anger, injury, and fear can bring out the worst in someone.

The night before they left for Cody, Paul led a special prayer service asking God to give them His divine protection. I surprised myself by adding an amen at the end.

A very loose plan was put together, a plan Donnie and Jerry are taking with them in hopes of organizing the people of Cody to shut Majors down. Realistically, we don't expect that to occur before we need to leave the ranch. So our plan is to head north to the community of Bakerville. Paul has a friend from high school who lives there, plus he knows many others from the community.

Sheriff Spieth says one of his deputies lives in Bakerville, and before the EMP wiped out communication, the deputy told him many of the neighbors were banding together.

It seems his deputy wasn't too impressed with that and thought the sheriff should tell them to stand down. But Sheriff Spieth thinks it's a good thing, telling his deputy to not only let them continue but to help them in any way he is able. He also thinks this group will be beneficial to us, provided they have continued. With Bakerville and Cody, maybe we can defeat Majors.

"Okay, everyone knows what the plan is?" There's a simultaneous nod. The sheriff gives his own nod. "Remember, during this operation, no voices over the walkie-talkies. Clicks only. Remember your click codes. Three clicks are a check in that all is well. Two clicks, potential trouble. One click means evacuate. We will confirm the clicks by repeating. You will then repeat your initial code. Those without radios, stay within voice contact of someone who has one, just like always."

"Okay, folks," Paul says. "This is the first of what we anticipate will be many steps toward taking back our town. Richard Majors might believe the Constitution was suspended after the EMP, but I, for one, do not."

There's a chorus of agreement.

"Besides . . . " Paul clears his throat and says a little louder, "Besides, the natural rights our Constitution protected weren't given to us by our forefathers. They were given to us by God. And no man can take those rights away."

That proclamation isn't just met with agreement, it's met with applause and cheers. Tears sting my eyes as I look around the room. I'm not the only one visibly moved. Fear and hope combined make it hard to know exactly how to feel.

"Let's go to Him in prayer and ask for His help and guidance during this time." Paul bows his head and begins his petition for assistance.

While I try to focus on his words, my mind slightly wanders as a feeling of peace washes over me. The prayers, the songs of praise, the references to God no longer stir up animosity in me. Instead, I find myself gravitating toward Him, toward God. Each night there's a family Bible reading. I try to feign disinterest, but I can't help listening—not only to the words but to their meaning.

As Paul prays, I feel the passion of his words. The fervent belief that God's hand is in our assault. It's hard to think God would be okay with taking the life of another person. And there was a substantial amount of debate over whether we should fight or simply try to live peacefully.

In the end, it was decided that Richard Majors's desire to take over the region was unacceptable. None of us could live in peace with that threat. He'll eventually come for us. If his army of goons is slightly smaller when that happens, we might have a chance.

Chapter 28

Our fighting team left several hours ago. Our usual sentry teams have increased to make sure we have the earliest possible notice of invasion. Paul's friend Angelo's daughter and I are watching the children: her two, Kirstin's two, and a little girl belonging to another couple who escaped Prospect. The two quads with attached trailers are at the ready in case we need to evacuate. While Tricia rambles on about some lady she knew when she and her husband lived on base, I think about the busyness of the last several days.

One advantage of owning and operating an outfitter's business is a ready supply of rifles and handguns. While elk and deer hunting are usually done in the mountains outside of Prospect, Cody, and near Dubois, the Camerons take their clients antelope hunting on the eastern side of the state. Those wide-open areas are perfect for specialty rifles designed for long-distance shooting. PJ and Dusty each had one custom built from a company in nearby Cody, while Dax has an only slightly less expensive off-the-shelf model. Grant said these rifles are designed to shoot one thousand yards out of the box—that's the company's motto and claim to fame, anyway.

When they were making the plans for the assault on Majors's people, Paul said they wouldn't need to shoot more than six hundred yards, but that the extra capability could come in handy.

In the two weeks we've been here, I've learned how to shoot. Sort of. Only the basics and just enough to be able to defend myself. While I never had any desire to handle a real firearm, I've realized the importance of being able to defend myself. I don't like it, but I'll do it.

Pamela was put in charge of my training. We spent most of the time just familiarizing me with how a revolver worked, then a shotgun, and finally a rifle with—what she called—open sights. When it was time for me to fire the gun, she was reluctant. With my advanced pregnancy, she was concerned the noise of the gunshots might bother my baby.

We ended up shooting only two times with each gun. This was enough for me to get the feel of it without bothering my baby too much. The handgun and rifle went fine. But with the shotgun, he didn't like that and was moving around more than usual. Pamela was also worried about the lead from the ammunition, so she made sure I immediately washed my hands after we were finished.

The next day, Paul came to me and said, "How do you feel about archery?"

I must have given him a strange look because he said, "You know, bows and arrows?"

"Oh! I, uh, I'm not sure I have any feeling about archery. I've never really given it much thought."

"My wife loved archery hunting. She'd sit for hours in her blind, just waiting for the perfect specimen to walk by. Many of those mounts in my den are from her."

"That's . . . nice," I said, giving an encouraging nod.

He had a small smile on his face as he gazed into the distance. "Yep. Quite a woman she was. A little like you. Always made sure she looked her finest."

I subconsciously reached for my hair. It had been pulled up in a ponytail or bun since we arrived here, and I hadn't even bothered with makeup.

"Oh, you still look pretty." Paul gave me a wink. "Anywho, Pamela told me about the worry of you not shooting enough to become proficient and it bothering your baby."

"Yes?"

"I thought you might like to try archery. It's silent, yet deadly. The compound bow my wife bought a few years ago, before she got sick, would be easy for you to use. When she was younger, she used either her recurve bow or longbow. But the compound was easier for her to use in her later years. She had a crossbow too—we both do. They have serious power, but I don't think you'd be able to cock it in your condition. Your belly would get in the way."

I gave a nod, not really understanding what he was talking about but figured he was probably right. My belly gets in the way with just about everything. Within a few minutes, Paul had the bow—a futuristic looking thing with these little wheels at the top and the bottom and a whole bunch of strings—and several arrows out.

"Now this here is a hybrid cam system. It's nice and light. Here, hold it."

He thrusted it into my hand. "Oh . . . okay." I fumbled with it slightly as he handed it over to me. "Yeah, it's . . . fine."

Paul gave a proud smile. "Katherine was quite fond of it. I suspect you'll learn to love it also. We could try the recurve, but" —he removed his hat to scratch his head— "this compound does some of the work for you so the arrow can fly a little faster. With the recurve or longbow, you're doing most of the work." He put his hat back on, pushing it down slightly before tilting it back into position. I couldn't help but smile at his distinct mannerism.

"Yep," he said. "This is going to fit you right nice. I think I'll have that quiet little Annette look at the recurve. The noise from a firearm bothers her, so the bow would be a good choice."

I gave a combination shrug and nod in response.

"So, let's see how this fits you. It'll need some adjusting—you probably have a longer draw length than Katherine did."

He took out a tape measure and had me put my arms out, measuring from fingertip to fingertip—he called it checking my wingspan. Then he made an adjustment on the bow. After that, he had me pull the bowstring back and look through a little hole on the string—the peep sight. The entire process seemed to take forever. Finally, he said, "That should do it."

He spent a few minutes going over the basics before letting me shoot. The first arrow didn't even hit the target, instead flying to the far left.

"I think your death grip on the bow might be the problem," he said, instructing me to barely hold the bow.

The next shot was better but not great. Trying to remember the light hold on the bow, drawing the string all the way back to the same spot each time—what Paul calls my nock spot—lining the peep sight up with the sight pin, keeping the bubble on the sight in the level position, and remembering to breathe—and then not breathe—took every bit of my concentration. I only sent half a dozen arrows toward the target that first day before I was mentally and physically exhausted. He did something to the string to make it easier for me to pull back, then I tried a few more times. It was still a lot of work but easier than before.

"Not the draw I'd prefer you have but better than nothing," he told me with a nod. "We'll get you good and accurate and then add weight."

I wasn't anywhere near accurate that first day. Or the second. But we've worked together a little each day, and now I'm a decent shot. He even made an adjustment to the bow, increasing the draw-weight slightly as my strength increased and I got used to the motion and all the details. Besides for learning how to use and fire the bow, he taught me about staying behind cover. Something sturdy that a bullet can't get through is best. At the very least, I should be thinking about concealment, something that hides me. While concealment may not stop a projectile, it may keep me from being detected. It's all great information, that I hope I never have to use.

"Earth to Shelby. Are you listening?"

"I—I'm sorry. What?" I ask, trying to focus on Tricia instead of thinking about my new archery skills.

"I said, do you want me to hold Caleb? Jeez. You were a million miles away. My story must have been completely boring to you," Tricia says in a pouty voice.

"I'm sorry, Tricia. I was just going over my archery stuff in my head. I'm fine holding him. He's almost asleep." I give him a slight bounce. Kirstin, proficient with a rifle, is part of the sentry crew. Tricia can also shoot and takes turn on watch, but five children is too many for me to handle on my own, so she's with me. This is helpful, considering her little boy has more energy than the other four put together.

I'll admit, Tricia is not what I expected as Grant's first crush. I guess I thought she'd look a little like me. She doesn't, not even a bit. Where I'm tall and voluptuous, she's short and scrawny. Even after having two children, she probably still weighs under a hundred pounds. She's pretty, with shiny black hair and almost black eyes, but she's not terribly nice. She makes a point of talking about people, even those I don't know, in an uncomplimentary way. Even her dad is fair game for her badmouthing.

I mostly tune her out, giving the occasional nod or "uh-huh" when it seems appropriate. Apparently, I completely tuned her out this time. And she's still pouting about it, as evidenced by her muttered, "Fine."

Caleb lets out a sigh, finally yielding to sleep. I give him a kiss on top of his head. It won't be long until I'm holding my own baby. My heart sinks at the thought of delivering without a hospital. Pamela has assured me my body will know what to do and she'll be there to help.

I take a deep breath, marveling at how clear my lungs have been lately. I've hardly had a wheeze since that day in the basement of City Hall when Harry practically scared the life out of me. The few times I've thought an attack was starting, I remember how he prayed for me, replaying his words in my head while not actually praying myself, and it seems to ease off. Could Harry's prayer have healed me? Nah . . . that can't happen, right?

Tricia must be over her feeling of insult because she starts in on another story. I focus in on Tricia as she says, "And then you know what she did? She told me I was the problem. Can you believe that? Just because I pointed out to her that she's too closedminded to realize what is right in front of her. And another thing— "

A horse whinnies in the distance, a welcome distraction from Tricia's complaining. Another advantage to owning an outfitter service is the horses and other gear. Many of the places they take hunters to are in the mountains and only accessible by horseback. They go in advance to set up camp, leaving a couple of the guides there to watch over everything, then bring the hunters in when it's time. Grant's family has a variety of horses for riding and packing.

I've never been on a horse—and have no plans of getting on one now—but several people in our group will ride if we need to evacuate. I've been assigned a seat in the trailer being towed by the quad, along with Kirstin's boys and the other couple's little girl.

Until a few years ago, in addition to the outfitter's business, Paul and his wife would do summer trips with people. They had daylong and overnight trail rides that took people to an already established camp. They even own a couple of wagons for hayrides and an old-fashion chuckwagon. For those, they'd ride across a flat section of public land with one wagon loaded with people and the other with gear. They'd set up camp, make meals out of the chuckwagon, and stay overnight. They'd often move to a new location the next day to give folks an experience of pioneer life.

Right now the wagons, pack horses, all their cattle and adult poultry, and everything else deemed essential have been moved to a nearby location the family refers to as The Bowl. When Grant's great-grandpa John first bought this land, it was a working cattle ranch. The Bowl, named because it's in a depression surrounded by three hills, was set up with fencing to form a couple of corrals. I have yet to see it, but I'm told it's a beautiful area with a natural spring and an almost lush environment.

The family got out of the cattle business almost twenty years ago, the year John turned eighty. The family service station was less hassle and a bigger moneymaker, so that along with the guide service and trail rides became the focus. Grant and his brother would raise a steer or pig for 4-H, but that was the extent of it until a few years ago when Dax started raising cattle seasonally. He buys two dozen head in the spring and sells them in the fall.

Pamela has chickens and ducks for eggs plus orders in turkeys and meat birds—both chickens and ducks—every spring. She started a tradition of a turkey dinner for every birthday. She says she got the idea from a book she read about a woman homesteader in Wyoming. She's been doing turkey birthday dinners every year since Grant was three.

This year she added a turkey for me. I knew I was a part of the family when her order of poults arrived and she made sure to tell me one had my name on it. Part of me was a little weirded out by thinking she's raising something from a baby that she plans on me eating for a special occasion, but mostly I felt loved. Even during the years Grant was away from home, she made sure there was a turkey for him. Bryce said she would still cook up the turkey feast on Grant's birthday without him there.

This morning, Chaplain Rick and Toby James went to The Bowl to tend to the horses, cattle, and poultry. Pairs rotate going a week at a time, camping while they're there. They've set up a big tent used for outfitting, in addition to a smaller tent, along with the chuckwagon to use for cooking. Next week, Grant and I are staying at The Bowl. I'm very much looking forward to it. It's going to be like a mini vacation with my husband. We didn't have a honeymoon, so maybe I'll pretend this is it.

The day passes very slowly. It's almost four o'clock when Pamela comes rushing over.

"Quick. Take the children to the root cellar." Pamela picks up Mason and grabs the little girl by the hand.

"What's going on?" Tricia asks. "Are we being attacked?"

"I don't know. I don't think so. Angelo came rushing in and told me to get you all locked down."

"We don't need to evacuate?"

"Please, let's just get to the root cellar," Pamela says, moving quickly in that direction. Tricia takes her children while I carry Caleb.

The old cellar door, which swells with the moisture, sticks. It takes both Pamela and Tricia to get it open. Once we're inside, Pamela turns on a battery-operated lantern, then says, "I'll be back when I know more."

"Where are you going?"

"To my lookout spot. Don't worry, Shelby." She gives me a weak smile. "All will be well. Lock this door behind me."

I set the lock as she quickly leaves the cellar. While not an *actual* underground root cellar, this space is carved into a hillside and functions the same. The shelves were well laden with food, most of which has already been moved to The Bowl, but there are still jars of home-canned goods. It was determined the jars should be used up while we're here so we don't have to worry about glass breakage when we leave.

"What do you think is going on?" I ask Tricia.

"Not sure. But my dad wouldn't have us come in here if it weren't safe to stay at the ranch."

"Okay. If you're sure."

"I'm sure. Don't worry. Would you like to meditate?"

"Uh, no. That's okay."

A few camp chairs have been put in the root cellar, along with a tarp to allow a play space on the dirt floor. I set Caleb on the tarp, and he immediately begins babbling at Mason. Tricia and I wait in silence. Thankfully, it's not long until there's a knock on the door.

"Shelby? It's Grant. You can come out now."

I struggle to get up from the camp chair. "Let me," Tricia says.

She has the door unlocked and Grant is inside before I'm even out of the chair.

"There was a small problem . . . well, maybe *problem* isn't the right word," Grant says.

"What happened?" Tricia asks.

"Someone followed Annette out of town."

"Followed her?" Tricia asks in a near whisper.

"Who?" I ask.

"I think it was that attorney. The one who challenged Richard Majors when he was going to— " Grant gives a side tilt of his head, motioning toward the children. He doesn't want to say it in front of

173

them. When Richard Majors was going to hang Milena, the sheriff, and the others.

"What attorney is that?" Tricia asks.

Grant scrunches up his face. "Umm . . . Jude, maybe? I think that's his first name."

"Jude Poppe? Oh, great. He's just what we need here."

"What do you mean?" I ask, again concerned for our safety.

"He's one of those crazy right-wing nutters. He's so conservative he makes my dad look liberal."

"I'm not sure that really matters right now," Grant says.

I nod my agreement. "As long as he's not with Majors and his goons, I'm okay with it."

"Well, I'm not. While my dad and everyone else here has been respectful about me being" —Tricia pauses and looks toward the ground— "of different beliefs than they are, Jude is anything but respectful. He came into my store one day and totally laid into me, telling me I was an abomination. Can you believe that?"

"What kind of store do you own?" Grant asks, his voice laced with confusion.

"Mystic Moon. I sell metaphysical supplies."

Grant gives a single nod.

"The little place next to the sandwich shop?" I ask. I almost stopped in there once but decided against it. Just like Christianity and all its trappings held no appeal for me, the religions she advertises aren't any better. I think back to my mom and how she said all the mainstream religions were nothing but a form of control. Now I wonder about that. I wonder if her experience during the one and only time she attended church fully tainted her opinion. When I think of the way Annette sings, sending praises up to God, and the fervent way Harry prayed for my healing, I don't feel controlled. I feel loved.

Tricia nods. "That was it. And that's where Jude Poppe harassed me. Too bad, too. The first time I met him, I thought he was kind of cute. That was before I realized he's just a smallminded bigot. I hope they're sending him back to Prospect."

"We can't do that," Grant says. "We can't risk him telling them about us, about what we're doing."

"Did the attack go okay?" I ask.

"I'm not sure. Bryce was walking up to the rendezvous spot when he heard Jude practically yelling at Annette. They heard the explosion followed by the shots. Jude flinched at the noise, which allowed Annette to take him down."

"Annette took him down?" I ask, my voice full of awe.

"That's what Bryce said. Then he helped her subdue him. They hogtied him, blindfolded him, and brought him back on the quad."

"Where is he now?" Tricia asks.

"Locked in one of the outbuildings."

"Do you think he knows where he is? Who we are?" Tricia asks.

"I don't think so. Bryce doesn't think he recognized him."

"So we could just let him go," Tricia says.

Grant shakes his head. "Doubtful. And it's not my decision to make. Anyway, you all can come out of here now."

The rest of the day passes without incident. It's decided to keep Jude locked in the shed for now, at least until we can determine his motives. Paul has talked to him through the door. Jude insists he wasn't really following Annette, just looking for a way out of town. He has family up near Glacier National Park in Montana and wants to go there. He says now that he's out of Prospect, that's his plan, to just head north. And that our secrets are safe with him. I don't think anyone trusts that.

Our evening meal is stressful. We're all wondering how PJ, Dusty, and Dax are doing. Did they escape from where they were shooting and find a safe place to spend the night?

Pamela and I are cleaning up when Paul comes in from outside.

"Thought you'd like to know, the spotter they had on the hillside at the Vasquezes' ranch reported in."

"Yes?" Pamela says, hands wringing the material of her apron.

"At least a dozen of Majors's people are dead. They sent a group out looking for our boys. They returned to town a short while ago. The spotter doesn't think they found them."

"Praise the Lord!" Pamela cries, giving me a hug.

"Now what?" I ask.

"We'll see them tomorrow. And we continue with the good fight. You busy this evening, Shelby?"

"Not that I know of. Pamela?"

"I'm going to go out and weed the garden. Don't have her do anything too exhausting," Pamela says to Paul.

"I need a secretary. Think you're up for that?" he asks me with a wink.

175

A half an hour later, I'm sitting in the living room, notebook in hand. Paul and the sheriff, with Harry's input, have been working on plans for our next attack. I'm the notetaker.

"I sure wish we had people who are better trained for combat," Sheriff Spieth says with a shake of his head.

"Angelo's daughter, Tricia, is Army Reserve," Paul says. I'm surprised by this. She didn't say anything about that to me. She did tell me her husband was killed while serving in Afghanistan, but she didn't say anything about being in the military herself. And with the way she talks, I'm surprised.

"Yes, I've spoken with her. Even though she did have weapons training, her MOS is in supplies. She'll still be a help, but for the most part, we only have ranchers and hunters."

"Rick is retired Army," Paul says. "But as a Chaplain, he had a noncombatant status."

"What's that mean?" I ask.

"He went to school to be a preacher but decided he wanted to be in the Army," Harry says.

"Okay. So he was a preacher in the Army, but he didn't go to war?"

"I wouldn't say that. It'd be more accurate to say he wasn't directly in combat," Paul says.

"And he wasn't trained for combat," Harry adds. "Though, he has had plenty of weapons training in his personal life. He's comfortable with firearms."

"But for our purposes," Sheriff Spieth says, "he doesn't count as retired Army."

"You've spoken with everyone at the other ranches as well?" Paul asks.

"Yep. As I said, ranchers and hunters."

"What about Jude?" Harry asks. "Wasn't he in the military?"

"The lawyer who was sneaking up on us?" I ask.

Harry and Paul exchange a look, and Sheriff Spieth nods before saying, "Seems he was in the military before he went to law school. We'll have to see if he's with us. If not— " He clears his throat.

Harry and Paul nod, then Paul says, "I still think Dax was right. We should just kill Majors and be done with it."

"I'd agree, but someone else would just step up. These guys have suddenly had a taste of control, and they like it. When they had me— " The sheriff clears his throat again. "When they were

176

interrogating me, it was obvious several of them had suddenly found what they believed to be their calling. Sure, there's a few joining in because they think it'll give them some safety. But many are enjoying the experience. We kill Majors, and his son Scott is suddenly in control. We kill Scott, and another idiot steps up. We need to seriously reduce their numbers, then we take out Richard and Scott."

"So what's next?" I ask.

"Next, I think we should simultaneously eliminate all the guards watching the roads going in and out of town," Paul says.

The sheriff stares off into space, scratching his chin. His shoulders sag. "It's the next logical step. It could put some good fear into them if we take out all his guards at one time."

"The road to Wesley will be a challenge," Harry says.

"No doubt," the sheriff agrees with a nod. "It's pretty wide open there with the east side of town opening up to the valley. We're good on the other three sides with the foothills and mountains helping provide cover, but that side . . . " He rubs his chin again. "I think I could get close enough."

"How?" I ask.

Paul shoots me a look and gives a slight shake of his head. I return his look with a slight shrug of my shoulders. I thought it was a legitimate question. I'm not sure why he's acting like it wasn't.

"Can't happen," Harry says. "Especially not by you. Everyone knows who you are, and my guess is there's a bounty on your head. Maybe Dax could get close enough to— "

"Nope," Sheriff Spieth interjects. "We're not putting that boy in danger. You know I wasn't on board with him being one of the snipers this time. That should have been my place."

"And, my old friend, you are well aware that you're still not physically able to move fast enough to get away if they're chasing you," Harry says.

"I will be by the time we do our next strike. And I'm thinking, maybe a slight disguise might be just what I need to get in and do what I need to do. Paul, did your wife have any wigs big enough to fit over my noggin?"

Paul looks down at his lap. "You're sure about this, Jason?" he asks Sheriff Spieth. "We could just hit the other sentry points and not worry about the road to Wesley. It wouldn't make that big of a difference."

"It's symbolic."

Chapter 29

It's day two of our honeymoon camping adventure. Being here with Grant is great, but The Bowl has its challenges. Everything was set up nicely, but the beds—little cots—weren't as comfortable as I thought they should've been. And while the complete silence here away from everything and everyone is wonderful during the day, at night it's annoying and makes sleep difficult. The cricket, which started chirping about an hour after we had gone to bed, is not the kind of noise I welcome.

Our job while we're here is to take care of the livestock, which includes not only feeding and watering but also exercising the horses and gathering the chicken and duck eggs. It's not a full-time job, so we have lots of downtime. We brought several more things from the ranch that will go with us when we evacuate, so we spend some time organizing those items.

I also spend time practicing my archery while Grant does different drills with his handgun.

Grandpa Paul, as I'm now calling him instead of just plain Paul, gave me a sling thing to wear on my back for carrying my compound bow. The sling has two parts to it and gives the option of carrying on my front also. With my baby bump, the fit isn't quite like it's supposed to be. Grandpa Paul suggested I practice with the sling, both wearing it on my back and on my front, so I can quickly get into position and nock an arrow. The quiver on my bow holds four arrows. He gave me a quiver bag for additional arrows, which can hang off my belt or back. Ideally, he'd like me to have the bow across my front and the quiver bag on my back. So far, that's not working out so well. There's just too much of me getting in the way.

I keep at it, practicing the movements, working at getting my bow from its carrying position to an arrow in place and accurately shooting. It's frustrating to feel so clumsy. The actual shooting, when I can take my time and line up my shot, is fine. But everything else is still a challenge.

After I'm finished, Grant says, "You're getting surprisingly good at that. And you seem really comfortable."

I smile my thanks before taking a long drink of water.

"My release thing slipped a few times, and I still feel super clumsy with all of it."

"Anything new is like that. You're shooting both field tips and broadheads?"

"Three of each," I say with a nod. "Just like your grandpa told me to do."

"What distance are you at now?"

"Sixty yards, but my grouping isn't particularly good at that distance. I'm afraid to go back any farther for fear of messing up the broadheads—I know we don't have enough of them."

"We don't have enough of anything these days," he says with a small smile. "You want to practice with the pistol?"

"That's a different gun than you've been carrying," I say, pointing to the handgun on his hip.

"It is." He unholsters it so I can look.

"Where'd you get it?"

"My dad gave it to me yesterday."

"Really?" I say with a squeal. "Why didn't you tell me?"

He shrugs. "It's not that big of a deal."

"Grant," I say, crossing my arms, "your dad hasn't spoken to you— "

"He's spoken to me. Or at least grunted in my direction." He raises his eyebrows.

I shake my head. "You've said barely two words between you both, and now he gives you a gun. A nice looking one at that. Seems like a big deal to me."

He tilts his head. "You're right. It is a big deal. I'm making light of it, but it means a lot to me. We talked, and I think things are going to be different—things already are different. We're good. So, you want to try it?"

"I don't want to actually shoot." I place a hand over my stomach.

"No, we're not shooting while we're here. It's better to be silent."

"So it's different from the one your mom showed me how to use?"

"Yeah. That was a revolver—an S&W .38 Special. This is a semi-automatic."

"Mm-hmm."

"The magazine is out." He motions to a black box looking thing sitting on the camp table. "And the chamber is empty." He does something to the top, pulling apart the gun and showing me the inside. "Empty," he says, placing a finger in the opening.

"Okay. That's good."

"My mom told you about checking for yourself and not taking someone's word about it being empty, right?"

"She did, but not with that kind of gun. She opened up the little wheel." I motion with my hands, trying to replicate how Pamela opened the gun. "Then she said to do a visual and a physical inspection."

"Right. The physical is because sometimes our mind sees what it wants to see."

"She said that."

"Okay." He nods. "So this is different from Mom's gun. The ammunition is kept in the magazine"— he motions again to several black cases on the table— "and feeds from there. Mom's revolver holds six?"

"Five."

"Right. The shorter magazines hold fifteen rounds. I can put another in the chamber for sixteen."

"Jeez. I hope you never need that many."

"Same here. The two longer magazines each hold thirty-one."

"What? That's crazy. And you can still have another bullet in the gun?"

He nods. "Right now I'm using a magazine loaded with dummy rounds. It doesn't actually shoot, but it gives a good replication to help with improving my skills."

"So your dad gave it to you? With all this stuff? To keep?"

"I don't think he's going to ask for it back," he says with a wink.

He spends several more minutes showing me the different parts and how it works.

"Remember, it's a Glock, so there isn't a safety."

"Okay. Your mom said her gun has an internal safety. So, the same thing?"

He tilts his head from side to side a few times. "Not really. With this weapon, I am the safety."

"You are the safety? Okay, that sounds nice."

"Basically, there's a trigger safety, so keep your finger off the trigger until you're ready to shoot."

"Well, duh. I think I already knew that. And your mom did go over those safety rules with me."

He has me move into a proper stance and helps me line up my shot. We spend quite a lot of time pretending to fire at different targets.

"Okay, I've had enough," I say, more than ready for a break.

"You've done well today."

"Thanks. I hope I never have to shoot a gun or use the bow and arrow."

"I know, me too." Grant nods.

"The day after tomorrow is when they'll attack the sentry posts in Prospect," I say.

"Yes. It should go well. Pretty much the same concept as the last attacks," Grant says.

"Except the road to Wesley."

After PJ, Dusty, and Dax returned from their sniper attacks, there was more planning done for the second onslaught. The new plan is better than the original, but it's still risky. And Sheriff Spieth still insists on being the one to execute the attack. He'll be making his way to an abandoned house and then, at the appointed time, use the roof of the house as his platform. The big question is, will he be able to get away afterward?

We'll have to be extra alert when the attacks happen. If anything goes wrong and we're discovered, our group and the people from the other three ranches will all meet here. Then we'll make our way to Bakerville, where we hope to be safe from Majors. At least for a little while.

Chapter 30

Today is the day. Grant slipped out of our tent before the sun was even fully up. I followed a few minutes later. It's chilly this morning. I know it'll be plenty warm later once the sun comes up, but right now I'm wearing a hoody and light gloves. Pamela made sure I packed things like gloves and hats. I'm glad she did.

"You're up early," I say, carefully picking my way to where Grant's caring for the horses. While the area around The Bowl has lots of brush, thanks to the natural spring, where the corral is located resembles the desert with rocks and cacti.

"I wanted to make sure everything was ready." He turns toward me, his head lamp catching me in the eyes. "Oops. Sorry," he says, quickly looking down after I let out a small squeal and cover my eyes.

"I always forget how bright those things are. I thought we got everything put in order yesterday?"

"It'll be good to have the chores done."

"What time is the assault?"

Grant looks toward the east. "Won't be long, as soon as the sun shows its face. Part of the hope is the rising sun will blind the guys on the east side, giving Jason more of an opportunity to get away."

"It sounds weird when you call him Jason."

"Well, that is his name."

"I know. But calling him Sheriff or Sheriff Spieth fits. Jason doesn't."

I help Grant finish the chores, then make us a breakfast of eggs. With the laying hens and ducks here at The Bowl, we eat a lot of eggs. When we return to the ranch—after Angelo, Tricia, and her children relieve us—we'll take eggs back with us for them. But while we're here, they're ready and available food.

I was weirded out by the idea of eggs being kept here all week before being taken back to the ranch. Without a refrigerator, or at least the coolness of the root cellar, it seems they would spoil. Pamela assured me if they were gathered and kept unwashed in a cool spot, they'd be fine. Eggs have a natural covering, she called it the bloom, which helps keep the eggs fresh.

Last night, after sundown, we put all the chickens, ducks, and turkeys into crates. Grant wants to leave them crated until late morning so they're ready to go if we need to evacuate. According to Grant, loading them into crates during daylight isn't easy, at least not the laying hens and ducks. He says the meat birds still move slow during the daytime, but the turkeys can be mean. I think he's right about that. The turkeys were mean last night when we put them in the crates—an assortment of dog kennels and laundry baskets bound together.

The day passes slowly and without incident. Late afternoon, I notice Grant begins to visibly relax. A few minutes later, he says, "It probably went well. I think we'd know by now if it didn't. Just in case, we'll make sure we're ready. You feel like doing some weapons practice?"

"Handgun?"

"I thought we could work with the rifle and the shotgun, get you comfortable holding them."

After an hour or so of practice, we call it good and relax for the evening. Even though we don't really do much here at The Bowl, I'm always exhausted by bedtime.

We've been asleep for several hours when Grant shakes me awake.

"What's going on?" I ask groggily.

"Shhh," he warns, then whispers, "I think someone's out there. I want you to stay in here, but be ready. The pistol is loaded. Shoot anyone entering the tent that isn't me. If it's me, I'll tell you."

"What? What's happening?" I hiss, listening as the cattle and horses stomp and snort. Even the chickens, usually asleep and quiet at night, are making clucking sounds, and the ducks are quacking.

"I'll find out. Just be ready."

"No, don't leave."

He kisses me, grabs the rifle, and slips out the tent door.

My hands go to my throat; I feel it tightening. My chest constricts. *No. Not now. Please, not now. God, if You're there, I beg of You, please keep Grant safe. And please don't let me have an asthma attack right now.*

With my breath becoming ragged, I slip on my shoes and hoody. Grabbing the handgun, I move behind a folding table. There's a small amount of ambient light from the moon coming through the tent— just enough for me to see. I quickly clear the couple of things off the table and silently flip it on its side. It won't protect me from someone

184

shooting at me, but it could conceal me enough so I have a slight advantage. *Please, God, help me.*

I'm completely quiet for many long minutes, minus the occasional wheeze. The livestock continue their cacophony. Soon, I hear Grant speaking in a low, calming voice. At first, I think someone's out there and he's trying to talk them down. Talk them into not attacking us. Then, I realize he's talking to the horses and the cattle. I feel myself begin to relax.

"Shelby? It's me. Everything's okay. I'm coming in the tent."

"Okay," I answer, moving from my hiding place behind the table. When he's inside, I rush over to him. "What was it?"

"Coyotes. Or maybe wolves. I'll be able to tell in the morning. They were harassing the Pekins. I guess they thought duck sounded good tonight."

"Wolves? Will they hurt us?"

"Not likely. But given the chance, they'd take the poultry. I'll double check the housing tomorrow."

"Maybe we should crate them every night, like we talked about."

"That was only so we could leave quicker in case the ranch was attacked. I'm not sure it'd be any safer for them, but we can think about it. Oh, hey" —he motions to the table— "good thinking."

I shrug. "Your grandpa mentioned finding something to hide behind. Something bullets can't get through is best, but I didn't have anything like that in here, so . . . "

"You sound a little wheezy. Do you need your inhaler?"

"I think I'm okay. It started to come on but didn't develop into a full attack. I'm feeling better now."

"You haven't needed your inhaler much. Maybe the symptoms are subsiding."

"They seem to be. Are you going back to bed? I don't know if I'll be able to sleep after that."

"I'm not sure I can either. And it's probably best to stay awake in case they come back. I think we need to consider additional people here. That way, someone can be on watch while the others sleep."

"Do you think that would've kept the wolves away tonight?"

"Possibly. Why don't you go back to bed?"

"You're going to be tired tomorrow. Or today, whichever it is."

"I'll nap, then. You can hold down the fort."

185

The rest of our time at The Bowl is spent with Grant and I sleeping in shifts. He lets me have actual nighttime sleeping, and during the day, he catches up on his sleep while I try finding things to occupy my time. I keep up with my archery and weapons practice and play lots of Solitaire—a first for me. I've played it on my phone before, but never with real cards. I like the real cards much better.

The day we're to be relieved, Grant stays awake. We get everything looking good and package up the eggs to take back with us. It's early afternoon before Angelo and Tricia arrive.

"Hey, girlfriend," Tricia says, wrapping me in a hug. "You've grown." She gives my stomach a pat. The whole touching a pregnant belly thing is weird to me. I've never once had the urge to pat anyone's stomach, but mine seems to be fair game.

"Where are your children?" I ask. "I thought they were coming with you."

"Milena and Kirstin are watching them. It seemed easier than bringing them here."

"The raid went well?" Grant asks, after shaking Angelo's hand.

A cloud passes over Angelo's face. "The mission was successful."

"Jason didn't make it back," Tricia blurts. "Bryce said he thinks they killed him."

I close my eyes.

"Bryce is okay? Dax? My dad?" Grant asks, his voice raising an octave with each name.

Angelo puts his hand on Grant's shoulder. "Everyone else is fine. Let us get our stuff put up, then we'll give you the details before you head back to the ranch."

While they organize their gear, I sniff back my tears as we finish loading our quad.

"C'mere." Grant opens his arms, and I melt into him.

"I can't believe they killed the sheriff. We all told him not to go. He shouldn't have gone."

"It was necessary," Grant says, smoothing my hair.

"Necessary for him to die?"

"Necessary for them to do the assault. We have to lessen their numbers."

"Why? Why can't we just leave? Go to Paul's friend's house."

Instead of answering, he pulls me closer. We stay that way for many minutes, until I finally dry my eyes.

"You okay?" he asks.

"No. I'm quite sure I am definitely not okay. And I wonder if I ever will be."

He nods and returns to the quad, tightening straps and doing whatever. I straighten slightly when I see Tricia striding toward us.

"We brought a few more things for the wagons," Tricia says. "Seems Paul is always finding more stuff he doesn't want to leave behind."

"Understandable," Grant says. "He's lived there his entire life. Did you know he was born in my great-grandpa and grandma's house?"

"Oh, yes. I've heard the story," she says with a smile. "I guess the days of homebirth being common are now brought back."

I lay a protective hand over my stomach.

"Well, I guess we're set," Angelo says.

"We had some trouble one night," Grant says. "Wolves were trying to get at the ducks."

"Really? Guess I shouldn't be surprised."

"We've been taking turns on watch. I thought I'd suggest another couple, or at least one more person, to come out and help. You okay with that?"

"Sounds smart. You two must be exhausted."

"They could send Jude out," Tricia says. Jude was kept locked in the shed until the day before we left for The Bowl. I guess there was some disagreement on what should be done with him, and I don't know what he did to convince them he wasn't a threat, but it was a long, drawn-out thing. Tricia was the most vocal about not allowing him to join us.

"Jude Poppe?" I ask. "The guy you hate?"

She gives a small, shy smile. "He's not so bad. At least not at the ranch. It seems some of his pretentiousness may have been for show."

"I thought he had a problem with you not being a Christian."

"Who said I'm not a Christian?"

"Umm. Well, I just assumed. You know, since you sold things like Ouija boards."

"Yeah. I can see why you would think that. And maybe it's true. Maybe I'm not. Or wasn't. Now . . . I just don't know."

"How can you not know?" I ask.

"Well," she says indignantly, "my dad and mom are both Christians. I went to church until I left home. How could I not be?"

"It doesn't quite work that way," Grant says gently.

"Oh yeah? Well, no one really knows for sure. We all just do the best we can and hope it's enough when we die."

Angelo gives Tricia a sad look and shakes his head.

Grant looks down at his shoes and then straightens up and takes a breath. "I used to think that way too. The last several years, I figured if I did more good things than bad, it'd be fine. Of course, I didn't really believe in God during that time. But now, now I realize— "

"Oh, I know all about that," Tricia interrupts, waving her hands. "My dad's always telling me I won't get to heaven on his coattails. And just because I think I'm a good person—and I am—doesn't mean I can escape God's judgment without having accepted Jesus. You don't need to worry about me. I've done all that. You don't need to preach at me about it."

"I'm sorry if you thought I was preaching, Tricia. That wasn't what— "

"No worries. Anyway, as I was saying, Jude isn't so bad. He'd be a help to us."

"He'll have his own tent," Angelo says gruffly, shooting a look in Tricia's direction. I watch as the color creeps up her neck.

I want to ask her more about the Christian stuff, but I know that's a conversation we should have in private. My biggest question is, how does she know whether or not she's a Christian? I would think someone who sold the things she sold would be forever ostracized by God. I mean, really, some of that stuff was for his direct competition.

"About Jason," Angelo says, returning to our earlier conversation, "the exact details are unclear, but here's what we know. You know Bryce was set up as a spotter and support for the sheriff?"

We nod. The plan was for Bryce to be on a small hillside southeast of town. He and the sheriff left for the location the same day Grant and I came to The Bowl. They had to take a long route to the hill, then they planned to set up camp on the southside. The sheriff wanted at least one day of observing the roadblock and sentries on the road to Wesley.

"Bryce said everything was going as planned. They made sure the house Jason wanted to use for his assault would work for how the sentries were positioned. He left right at dark. As soon as it was time, he easily took out each of the men at the roadblock. He moved from that shooting position to a secondary location he'd chosen, with the plans to make his way back to Bryce after nightfall. Someone must have seen him because it wasn't long after he arrived at his hiding spot when the goons started showing up, surrounding the house."

I let out a gasp. Angelo nods and continues, "And, of course, Bryce's first instinct was to go in and help him. But the shooting started right away. He never saw anyone come back into view. He also didn't see Jason again. He stayed on watch. At one point, Majors and his son showed up. They were visibly angry. They drug out a body, and Bryce was almost certain it was Jason. He waited another two days after that just to be sure the sheriff didn't show up."

"So that's it then?" Grant asks. "We're sure?"

"Yeah. Seems so. But it gets more interesting."

"How so?"

"One of the people from the Vasquez ranch was watching on the west end of town when it seemed they were setting up for a town meeting midday. They had someone sneak in close enough to be able to listen and observe. Majors announced the sheriff was dead and had been responsible for the recent acts of sabotage. Right then, a small bomb went off at City Hall. All the glass in the windows blew out. It wasn't our group, so all we can figure is we're not the only ones trying to bring Majors down."

Chapter 31

After we checked in and gave our report, I went straight to the bathtub. Today's bath is not overly luxurious by any means, but it beats the sponge baths we had while staying at The Bowl. Hot running water at my fingertips is probably what I missed the most. As I recline in my shallow bath, I think about others in Wyoming, in the more arid regions. How are they doing? We're fortunate to have the creek here and the natural spring at The Bowl, plus several other small creeks and streams coming out of the mountains. Paul says there's a stretch on our way to Bakerville that won't have water for several miles. We'll have to carry what we need during that time.

I used to think the idea of going to Bakerville was just a backup plan. We'd be able to defeat Majors and take back Prospect. But everyone is so sure we'll have to leave—bug out is the way Uncle PJ refers to it—that I've come to fully accept it also. And now, with the sheriff dead, we've lost our main strategist. There's hope that the other people who are fighting against Majors, the ones who set off the bomb, can combine with us and we can really do some good. And we still have Donnie and Jerry seeking help from the town of Cody.

When we gave our report, everyone agreed with our suggestion of needing more than two people at The Bowl. They asked Jude Poppe if he'd like to spend the week with Angelo and Tricia, and he practically jumped for joy. I guess Tricia's fondness for him isn't one sided. He'll have to take what he needs on his back; we don't have a spare quad or dirt bike to send with him, so he'll be packing light. He said it wasn't a big deal. He hiked the Colorado Trail a couple summers ago and is comfortable with carrying only what he needs.

I think back to my conversation with Pamela as she walked with me back to the house. "I guess he's sweet on Tricia," she said. "When did that happen?"

"I have no idea. The day they brought him here, she said she hated him and that he was always harassing her."

Pamela shrugged. "I'm surprised. He's always seemed so strong in his faith. I wouldn't think he'd want to yoke with an unbeliever."

I gave her a questioning look.

"Oh! I know it's different with you and Grant."

"I'm sorry, Pamela, but I don't know what we're talking about."

"About being unevenly yoked. Christians and non-Christians."

"Christians aren't supposed to date non-Christians? That seems rather . . . elitist."

"Elitist? No, I don't think so. It's from scripture, a parable about how two oxen that are not similar but are yoked together—joined by a wooden bar to each other and to whatever they are pulling—should be similar."

"And what does this have to do with people?" I could hear my voice sounding much snottier than I intended.

"The unequally yoked team has one oxen that is stronger than the other, or maybe taller or something. The weaker one will walk more slowly and can cause the load to go in circles." She gave me a look and a nod. "Understand?"

"Umm, I guess. But you're talking about oxen. Those are cows, right?"

"Usually castrated cattle, yes. They're trained to pull a plow or lead a team, quite common in years past. Might be again soon."

"And? What does that have to do with Jude and Tricia?"

"If the oxen are unequally yoked, they can't work together. They go in circles, at odds with one another. It's the same with people."

"I thought being different from each other is a good thing. My grandma always taught me to embrace people's differences, saying it makes the world go 'round."

With a smile, Pamela said, "There certainly are plenty of differences in the world. And I'm not saying we don't still become friends with those who have different beliefs. We can certainly like people, even respect them. We're just cautioned not to form strong bonds. Jesus was a friend to all, even those who were blatantly sinning, but he didn't form tight bonds with them. Things like business partnerships and marriage will be more difficult if we're unevenly yoked."

"That sounds kind of . . . " I shrugged. "It sounds very snobby." Even though it sounds snobby, I do wonder if this was a problem for my parents. Was my dad being a Christian and my mom being kind of anti-Christian an issue in their marriage?

Pamela's smile increased. "I guess it might be. And I'm sure it makes little sense to you."

"So, is that what you think of me?" I felt the tears stinging my eyes. "Do you think I'm not good enough for Grant?" My voice cracked on his name.

"No, no. Not at all," she said, wrapping an arm around me. "Oh, I haven't explained as well as I should have. It's not about being good enough. It's about having a match that works. With you and Grant, it's different. Grant made it clear he turned his back on his faith. When the two of you met, you had consistent faith and neither of you were believers."

"So, you do think we're a good match?"

"Faith wise? I think when you met you were evenly yoked, yes."

"And now?"

"And now . . . what do you think, Shelby? Do you feel like you're well matched as far as faith is concerned?"

It was several beats before I said, "I'm not sure what to think."

Replaying the conversation in my mind, I wish I would've told her Grant and I are perfect together. He loves me, and I love him. We don't need anything more. But is that the truth? In some ways, I can feel Grant slipping away from me. He participates in all the group church services. He sings along. He prays. And he's started reading a Bible. I caught him when we were camping when he thought I was resting. And I heard him talking to himself. At least, I thought he was talking to himself, but he was praying. *Alone*. With no one else around to impress. What was he saying to Tricia? If she does more good than bad, what's the problem? And he was almost sounding preachy. What is he thinking?

I feel myself getting angry at him. I feel betrayed. Then I remember I've been kind of praying too. Not out loud, but silently. Ever since the day in the basement when Harry prayed and my asthma attack stopped, I've asked God for help when the attacks start or when I'm scared. Is that praying?

When Grant was doing it, or when Grandpa Paul or one of the others prayed, they just talked. Almost like they're talking to each other. There's not a lot of fancy words most of the time. But they do end it with amen. Since I don't end with amen, maybe I'm not praying. I don't think I want to pray. I mean, if I did, that would mean . . . no. I won't betray Mom's memory. I won't betray my grandparents. Dad was wrong to believe in that stuff. Grant is wrong if he's starting to believe it again. I must talk to him and make him stop. Otherwise, we might be like the oxen, and that won't be okay.

I hop out of the tub—as much as a woman of my advancing pregnancy can hop—and go quickly to my room. I'm going to find Grant and talk with him right now. I dress in a knee-length skirt and tank top along with my hiking boots. I'll put a button-up shirt over the top before I go. I'm tying my shoes when Pamela bursts through the door.

"There's a squad leaving town and heading this way. We're going to our assigned places."

"Right behind you," I say, throwing my daypack over my arm and grabbing my bow and quiver bag. "Where are the children?"

"I'm not sure. I think the sisters have them today. They should take them to the root cellar," Pamela says as she jogs away from me toward her own assigned location.

I turn the corner of the house and see the younger sister with the children. She's holding Caleb on her hip and trying to open the door to the root cellar.

"Amy! Let me help."

"Shelby, I was hoping you'd get here. The door's stuck again." It takes both of us to lift the door enough for Tricia's son to push on it until it gives.

"Okay, everyone inside," I say, leaving the door open so there's enough light to turn on the lantern.

"You brought your shooting stuff?" Mason asks, pointing at the bow I've haphazardly slung over my shoulder.

I try to smile at him as I say, "Just so I'd have it."

"Bad guys come." Mason gives a solemn nod.

I close my eyes, wondering what kind of damage these children may have long term. Will the life we are currently living scar them? Not long before the planes crashed back in June, Grant and I watched a PBS show on The Dust Bowl that happened in the 1930s. There was a man interviewed who talked about how every morning he'd wake up and all his dishes would be covered with dust. For the rest of his life he had to wash a plate or a glass before he could use it. That childhood memory of dust covering everything was embedded.

Will the same thing happen to these children? Will something we have to do now affect them forever? Will things ever return to normal so they can have the childhoods they deserve? What about my baby?

"We'll be fine, squirt," Amy says. "There's lots of people looking out for us."

I shiver in the cool dampness of the root cellar. My still wet hair, bundled loosely on my head, doesn't help. It's plenty hot outside, but the root cellar is always cool. Too cool for my wet hair, short skirt, and sleeveless top.

"Do you need a blanket?" Amy asks.

"Please. And let's put the tarp on the ground for the children to play on."

Amy hands me a small, thin blanket, which I wrap around my shoulders after propping my bow against the wall, then she spreads the tarp out. She puts Caleb on it and then turns to me. "How long do you think we'll be in here?"

I shake my head. "It's hard telling."

"If they have to fight them, will they leave us here? Or will someone come and tell us to leave? To go to The Bowl?"

"I guess it just depends on what they decide."

"Do you know how to get there? If we need to leave? I've never been there, and I'm not sure— "

"We're fine, Amy," I say with as much patience as I can muster. "We just need to wait and . . . and watch the children." I motion to the gun on her hip. "You know how to use that?"

She gives me a look. "Of course. You think I'd be wearing it if I didn't?" She bites her lip and drops her eyes. "I'm sorry. That wasn't— it wasn't necessary for me to snap at you. I'm just . . . "

"Scared?" I whisper.

Head bowed, she nods. I watch as a tear drops onto the dirt floor of the root cellar. I move over next to her. Wrapping my blanket–clad arm around her, I pull her close. All five children are looking at us with wide eyes.

"I'm scared too," I say softly. "It's okay to be scared. Amy, let's you and I sit on the floor with the kids."

Mason nods. "Sit by me, Shelby."

"I will. But someone might have to help me get up."

"Can you read us a story?" Tricia's daughter asks.

Amy gets a book from the toy box, left in here for this purpose, and we settle in for the story. It's not long until all but Tricia's son have fallen asleep.

"Do you want me to keep reading?" I ask.

"Nah. But I might as well sleep too. Nothing much else to do." He curls up next to his sister. Amy and I are silent until his soft snores indicate he's asleep too.

"Must be nice to be able to just fall asleep without worry," Amy says. "I haven't had a good night's sleep since the planes crashed. I know I worry too much. It's something I'm working on."

"It's hard not to worry when there's so much uncertainty and with— " I bite my lip.

"With all the death?"

I nod.

"It's hard. Especially since my parents died. It wasn't so bad before. I still worried, but my mom and dad were so strong. They made everything seem better. When they were killed— " She lets out a small cry, then covers her mouth.

After many minutes she says, "You know, the only reason Emily and I didn't die too was because we were standing in the back with our friends. When the shooting started, I saw my mom turn and look for us. She met my eyes and motioned for me to get on the ground. My dad repeated the motion as he started to pull her down. Then the explosion happened, right next to where they were standing. I tried to go toward them, but Emily yanked me down, telling me there was nothing I could do. I didn't— " She stops midsentence, turning toward me. "Is that gunfire?"

I tilt my head to the side. "I'm not sure. I'm going to open the door to see if I can hear better."

"Let me. I can get up easier," she says, already on her feet and walking toward the door. There's a loud creak of protest as the door slowly slides open. The sound of gunfire is immediately apparent. "We're under attack! We have to go."

"No, it's not here. Down the road, I think. Maybe at the Vasquezes' place?" I say.

"But they'll come here!"

Mason stirs slightly from Amy's yelling.

"Shh. Let's not wake the children. We're fine for now. Close the door. If we need to evacuate, we will."

"What if they forget about us?" Amy asks.

"Do you think Kirstin will forget her boys? You think Emily will forget you? I know Grant won't forget about me."

"They will if they end up dead," she snaps. I meet her glare with—what I hope is—a calm, even gaze. She lets out a huff and closes the door.

Even though I'm acting calm for Amy, I feel anything but. Like her, I'm scared and want to run. But not knowing exactly what's happening makes the root cellar our safest option, at least for now.

Amy stomps back over toward me, stopping a few feet away. "What's wrong with your neck?"

I pull my hand down from my throat and take a wheezy breath. "Nothing, it's just sometimes when I feel an asthma attack coming on, I, um, I claw at my throat. It's fine."

"Do you need one of those breathing things?"

"I'm probably fine. Just . . . can you help me up into one of the camp chairs?"

Once I'm sitting in a better position, I catch myself doing it again, starting to ask God to keep my asthma attack away.

Instead of sitting, Amy paces and lets out numerous sighs. Just when I'm close to asking her to sit down and shut up, there's a knock at the door. She rushes toward it.

"Wait," I say. "Ask who it is."

With a nod, she says, "Uh, yeah. Who's there?"

"It's Emily."

Amy slides open the door. "Are we okay?"

"I . . . I don't know. For now, yes. We're okay. They said to come and get you. We're going to meet in the house so they can tell us more."

Chapter 32

It's many minutes before those not on watch return to the house. Even though Grant isn't on watch right now since we just got back from The Bowl, he's been put into the watch rotation. When I ask Grandpa Paul what's happening, he tells me he'll explain once everyone arrives.

When Dusty and PJ come into the house, Paul asks, "Did everything go okay?"

"As well as can be expected," Dusty says. He makes a point of looking for Pamela, then glances toward me. He gives me a nod and a pained smile. I tilt my head in response.

"Okay, so here's what happened," Paul says in a booming voice. "Majors sent a group of six out. We had enough warning to get everyone in position. They stopped at Trey Vasquez's place and demanded all their livestock and to search the property for anything usable—for the good of the community."

There's much talk among the group about how unfair this is before Paul continues, "I know, I know. I don't like it either. And, well, those guys won't be taking anything. It went . . . things changed abruptly. Unfortunately, Bradyn Vasquez was shot and killed." There are several gasps. "And the six that showed up are also dead." Paul nods. "We suspect—*we know*—Majors will send out someone looking for them. He won't find them, at least not easily."

"The other families are packing up," PJ says. "We'll use this ranch as our base for the next day or two. We'll have a few . . . *surprises* set up for Majors at the Vasquez and Smalls ranches. Then, when they get here— " PJ looks to his dad. Tears are traveling down Grandpa Paul's face.

"Then, when they get here, we'll blow this place to smithereens," Paul says.

"No," Pamela says in a gasp.

wrap my arm around her shoulder.

"Let's get on with it," Paul says. "There's lots to do before Majors's people show up again."

"Do you think Richard Majors will be with them?" I ask.

PJ snorts. "That wuss? Not likely. He's more of the type to sit in an ivory tower and send others to do his bidding."

"But he did go to the house with the sheriff—when they killed the sheriff," Bryce says.

Paul nods. "That's true. And maybe he will. If he does, then we can possibly cut the head off the snake. And if we take out enough of them, including his son Scott, then perhaps we can take our town back. But that will be a big if. Richard Majors is scum, but he's smart. I'd be surprised if he sends more than a dozen people. And he and Scott will not be in that group."

The meeting breaks up after everyone's given assignments on what to do. We're not expecting trouble until tomorrow. The thought is it'll take Majors some time to realize his people aren't coming back. Then he'll send a team out to look for them. They'll go to the Vasquezes' ranch first since its closest to town, and where the guys from yesterday met their end. The ranch will be abandoned, so they'll move on to the next ranch—also abandoned.

Between the second ranch and our place, the road tightens into a bottleneck. That's where they plan to take out the group of goons. Once they're disposed of, booby traps will be set at the other three ranches. We'll rest and regroup, then head for The Bowl. A few will stay behind to set up more concealed dangers at our ranch.

After that, we'll stay at The Bowl until nightfall and then we'll begin our journey to Bakerville. It's about thirty miles by road from Prospect to Bakerville. Paul says it's slightly longer going overland. With the wagons, horses, livestock, and all the people, he expects it to take us five nights of traveling. He also says, unconvincingly, it's best we are leaving now. If we wait until winter, we'll have a harder time getting to Bakerville. He reminds us that, since we'll be traveling at night, it can be chilly and to dress accordingly.

There's some opposition to traveling at night. It'll be harder with the livestock and wagons. It's not like we have headlights, plus we wouldn't want to use them if we did. The entire reason for traveling at night is to be unseen. Between here and Bakerville, once we leave Cameron land, it's mainly BLM and state land—all public with full access. There's one spot of private land, an island within the BLM, which we'll skirt to prevent trespassing.

For the most part, everyone seems in agreement with the plan. But will it work out as outlined? We know it can all change based on Majors and his goon squad.

"Shelby, do you think you can take a turn on watch?"

"What? Yes, of course."

"No, Paul," Pamela says.

"She won't be in danger. We'll put her in that tree stand at the edge of the driveway."

"She shouldn't be climbing that ladder, not in her condition. I'll do it."

"You need to get all of your little chicks and ducklings ready to go. She'll be fine. Once she's up the ladder, she'll strap herself in. We need her. We've got a lot to do, and she's the logical choice for that spot."

Pamela shakes her head. "She can't stay up there for hours and hours. It's not good for her not to be able to move around."

"She'll be there just long enough for us to take care of the necessities. Once we get some of the other families here, we can relieve her."

"I can do it," I say. "I want to do it."

"Bring those arrows with the new broadheads, not the practice ones," Paul says.

Pamela shakes her head before embracing me in a hug. "Be careful."

"Of course she will," Paul says as he leads me away from the house. It's only a few minute walk to the spot on the edge of the driveway.

"Okay, now, with your bow on your back, you should be able to climb up. You ready?"

He makes sure I'm in the stand and secured to the tree by a little belt thing. That way if I lose my balance, or fall asleep, I won't fall twenty feet and plop on the ground like the goon in Prospect did. I shudder as I think about a fall like that.

"Now remember, you're just watching," Paul says, standing safe on the ground. "There's a lot of people watching between here and town, so the odds of anyone getting past them and to you is slim. Beyond slim. But if they do, if you see someone who shouldn't be out here, use your radio. The code is blueberry followed by elm tree."

"Blueberry followed by elm tree?"

"Your location is elm tree. Blueberry means you see a possible goon."

"So I say blueberry elm tree?"

"Right."

"Okay. I've got it."

I try and get comfortable on the little stool in the stand. I have an amazing view of the driveway and the road beyond. There's a slight breeze, making it cool but not cold. It's almost pleasant, and I'm happy to be contributing in this manner. After a short while, the novelty wears off, then it's just boring.

When I hear footsteps in the brush, I tense up. A voice quietly says, "Elm tree, I'm here to relieve you."

"Harry?"

"Yep." He steps out from a tree so I can see him.

"Did they get everything finished? I thought the other ranch families would show up by now."

"Some have. They cut through the properties instead of using the road. No reason to drive since we can't take vehicles with us. Other than the motorcycles and quads."

"I didn't realize we were taking those. Thought we were just riding horses and walking once we got to The Bowl."

"We'll take as many as we can. The fuel is more of an issue than anything, but we should be able to carry enough. Being able to pull the quad trailers gives us more supplies. Plus, it might be good for you and the children to have an option to ride occasionally. So, do you know how to get out of that thing?"

"Unhook the safety harness and climb down? Is there anything more to it than that?"

"Don't fall."

"I don't plan on it!"

When I return to the ranch house, the area has been transformed. There are tents of all shapes and sizes dotting the landscape. A woman around Pamela's age gives me a small wave. There's at least a dozen more children than the five we previously had. Tricia's son and daughter are playing with a few of similar age.

Grant finally shows back up after dark. I'm getting ready for bed when he knocks on our door.

"Shelby? It's me. Can I come in?"

"Of course you can, silly."

He enters, giving me a small, tired smile. "Boy, that bed sure looks comfortable."

"I'm looking forward to it. The cots we've been sleeping on for the last week left a lot to be desired."

"I heard they put you in one of the tree stands today."

"They did. It was fine. Kind of boring."

"Yeah. Sentry duty isn't too exciting. But it's necessary. At nighttime it's boring and hard to stay awake."

"I guess I never thought about that before I was in the stand today. I'd have a terrible time at night. Good thing they have that harness to keep you from falling out."

"Ask my dad about the time he fell out of a tree stand. He was fortunate he wasn't killed."

"What time do you think the goons will show up tomorrow?"

"*If* they show up."

"You don't think they will?"

"Probably. But who knows? Figuring out Richard Majors and his plans might prove to be a challenge. He doesn't think like the rest of us."

We settle into bed, sleeping in the same space for the first time in a week. I cuddle up next to him and immediately hear his rhythmic breathing turn into light snoring.

It feels like we've just fallen asleep when there's a banging at our door. "They're on their way. Get to your stations!"

I dress quickly in clothes warm enough for staying in the root cellar with the children, while Grant—already wearing sweatpants and a T-shirt—simply slips into his boots. He kisses me and says, "I'll see you soon."

Pamela is in the living room tying her shoes when I walk out. "Where are they?" I ask.

"They were just leaving town when our sentry saw them. He said they're traveling lights out."

"He said that? I thought we only use codes on the radio?"

"Yes, he broke protocol to give us extra details. Useful details." She stands up and goes for a rifle sitting in the corner of the room. "He also said there's at least fifty of them."

I feel the blood rush from my face. "Fifty?"

"They'll be here right as the sun's rising. With it behind them . . . it was smart of Richard. Too smart."

I give her a look.

She shrugs. "Let's go."

When we get outside, instead of being at their stations, everyone is standing in the yard—our group plus the people from the three other ranches. Paul looks around and says, "This is it, folks. Take down the tents and get everything you need. Head for The Bowl. We've called in the sentries. Those of you assigned for the bottleneck, go there. The rest, we'll see you soon. Once you get to The Bowl, Dusty will give assignments for sentries there. The plan is to stay there until dark and then start toward Bakerville. Hopefully, Majors's people will follow our plans and won't be a threat to us for long. All right. You've got fifteen minutes before you need to head out. Bottleneck crew, let's go."

I look for Grant. He gives me a small smile and a nod. I blow him a kiss. He's part of the bottleneck crew. He'll be expected to kill the people who want to kill us. He lifts his hand toward me as he follows the rest of the group.

"Let's get these tents down," Dusty says.

It feels like much longer than fifteen minutes before we're loaded and heading for The Bowl. The trailers attached to our quads are filled with tents and other supplies. Dusty's radio sounds and Paul's voice comes across. "Head out," is all that is said.

"Let's go," Dusty says.

Pamela takes my hand. "Are you okay to walk?"

Walking to The Bowl in the dark, as opposed to riding on a quad in the light, is a bit of a challenge. There's plenty of branches and rocks, which seem to reach out and grab us. Once we're beyond the lushness of the creek, the rocks continue and combine with cactus. More than one person cries out as a spine attacks.

Thankfully, as the sun begins its ascent, the travel becomes slightly less treacherous. The bright green of the natural spring comes into view. I let out a sigh of relief. The sound of gunfire immediately causes me to tense. It's only a couple of shots and then it ends.

"That's it?" I ask Pamela.

"I don't think so. I'm not quite sure what that was. Maybe Richard's people are firing on one of the houses, testing to see if there's any return fire."

"What about the booby traps?" I ask.

"They'll be set after the group moves on. Dax is with PJ and a few others to make sure they're in place."

"How is it they know how to make those things?"

She lets out a small chuckle. "Oh, you know. Country boys know things. Just like the small detonations we used in our first attack, they're very basic. They won't do the damage the bomb Richard used did when he took over the town, but they'll do what is needed."

When we reach The Bowl, it's obvious a few things have changed. The tent Grant and I stayed in is now accompanied by four others. And the amount of livestock has increased. There's a beautiful brown cow with a calf.

"The neighbors brought these over?" I ask.

"Yes. Like us, they don't have full working ranches but did bring their horses and what little livestock they have. Including a milk cow."

"The brown one?"

"Yes. There's a couple of goats here somewhere too."

Dusty goes around to different people, talking to them quickly. I watch as each person nods as he points. Then they take off. He walks off with a few people, returning many minutes later. Eventually, he comes to Pamela and me. "Are you doing okay, Shelby? Feeling fine after the walk?"

"I'm okay."

"I've set our first watch up. Do you think you can take watch later?"

"Dusty," Pamela says, a note of caution in her voice.

"The watch is just a precaution. You'll have watch too. We'll pretty much all need to take turns until we reach Bakerville. That's just the way it has to be." Dusty speaks quickly, getting out all he wants to say.

"I can do it," I say. "Here and on the road. Or trail. Whatever."

"I'll put her in my mom's antelope blind. It has a nice view of the game trail. And it's comfortable. You know how my mom liked that spot."

Pamela's face is tight as she gives a single nod.

"Will we be able to hear the bottleneck shooting from here?" I ask.

Dusty tilts his head. "I'm not sure. The way they'll be positioned will dampen a lot of the sound."

"We heard the shots earlier," I say.

"Yes, but that's a more wide-open space. Sound travels differently in open areas than in the hills."

"So how will we know when it's over?" I ask.

"When our people arrive here."

Pamela closes her eyes. All three of her sons are part of the bottleneck crew. Dusty wanted to be in that group, but Paul said he needed him to make sure all of us made it to The Bowl.

Grant and the others have yet to return when Dusty takes me to my watch spot. I'm expecting to need to climb up in a tree again, but instead there's a brushy area he walks me to. As we start getting close, he says, "Cherry blossom."

"Understood," a voice replies.

"This is it," Dusty says as we move closer to where a man is stepping out from behind some brush. "My mom's old antelope blind."

"Isn't this just some sagebrush?" I ask.

"Perfectly situated Wyoming Big Sagebrush," Dusty says with a smile. "Well tended over the years to blend into the environment, while offering the perfect camouflage and having a clear line of fire. I've lost track of how many antelope she harvested from here over the years. She didn't draw a tag the last few years, but before that . . . " He shrugs. "Anyway, make yourself comfortable."

The guy who was in the blind—that must be from one of the other ranches since I don't know him—hands me a whistle. I give him a look.

"We don't have enough radios," Dusty says. "If you see anyone, blow the whistle."

"That doesn't seem very . . . stealthy."

"Nope. Not at all. But we'll know there's a problem. If it's someone from our group, they'll respond with cherry blossom. In that case, blow the whistle again. If they don't respond with cherry blossom . . . make yourself small. We'll come running."

"Others have whistles too?"

"Other sentries? Yes."

"How will you know it's me?"

"Don't worry. We'll know."

I'm under no illusions sitting in the blind will be any more exciting than the tree stand was. The intense bouquet of the sagebrush fades as I'm in and settled. I make a point to remember not to touch the aromatic bush. While I like the smell, a little goes a long way. An upended log acts as my chair. Dusty was right, this is a well-hidden spot. The sagebrush is varying in height, with all of it at least as tall as

I am. Sections are a tangled mess, but there's several little holes, or what Dusty called ports, for shooting.

Before Dusty left, he said I would be here for four hours, that I should wear my trigger release just in case, and to remember the code of cherry blossom. What is it with their codes? Elm tree, blueberry, cherry blossom? Weird.

It feels like it's been just about forever since I was put in this blind. Next time I'm supposed to be on watch, I'm going to ask if I can bring a book. I can't help but smile at the thought of getting lost in a book when I'm supposed to be looking for bad guys.

My smile instantly fades when I hear the rustle of brush. At first, I think it's from behind me, my watch relief arriving early, but I quickly realize it's coming from the direction of the game trail. I keep my eyes on the spot until I see a bearded man appear, carrying a rifle. There's three more men right behind him bunched up on the small trail—all bearded and armed.

The front man looks slightly familiar, but I can't place him. Maybe from one of the other ranches? I slowly lift my bow and nock an arrow. I set the lower limb of the bow on the ground while holding the arrow in place. With my heart pounding in my ears, I put the whistle to my lips. The shrill sound hits my ears. The four guys dive behind trees and brush. I strain to hear the word cherry blossom, the code to let me know all is well.

Nothing. I lift my bow into position. One of the guys steps out slightly from behind a tree. He lifts his rifle. That's when I see the bandanna tied around his arm. A goon for sure, right? They didn't respond with cherry blossom and he's wearing a bandanna. Our people know better than to wear a bandanna.

Is it . . . is that Ellis, the loud guy from our apartment building who we sheltered with? He joined the goon squad. I can't tell for sure because Ellis was heavier, but I think it might be him.

I sit as quietly as I can as each of the others steps out. Dusty said they would come as soon as I blew the whistle. It only took us about five minutes to walk here, and I assume he'll move quicker than a walk. All four goons are in view and begin to slowly move up the trail, in one tight group, with the one who may be Ellis in the lead. They stop a moment, and all of them look around. One shrugs and starts moving.

He stops abruptly as a voice calls out, "You're surrounded. Drop your weapons." Dusty!

Instead of dropping their guns, they scatter. The one I think is Ellis stays on the game trail, running in my direction. He lifts his rifle, aiming off to his left—where I'm sure Dusty's voice originated. There are several shots fired before I can draw back my bow string to my nock position. *Please, God, help me.*

Lining up my peep sight with my middle sight pin, I take a deep breath and start to exhale, pausing my breath as I squeeze the trigger on my release. The lead guy's rifle lifts slightly just before the arrow hits him in the bicep. I quickly nock another arrow, forcing myself not to watch as he falls to the ground screaming in agony.

I wait at the ready, but the shooting soon stops. The screams from more than one person continue.

"Cherry blossom!" Someone yells out, maybe Dusty. "Cherry blossom, confirm!"

"Um, yeah!" I say. "You're a cherry blossom."

Two other people say, "Cherry blossom. Confirmed."

I watch as Dusty and the other guys step out, weapons raised. The three approach the goon farthest down the trail, then slowly work their way toward my location. I haven't heard the guy I shot with the arrow for several minutes. I know it went into his arm, so I assume he's okay.

When Dusty and his group get to the spot where my goon went down, one of the other guys shakes his head. Dusty looks toward the blind, searching me out.

"Is he going to be okay?" I ask.

"Ha," the guy who was shaking his head says.

Dusty says something to the two guys, then walks in my direction.

"Is he okay?" I ask again.

Dusty lifts a single finger in a one moment gesture.

My heart is once again pounding in my ears, and my mouth is dry. I take a sip from the water jug in the pocket of my daypack.

At the entrance to the blind, he says, "You did well, Shelby. Your signal and response were perfect."

"And the guy? I think I might have known him. He might have lived in our building."

"Your shot was true."

"I shot him in the arm. Just to keep him from shooting."

"Yes. The arrow embedded."

"In his arm?"

"Through the bicep and into his chest. He, uh . . . he didn't make it."

"I killed him?" The antelope blind starts to close in around me, the smell of the damp dirt and brush making me feel a little sick. *I killed him?* That can't be right. I was aiming for his arm.

"You did what you had to do," Dusty says, offering me his hand. "Let's go back to camp."

I feel completely numb. "I killed him." I step out of the blind and feel my knees buckle slightly.

Dusty wraps his arm around me, propping me up. "Do you need to puke?" he asks.

"I don't—no. Why?"

He lets out a breath. "When I went into town the first time and we . . . we shot, I puked afterward. All of us did. When Grant gets back, you'll probably find out he did too."

"Are there only the four? Is everything okay now?" I ask.

"The two that were with me will make sure."

"Can you—I need to know. Was it Ellis?"

Dusty nods. "We can find out." We walk within several feet of the fallen man. I can't see him, because of the foliage. Quietly, Dusty says, "Any idea who that guy is?"

"I recognize him. Can't think of his name. Think he might have been one of your hired hands before."

"What? One of my hunting guides?"

"Could be. The whiney one who went on and on about his wife being a nag."

"Ellis said he worked with you as a guide," I say.

"Yeah, I think that's his name."

Dusty motions me to stay put while he steps forward. A look of recognition crosses his face. "It's him."

I nod. "Can I . . . can I be done now?" I ask.

"Absolutely. Let's get you back to camp."

Dusty supports me as we make our way back. As soon as we're seen, Pamela and several others run to us. Dusty sends someone to take over for me in the blind while helping me to a chair.

"Is she injured?" someone asks.

"I killed him. Ellis. I killed him," I respond without emotion. Then everything goes dark.

Chapter 33

"Shelby? Shelb, are you okay?"

I scrunch my eyes. "Mm-hmm. Ti-zit?"

"What time is it? Around five, I guess."

My eyes pop open. "Grant?"

He caresses my arm. "It's me."

"Oh, Grant." I throw my arms up. "You're here."

He engulfs me in an awkward hug, crushing me into the cot. I squeeze him tightly as he says, "I'm here."

I close my eyes and whisper, "Did your dad tell you? Did he tell you what I did? To Ellis?"

"He told me you were amazing. That you did exactly what you were supposed to do. What you had to do."

"I killed him—Ellis."

"I know."

"You? Did you have to . . . "

"Yes."

"You guys, you got them all? Your ambush worked?"

"We got all that went into the bottleneck. We didn't know about Ellis. We don't know if there are others like him, so we have people on watch still."

I let out a big sigh. "Are we . . . what kind of people are we now?"

After a long pause, he says, "If a thief is caught breaking in at night and is struck a fatal blow, the defender is not guilty of bloodshed."

"Um, okay."

"It's from the Bible, in the book of Exodus, part of the Old Testament. Interestingly enough, 'You shall not murder,' one of the Ten Commandments, is also in Exodus, just a couple chapters earlier. Of course, the thief breaking in at night probably isn't a good example, because the next verse goes on to say if the break-in happens after sunrise then the defender is guilty of bloodshed."

"I don't—I'm not sure why you're telling me about the Bible."

"There's many verses in the Old Testament advocating for self-defense," he says with a nod. "And in the New Testament also. We know there's plenty of wickedness in the world. You and I, we've seen it with our own eyes, with Richard Majors and his goon squad, of course, including Ellis. But other times too."

"Yes, sure. There's good people and bad people."

"But that's just it, Shelby. There really aren't good people."

"What are you talking about? Of course there are good people. You're good. I'm g—well, maybe I'm not now. But . . . are you saying I'm bad because I killed that man?" I feel the tears welling up. I want to argue with him, tell him I only did it because I had to, because I didn't want Ellis to hurt his dad or any of our friends.

"No, no. Not at all. I'm saying— " He lets out a sigh. "I'm saying I was wrong. I was wrong to turn my back on my family. On God. I thought I was expected to live up to some sort of standard I couldn't adhere to. But that wasn't what was happening. I was hurting. My entire family was hurting after the car wreck and after my Aunt Marian and Melody died. I thought . . . " He stops and stares at the floor of the tent.

"I thought my dad was being unfair to me, that he should've supported me better, when he was really just trying to help me through my grief and guilt. Running away from here, from him, and turning my back on God didn't help with either of those. It just prolonged it."

I wait several moments for him to say more. When he doesn't, I finally ask, "And now?"

"And now, I can't take back what happened, but I know it wasn't intentional. And the accident wasn't caused by anything I did. It couldn't have been prevented. It truly was an accident. But today . . . today I specifically set out to kill people who may try and hurt you and our baby. And I'll do it again if I have to."

"So, you think we're—what's the word? Justified?"

"Justified? Maybe. I don't know. I do know that I'm a sinner and I've been living in sin."

"What do you mean *living in sin*? With me?"

"No. With myself. A sinful nature lives within me, and I acted on that sin when I rejected Christ. I don't want to live like that any longer. I don't want to be out of fellowship with Him. And I need you to know that I've asked God to forgive me. I want to be the kind of husband you deserve, a Biblical husband like my dad is. That's the kind of man you need, the kind of father our baby needs. That's what I'm going to be."

I stare into his tear-filled eyes and shake my head. "I don't understand. You're already the kind of husband I want. You're already good to me. Wonderful, in fact."

"By who's standards?"

"By, I don't know, society's standards. Everyone knows— " I bite my lip. "What exactly are you saying?"

"Nothing bad, I promise. Only that God is going to be a central part of my life—our lives."

"Are you—your mom said Tricia and Jude shouldn't be a couple because of the oxen. Are you saying we're like the oxen?"

Grant smiles as he shakes his head. "No, that's not at all what I'm saying. I think we're probably remarkably similar oxen. I see something different in you, Shelby. And that difference is probably what really drew me back to God."

I close my eyes. "I can't talk about this anymore. I did something awful today, and I don't think your God will be okay with that."

"I think that's where you're wrong. But we can stop talking now. We need to, in fact. I was supposed to come in here and wake you up so we can take the tent down. It's almost time to leave."

I start to sit up when, he says, "Slowly. My mom said you aren't to stand without me helping you."

"I'm fine. Besides, it'll probably be good if I can stand up on my own since I have to walk all night."

"Not tonight. You have a ride."

"A ride?"

"Yep. Grandpa says you're riding on the chuckwagon with him."

"In the back?"

"Nope. On the seat. It's even padded."

I nod. "Okay. That might be best."

He helps me up. I don't really feel too terrible, just a little foggy. As we walk to the tent, I say, "You don't think He's mad at me?"

"Grandpa? No, I think he planned on asking you to ride with him anyway. This was just a good reason."

"Not him," I whisper. "God."

Grant stops and turns me so I'm looking at him. "There's a story Jesus tells in the Gospel of Matthew. He talks about a man that owns a hundred sheep and one wanders off. He leaves the ninety-nine sheep and goes looking for the missing one. When he finds it, he rejoices.

He's happier about finding the missing one safe than he is about the ninety-nine he already has."

I narrow my eyes. "And? What's that have to do with how God feels about me?"

"You're the one, Shelby. He wants to have you safe. He doesn't want to see you perish."

Chapter 34

We're no sooner out of the tent than several people converge on it, taking it down. Grant walks closely with me, holding me in support. After a few steps, I realize I'm fine and can walk on my own.

All the tents that were set up earlier are gone. The two wagons, each designed to be pulled by a team of two horses, are loaded and ready. Several crates of chickens are at the back of one. I know Pamela is concerned about how her poultry will handle the trip. When it became obvious it was time to leave, she loaded up the small chicks she had been raising into boxes with air holes. The meat birds, turkeys, and hens are all in their crates.

"Where's the cattle?" I ask.

"Already on their way to Bakerville. Except the milk cow. She and her calf will stay with the walkers."

A loud *baaaaah* draws my attention. There are half a dozen goats of various sizes, all with collars and on leashes, being held by two teenage girls. A louder, lower *baaaah* answers from the other side of camp. A much larger goat is all by himself with a teen boy holding him.

"That's Tramp," Grant says. "He's the buck."

"Hmm. And they'll walk them like dogs?"

"I guess so."

"This is going to be a long trip. Where's your mom and dad?"

"Dad and Dax left a little while ago. They're the forward scouts. Mom's around here somewhere."

"Bryce?"

"He and a few others are still on sentry duty. They'll stay behind us, just to make sure we aren't being followed."

"Does anyone know where Ellis and the others came from? How did they get to the game trail?"

"Ellis knew our ranch from working as a guide. Grandpa said he brought him to The Bowl before. We don't know if he told Majors about it or struck out on his own."

"Did they set up the traps?"

"At our ranch? Yeah."

"So that's it then? We won't be coming back here—ever?"

"Not likely. But if they don't set them all off and we're able to defeat Majors, maybe."

"Got your horse ready?" Grandpa Paul asks Grant.

"Yeah," Grant answers. "Are we ready to go?"

"Looks like we're close. Your dad just radioed that everything looks good ahead. They have a spot they're watching. You need to go catch up with the cattle, help drive them."

"Where's the quads and motorcycles?" I ask, looking around.

"We decided against taking them. Too noisy. Found a hidey-hole to stash them. My truck and Jeep are there too. Maybe we'll come back for them sometime in the future."

"I thought we needed them, at least to pull the trailers."

Paul shrugs. "We'll be fine. With the wagons and the pack horses, we've got the essentials."

"How far will we go tonight?" I ask.

"Probably not far," Grandpa Paul says. "After the day we've had, we'll be blessed to make it more than a couple of miles. Ah, Rafe McCracken is signaling me. We're ready to move. I'll take care of your bride, Grant. You'd best get to your horse."

Grant kisses me goodbye before trotting off to the horses. Paul walks me to the front of the chuckwagon and helps me up. As promised, the wooden seat is padded and covered in leather or vinyl. The padding, while helpful, isn't overly thick. It's going to be a long night.

Before I know it, we're heading out. There's a horseman leading another horse, followed by the two wagons and then our chuckwagon. Grant walks his horse by my side as he says, "I'm not sure how much we'll see each other on this trip. I'll be with the cattle most of the time."

"Sneak away when you can," I say with a smile.

He gives me a nod before putting his horse into a trot.

"Pamela?" I ask Grandpa Paul.

"With the walkers. We're going so slow we won't be far ahead of them."

We've been on the trail for quite some time when Paul startles me by asking, "Are you feeling okay now?"

"I'm . . . I don't feel as weak as I did."

"You know you probably saved Dusty, right?"

"Saved him?"

"The guy had a bead on him. Dusty had just turned from firing on one of the others and saw him—felt for sure he was a goner. But then you took your shot and the goon's bullet went wide."

"Ellis. His name was Ellis."

"Yes, it was."

Is this true? Did I really save Dusty? And if I did, why don't I feel better about it?

After many minutes, Paul says, "None of us like the things we've done. And you may not know this, but there's been quite a bit of disagreement about our methods. If we thought Majors would've just let us live peacefully, we wouldn't have launched the attacks. Several just wanted to leave, head to Bakerville and not do any of the things we've done. But then we'd just be putting off the inevitable. Majors will gather more followers and become stronger. At least now we've taken away some of his crew."

"And the other people? The ones who caused the explosion in Prospect?"

"No idea."

"Do you think Donnie and Jerry could have made it to Cody and brought people to start the attack?"

"That wasn't the plan. They were supposed to get word to us before they started anything. Besides, I'd be surprised if he had time to get there and set up something. No, I think it's townspeople who've had enough. I just wish we could stay and help them. But like we talked about, with winter coming, it's time for us to get someplace safe. Speaking of, you warm enough? It's a chilly night."

"I'm fine," I say, pulling the collar up on my jacket. "Did Grant tell you about his . . . um, he's decided he's a Christian again."

"He didn't tell me, but I suspected. How do you feel about it?"

I watch the sky as the darkness takes over. "Will you be able to see okay?"

"Sure. The moon will give us some light. In a few days it might be a challenge. Tonight's fine, though."

"At first I felt betrayed," I say quietly.

"That's understandable. I remember my mom feeling that way when my dad wanted to start going to church."

"Your mom?"

"Yep. Neither of them really gave much thought to God. They were both too busy trying to build the ranch and just get through each day. Then my dad met this guy—not a real preacher, but he could have been."

"Okay, and?"

"And the preacher guy told my dad about Jesus, referring to Him as a sinner's savior. They ended up in a big discussion about how sin is all around and how everyone sins. My dad got mad at that. Not so much because he didn't think of himself as a sinner, but because he didn't like thinking of my mom or me as sinners."

"Were you a sinner?"

"Well, sure. I was— " He pauses for a moment and does something with the reins. "I was eight, maybe nine at the time. My mom and dad had taught me about right and wrong. And even so, I still did wrong. Purposely at times. Wouldn't you say that's sinning?"

"Well, I guess, but it's not like you killed someone." I balk as soon as the words are out of my mouth.

Paul looks over at me. "Sin is sin. And we all do it. We all sin. But that's one thing God can't stand for. He can't allow sinners into heaven."

I stare off into the darkness. If God doesn't allow sin in heaven and everyone sins, then how do people go to heaven. Grant once told me Christians believe Jesus is the only way to heaven. But none of it makes any sense.

It's a long time before Paul says, "That's why He's a sinner's savior. Jesus makes a way for us sinners to be able to go to heaven."

We ride for a long time in silence, with the occasional chitchat. The phrase "sinner's savior" sticks with me. Finally, I say, "My mom told me Christians are a bunch of hypocrites. You don't seem like that. Neither does Pamela."

"Hypocrite? I don't know about that. But I'm certainly not perfect. My wife could've told you some stories that—never mind. Suffice it to say, I'm flawed. I'm a sinner. God knows that, that's why He gave me the opportunity to accept His grace and Jesus. I certainly am not good on my own. And when I do fail, God helps me get back on track. This whole thing with Majors has definitely been a test of my faith."

"How so?"

"Sometimes I forget to go to God about it. Sometimes it's easy to think this is what needs to be done. And now I realize I've become complacent in my walk with God. I've been too comfortable. Maybe we've all become too comfortable and that's why— " He clears his throat. "Anyway, being a Christian doesn't make us perfect, and to some that may make us seem hypocritical. Admitting we've failed isn't always easy. I think if you talk to Grant, he'll be able to tell you about that. Dusty too. They both failed and had a lot of stuff to work through, not just with each other but within themselves. I'm proud of them both."

Am I a sinner? I almost snort out loud at the thought. Yeah, I've done some things. Oh, nothing too bad. But things for sure. Shortly before we stop, I realize that's what I need. I need a sinner's savior. Even though my mom thought it was all fake, I've seen it with Grant's family. With Grant. Maybe even in me. Things are different. Things are terrible and awful at times, but I have a new comfort.

Sometimes a song will float through my head, and I'll realize it's one of the songs Annette was singing, a song about God or Jesus. And when we pray, I no longer just pretend, I follow along. The words fill me. Somehow, when I wasn't paying attention, God made a difference, and I'm now drawing strength from him.

I feel a smile spread across my face. Something has changed in me. I don't know exactly when it happened, but things are different.

"Whoa, boss," Paul says, pulling back on the reins and bringing the chuckwagon to a stop.

"Why don't you hold up a minute and I'll help you down?" Paul says, standing and stretching.

"Wait," I say, reaching for his hand.

"Something wrong, Shelby?" he asks, sitting back down.

"I need to know more. I need to know about God and Jesus."

With a huge smile, Paul says, "I think that sounds pretty good."

"Will you pray with me?"

"I'd be happy to."

"What do I say?"

"Whatever's in your heart."

I close my eyes and bow my head. "Um, should I do it out loud?"

"If you want."

"God— " I clear my throat. "I thought You were nothing but a fairytale. And I can't believe I'm saying this, that I'm praying, but I need to know You. To know Jesus. I don't think You're fake. I'm sorry I didn't know. I believe . . . " I take a deep breath. "I believe in You. Help me to learn more."

I lift my eyes and look up to Paul. He gives me a nod.

"Oh!" I say, bowing my head. "Uh, amen."

"Amen," Paul whispers. "God's grace has been working for you, Shelby. You've accepted this free gift with your belief."

"Now what happens?" I ask. "Should I do something?"

"The Bible says you should repent and then be baptized. You've already done the repentance part, since you've realized your need for Christ and accepted Him. Now you just need to follow Him.

"How will I know?"

"You've been given a gift, Shelby, the gift of the Holy Spirit to help you. Plus, the more you learn about God and His son, the more you'll know about His ways. Not sure we can do the baptizing out here, but we can when we get to Bakerville."

"Okay. I need to tell Grant. He's going to be surprised."

"Wait, let me help you down." As he walks around the chuckwagon, he says, "There was a time I'd just bounce down from that seat. I guess those days are long gone. I'm feeling every bit of my seventy-eight years right now."

He lifts a hand up to me, and as I cautiously crawl down from the wagon, he says, "I don't think Grant will be as surprised as you might think."

"Why's that?"

"Because he's been praying for you. We all have. We prayed for Grant and Dusty too. God heard our prayers for them, so . . . welcome to the family."

"Um, I was already part of the fam—oh! Is this, like, a God thing?"

Paul gives his big booming belly laugh, causing several people to look toward us. "Go see your husband. He'll rejoice with you."

I step carefully toward where the cattle are. The sky is lighter, but the sun isn't yet up. I'm still a fair distance away when I find Bryce unsaddling his horse.

"Hey, Shelby. Did you have a good night?"

"I did. Really good."

"Really?"

"Mm-hmm. Where's Grant?"

"He's still with the cattle, making sure they're settled. Do you need him?"

"Not really. Maybe he could come find me when he gets a break?"

"Sure. I'll tell him."

While Grant and others are staying on watch with the cattle and wagons on the flat section of land, the rest of us are moving into the foothills to set up camp. This is a spot Paul is familiar with, having camped here many times with his dude ranch people. It was chosen because of the hills forming a similar shape to The Bowl, providing a hiding area for the cattle and wagons, plus a small run off coming out of the mountains so we can refill the water containers. Moving the rest of us behind another set of hills gives extra protection.

As soon as camp is set up, Dusty and Dax head out once again. They'll go during the daylight to look for other travelers and possible dangers, plus find us a spot to camp tonight. Paul told me he has a place in mind for the second night that's remarkably similar to this spot. When they reach it, they'll set up watch until we arrive tomorrow.

The morning warms up and makes sleeping difficult, but in the early afternoon it cools substantially when clouds roll in. I'm crawling into a small tent to wait out the storm when Grant comes running up. "Hey, beautiful," he says. "There room in there for a stinky cowboy?"

"Mmm. Probably not. But I can fit you."

"Oh, okay," he says with a smile. "I smell like a horse."

"C'mon in."

He takes his boots off, tucking them under the tent's built-in doormat.

"Will they be okay there?"

"Should be. I don't think we want them inside."

Once we're in the tent with the flap zipped, the horse smell hits me full on. He wasn't kidding.

"Maybe I should unzip the window," he says as he starts to open it.

"Don't you need to sleep?"

"Yeah, for a bit. I thought I'd use the hammock, but the trees are too small here. And with the rain . . . "

"I'm glad you're here, even if you do offend my delicate nose."

"Bryce said you were looking for me this morning. Sorry I'm so late getting here."

"It's fine. I know you had things to do."

"Man, I'm beat." He crawls on top of the sleeping bag. "What did you need me for? Are you doing okay?"

"I'm good. I wanted to tell you— " I let out a small laugh. "You know the oxen thing?"

"Oxen?"

"Yeah, you know, about us not matching up."

"Oh, yep," he says with a yawn. "But I still think we do."

I give a vigorous nod. "I spent some time thinking and talking to Grandpa Paul and— " I let out a sigh and glance over at him. His eyes are closed and his face is relaxed. I lean in a little. He's asleep.

A wave of irritation passes through me as I shake my head. I reach over to shake him, stopping midway. Is this a test? Is God putting something that would normally irritate me in place to see what I do? I shake my head. I don't really know much about God, but that doesn't seem right. Instead of waking Grant up, I curl up next to him. That lasts about four seconds until the smell is too much. I move to the other sleeping bag and wait out the storm.

Chapter 35

I'm helping pack things up for our new night of travel when Grant walks up behind me, wrapping me in a hug. "Sorry I fell asleep," he says, kissing my neck.

"You were beat."

"I was. And I realized when I woke up that I should've cleaned up before climbing in the tent. It might never be the same again."

"True," I say with a laugh. "It was pretty bad when I got out." I turn around to face him. "Can we walk for a minute? Or do you need to go?"

"I have a few minutes. I took the tent down and put the gear in the green wagon."

"That's fine. I'll make sure someone else gets that tent and sleeping bag tomorrow."

We both laugh as we hold hands and walk toward where the goats are tethered.

"What were you talking about earlier?"

"Me, you, and God. Or maybe it's supposed to be God, you, and me?"

He stops and turns me to face him. "Maybe you'd like to get to know Him?"

With a smile and a shrug, I say, "I think I already have been. Not on purpose. But somehow it's happened."

"You seemed pretty upset the other day. When you found out I was— "

"I felt betrayed."

"So what's changed?"

"Even though I felt betrayed by you, I still felt . . . pulled . . . I guess that's the right word. Pulled toward God."

Grant pulls me into a hug. "Things have always been good with us. But by putting God at the center of our marriage, things will be even better. I know they will."

"Just don't expect too much from me. I don't know the . . . you know, the stuff."

"The stuff?"

220

"The right words—the Christian things to say. I won't know it."

He kisses me on the nose. "I don't think you need to worry about that."

The next nights and days pass slowly, traveling at night and then sleeping or taking watch during the day. And everything goes much slower than anticipated. Paul thought we'd make better time than we have. The second night, Dusty found a camp spot about six miles from the first camp. It was full daylight before the last of us made it in. We decreased our distance to five miles the next night. Almost everyone has blisters on their feet, cactus spines in their shoes, and scratches or bruises on their shins. There's even been a sprained ankle and one lady has a swollen knee; those two people are now riding instead of walking.

The extra days have been hard not only on us humans but on the livestock. Pamela lost a duck and two of the small chickens. Tramp, the buck goat, got off his tether one day and had no desire to be recaptured. It took almost an hour before his owner was able to lure him back with a small snack of grain.

We're just about to begin our sixth night of travel. I've been alternating between riding in the chuckwagon with Grandpa Paul and walking. When I ride, I ask Paul questions about God. It's strange to not feel angry when talking and thinking about God. Sometimes I wonder why I had so much anger before.

Tonight is so dark Grant has asked me to only ride. He's afraid, even with the flashlights, I won't be able to see well enough to keep my footing. We haven't even been on the trail an hour when there's a thud and a wail. We stop the procession to tend to a scraped knee on one of the older children from the McCracken ranch. Once we get going again, we barely make another ten minutes before someone else falls.

While we're stopped, Pamela comes running to the chuckwagon. "It's too dark, Paul. Her wrist might be broken. It's too dark for us to tell, but this is dangerous. We need to stop."

"It might lighten up."

"And if it does, we can move again. A broken wrist is bad, but someone else could get hurt worse.

"All right. But we're stopping right here so we can easily start moving again. We're not camping up in the hills."

"No, we'd never make it. It's too dark."

While a couple of tents are set up for the children, we don't set up camp. It's decided the wrist is probably only sprained, not broken.

"Shelby, come over here," Pamela says, flashing a light on the ground in my direction. "Be careful and watch your footing. I have a spot for you." She motions to my sleeping bag spread out on the ground.

"You set up my bed?"

"Yes, now crawl in and get some sleep. I sent one of the Smalls boys ahead to tell Grant and the others with the cattle that we've stopped. Then he'll find Dusty and Dax. Sleep a bit. If the moon comes out, we'll start moving again."

I snuggle into the bag and fall asleep almost immediately. When Pamela gently shakes me awake, my eyes pop open.

"You slept well?" she asks.

"Mm-hmm. We're leaving?"

"We'll try to get in a couple of miles before camping for the day. It's not quite as dark as it was."

The sun is well up before we stop. Dusty and Dax are both at the camp. After talking with Paul for a few minutes, Dusty asks everyone to gather around.

"Okay, folks, I know last night was challenging. This whole trip has been challenging. We all expected to be basking in luxury in Bakerville by now."

There are a few courtesy chuckles.

"The good news is, we're close. Dax and I are going to go ahead as usual. We believe there's a good chance they have sentries set up, but probably only on the roads. Since we are traveling overland, we might just head right in."

"You think that'll be safe?" someone asks.

"Probably not," Paul answers. "Most likely, we'll want to head to the road where they have their sentries, introduce ourselves proper like. Dusty and Dax will determine where the best point of entry is."

"We'll travel tonight and then wait until daylight to finish our trek to town."

"So tomorrow we'll be in Bakerville?" Tricia's son asks.

"Yep. We should be," Grandpa Paul says.

After the meeting breaks up, we set up camp. Even though I slept for several hours last night, I'm exhausted. I can't wait to finish this journey. Being on the trail, whether walking or riding in the chuckwagon, is exhausting. My back hurts something awful, and my feet are swelling. Pamela says she thinks a nurse practitioner who used to work for one of the surgeons in Prospect lives in Bakerville.

"A doctor?" I ask.

"Similar. She worked for a surgeon, even having her own patients, but she'll know about babies."

"Do you think everything is okay? Is there a problem?"

"Oh, I think you're fine. A little swelling is normal when you're reaching the end of your pregnancy. We'll just keep an eye on you until she can check you out."

Since Grant is part of the team driving the cattle, I've barely seen him. Missing him, combined with feeling wiped out—I'm pretty much done with this trip.

The day is cool, like a late-September day should be, and perfect for sleeping. Even with my nap last night, I have no problem sleeping for several hours. Once I'm up, I get something to eat. When it became obvious we'd be leaving the ranch soon, Pamela started cooking and baking. The freezer, which was kept running with a generator, was emptied of all the meat. She turned most of it into jerky, but some was cooked and refrozen. We ate those along with bread and other baked goods the first few days.

Grant added all the non-cook foods we had cached in various places between the ranch and Prospect. Before we left the ranch, he also visited the final spot where Kirstin's clue for her husband was left, changing the coded note and directing him to the ranch for an even more cryptic note sending him to Bakerville. Kirstin is sure he'll know what this note means and will have no trouble deciphering it. She says they spent a lovely day picnicking on the river in Bakerville right before he left. The note that says *Last place we ate chopped olive sandwiches* will at least get him to the right area. I'd never heard of a chopped olive sandwich, so the note resulted in a huge explanation on what this rather unique sandwich filling was—and convinced me there are certain things that should not go between two pieces of bread.

But since Ethan loves those sandwiches, it's a perfect clue for him. We hope, once he reaches Bakerville, someone can help him locate his family. Of course, it's all an assumption that he can make his way to Prospect and then escape Majors's tyranny to be able to find the first tip in the apartment, which will start his quest.

Each time Grant left to visit our stashes, I faced a new test in patience and trust in his return. Was that part of helping me get to know God?

Our diet now consists mainly of jerky, nuts, and some hard biscuits Pamela made. She said they wouldn't be much for flavor—she's right—but would keep us going. Tonight, I soak my jerky in hot water and dunk the biscuit in before eating. This is the extent of cooking on the trail. We don't make actual meals for fear of odors—partly out of concern of being discovered by Majors's goons and partly because of bears. Since this is grizzly country, we take precautions such as not cooking near the tents and eating only in the designated food area by the chuckwagon.

After I eat, I take a turn at watch so someone else can rest. Taking a watch shift always gives me a knot in my stomach. While I do know I did what I had to do when Ellis and his men were sneaking up on us, I don't want to have to do that again. I will, but I pray I never need to. When it's finally time to break camp and start the final leg of our journey, I'm more than ready.

Shortly before dark, Dusty rides in. He talks to Paul for a few minutes, then leaves.

"Okay, folks, gather around," Paul says. "As expected, they do have guards on duty. In fact, a little more than we expected. Seems they have a guard station of sorts on this side of Bakerville. They'll see us long before we reach them. This is good news in many ways, but for our needs it does add a small wrinkle."

"How is it good news?" a lady from one of the other ranches asks.

"It shows they've set up defenses."

"Will they— "

"Hold on a minute," Paul says, raising a hand. "Let me tell you the plan and then we can discuss. We won't go as far tonight as anticipated. Dusty and Dax spent the day watching. We think the best thing to do is to go in as a group tomorrow morning. We'll stay back far enough to be safe, but we want to give them a good look at us. Make sure they can see we're families with women and children. We'll keep the cattle back until we make their acquaintance."

"And if they're hostile?" the lady asks.

"We'll have our own defense set up as a precaution."

"What's that mean?"

"It means we won't get too close until we know it's safe."

"And if they attack us or reject us?" the same lady asks, while at the same time Tricia cries out, "I thought you said this was a safe place."

Paul loses control of the group, and there are many similar questions and statements. I hear one guy mutter that he should've joined the goon squad, that he'd have been better off. I search over the group of three guys around my age and try to figure out if it was one of them.

"Okay, folks. I know we've had a long trip and this isn't what any of us expected. Let's just keep the faith. I don't think God would've led us here if it weren't a safe place for us. Let's pray, then we'll finish our journey."

Even though it's not quite as dark as last night, it's still hard traveling. I walk very little, choosing to ride most of the time. It's still quite some time before sunrise when we stop.

"We'll wait here until it's time to move forward," Paul tells me. "We're hidden from the sentries, but with the way sound travels, we'll need to keep it down. I'm going to go tell a few others so we can pass it around. Wait here for me, and I'll come back to help you down from the wagon."

When I'm finally on the ground, I search out Kirstin. She's sitting with Milena and Annette on a cluster of large boulders.

"Here's a spot for you," Annette says, taking my hand and helping me navigate through the rocks.

"I'll be glad to end this trip," Kirstin says, her voice barely a whisper. She has Caleb tucked in his carrier, close to her body. Annette is holding Mason in a similar manner, his legs sticking out the bottom of the almost too small baby pack.

While the cattle and other livestock aren't overly quiet, the people are—other than the rare murmur that carries gently on the breeze. There's not much to talk about until we know whether the community of Bakerville will welcome us.

The sky is just beginning to lighten when several gunshots sound in the distance. Kirstin lets out a slight gasp while others in the group ask where the shots are coming from. Within a minute or so, Pamela is walking around telling everyone to stay calm, that the shooting has ended and it wasn't very close, more near the road than the edge of the foothills where we are.

Just before daylight, Dusty, Dax, and several others move away from the group. They're going into the foothills to find spots to cover us. Grant is still with the cattle crew as they work at keeping them calm. My heart starts to pound as I think of what will happen next.

"Okay, folks," Paul says calmly. "We'll give them just a minute to get in position. Then we'll start moving forward. The beef cattle will stay here, but we'll bring the milk cow and the goats. Just walk them like normal. Remember, we won't get within range, so we won't be in danger. If—and I don't think this will happen—but if they're hostile, our guys will give us plenty of time to get hidden. Return to this spot, and we'll regroup."

We start to break up when I surprise myself by saying, "Can we pray? I mean . . . do you think we should?"

"We definitely should," Kirstin says, taking my hand.

After Paul prays, I follow him to the chuckwagon. We're usually behind the other two wagons, but this time those wagons are staying here. It's just us, a couple of people on horses, the goats, dairy cow and calf, and our people walking.

We move very slowly, letting the sun rise. When it's full daylight, Paul gestures toward a hillside. "That's their watch tower. We're pretty sure there's two people in there. And I think I see movement. Can you make out what's happening?"

"Should I use the binoculars?"

"I'd rather we didn't. Just your naked eye."

"Should we stop? Are we close enough?"

"A little farther. We're still good."

"Yeah, they're moving. And . . . I think I see dust in the distance. Maybe a truck or something?"

"Ah. Yep. Here they come. Whoa, boss." He pulls the wagon to a stop. "Okay, folks. Just stand still. We're fine." Paul reaches down by our feet and pulls up a pole with a white handkerchief tied to it. He lifts it in the air, waving it back and forth. "You take the flag, Shelby. I'm going to come around and help you down. Then you'll go back and find Pamela."

"Where are you going?"

"Pretty soon, they're going to send out a welcoming party. I'll greet them."

"By yourself?"

"Me and my flag. It'll be fine."

Once I'm on the ground, Paul motions to one of the teenage boys from the other ranches. He comes trotting over, and Paul says, "You sure you can drive this thing?"

"Yeah, I can do it."

"Okay. Hold it steady, and don't take off unless the shooting starts."

"Got it," the boy says, climbing up.

"Grandpa Paul . . . be careful," I say, as he starts to walk away.

He lifts a hand in acknowledgment. "It's going to be fine, Shelby."

I move to the back and find Pamela. She wraps an arm around me as we watch Paul move quickly away from us. A pickup and a quad are heading in our direction.

"Should we take cover?" I ask.

"We'll just stay near the chuckwagon," she says. "Not too close, in case he needs to move it quickly. We want to look . . . vulnerable. I think we're fine here."

We stand quietly for another minute, then Pamela says, "It looks like they're slowing down, keeping their distance from Paul. And Dusty and the others are ready."

The pickup stops with the quad behind it. Both doors to the pickup open and two men step out, staying behind the doors. Paul waves the flag slightly, lifting his other hand out so they can see it. His voice carries slightly across the high desert, enough to hear a noise of him saying something but not enough to make it out. One of the guys responds. The back and forth continues for many minutes. Eventually, Paul starts moving toward the pickup while both men from Bakerville start walking toward him. When they meet in the middle, there are handshakes all around.

"I think we're okay," Pamela says with a sigh.

There's a buzz among our group as we all hug and hold each other. We've made it here. We've made it to Bakerville. We'll be safe. At least for now.

"Thank you, God. Thank you for getting us here," I whisper.

Epilogue

I groan as I turn over and try to sit up. The weight of my stomach makes everything more difficult.

"Bathroom trip?" Grant asks, his voice laced with sleep.

"I—maybe. I just can't seem to get comfortable."

When we reached the edge of Bakerville on that day in late September, we were not exactly welcomed with open arms, but we weren't turned away. The community had set up not only a defense plan but a plan for their town's government. In order to become a part of the community, we had to either be approved by the council or sponsored by a Bakerville resident. Paul's high school classmate Sally-Ann agreed to sponsor everyone related to Paul. The McCrackens used to work with another town member, who was willing to sponsor their family. The Vasquezes and Smalls had to go through the approval process.

It seemed we arrived at an interesting time. The community was in the process of moving to a new location, up to a small ski resort on the edge of the mountain. Well, part of the community. Part of the town stayed behind, thinking the idea of moving to a new location was more trouble than an advantage. When I asked why they were moving, Sally-Ann said it was because of defense. They were all spread out too thin, and the way they were set up wouldn't work for winter. Sally-Ann was part of the group moving to the ski resort. As such, we moved to the ski resort too. The McCrackens' friend was part of the group staying behind.

Grant and I were surprised to see a familiar face in the Bakerville group. Jake—the man we met the day after the cyberattacks when he was stocking up at SuperMart—was helping transport supplies up to the new location. At first, he didn't recognize us. And I knew he looked familiar, but I couldn't quite place him. It was Grant who put it together. I know we owe so much to him. He and Grandpa Paul saw what was happening early on. Without their encouragement, I'm not sure we would've acted so quickly.

Because of the fracture in the community, the other two families who arrived with us in Bakerville were interviewed by representatives from both groups. In the end, the Smalls were asked to join the group staying in Bakerville, while the Vasquezes moved up to the ski resort with us. I think who went where was decided by the livestock. The group staying in Bakerville had several milk cows but no goats. The Smalls and their small goat herd were a welcome addition.

Grant and I were given a small room—just large enough for a double bed, dressing area, and small closet space—in the old ski lodge. Men's and women's bathrooms are down the hall, with toilets and sinks only. Makeshift showers are set up at the nearby homes and the old dude ranch across the road. Just like in Prospect, running water is a thing of the past. PJ and Dusty discussed setting up a system for bringing in water from the creek, but all the living spaces are at a higher elevation than the creek.

"Want me to go with you?" Grant asks.

"I'm pretty sure I can walk down the hall, you goof," I say, pushing him lightly on the arm.

"I'm sure ready for the feast they're planning today," he says, propping himself up on one arm. "What are you most looking forward to?"

"Ugh. Nothing. My stomach isn't feeling very good. Even thinking about the Thanksgiving meal we've planned—just ugh."

He gives a small laugh before lying back down. I hoist myself off the bed. As I do, a gush of water runs down my legs.

"Oh! I think—I guess . . . "

"What?" he asks, sitting up quickly.

"Either I just wet my pants or my water broke."

"Right now?"

"Yes! Can you—can you get me a towel? Everything is wet."

He grabs a towel from one of our hooks. As he's walking toward me, a pain grips my stomach. "Oh . . . argh," I say, trying to muffle my cry.

"I thought Belinda and Dr. Sam both said it would be unlikely for you to deliver on your due date. They thought it'd still be another week or so."

"I guess they were wrong."

After cleaning things up as best he can, Grant helps me dress. I'm almost ready when another contraction hits.

After it's over, Grant asks, "You want to wait here? I can get someone to let Belinda and Dr. Sam know we're on our way."

"It'll be Belinda and Kelley," I say. "Sam started running a fever again yesterday. Besides, he was never going to help with the delivery since he can't even sit up, but we planned on him being nearby. I'll go with you. I don't want to be alone."

Fifteen minutes later, after a bumpy ride in a four-person UTV, I'm in the small duplex being used as the doctor's office.

"This little one takes his suggested due date seriously," Belinda says with a smile.

"I'm sorry we woke you up," I say.

"You didn't. I was in with Dr. Sam when I got the call."

"Is he okay?"

She gives me a sad look before saying, "He's excited for your baby. He'll be within earshot if we need him."

From the room next door, a muffled voice says, "Open the door between the rooms so I can hear better."

Belinda shakes her head. "Yes, Sam," she says, moving to the door connecting the two cabins. She opens it and sticks her head in. "We're still a long way off from having the baby. Why don't you get some sleep? Maybe that fever will break."

Two months ago, Dr. Sam and his wife were shot at by a sniper. She wasn't injured, but Sam's pelvis was shattered and he had extensive internal damage. He's had many surgeries and many battles with infection. They thought he was in the clear, having been recovering well for the last month or so. He knows he won't walk again; he can't even sit upright. He does his doctoring—which is limited to consulting only—from a camping cot set up to wheel around. When he moves from his cabin to the doctor's office, he's carried on a stretcher. When word spread that he'd spiked a fever, it was a hard blow to the community. Infection is a huge concern for all of us. There's a hope he has only a mild virus, a cold that's circulating among the group, instead of a bacterial infection.

I feel the beginnings of a contraction. "It's happening," I say.

Belinda rushes over, putting a comforting hand on my stomach. As the wave of pain washes over me, she says, "Nice and strong. You're going to do just fine."

Several hours and many contractions later, Belinda says, "Keep breathing, Shelby. It won't be much longer now. Grant, can you wipe her forehead?"

I'm leaning against Grant, using him as a brace, as he reaches across my face. "Stop! My forehead is fine," I say through gritted teeth. I feel the wave of a new contraction beginning. "Argh! It's happening again."

"That's what we want. You're almost finished. Just let the contraction do its thing."

"Wipe my forehead, wipe my forehead," I cry out as sweat drips into my eyes. "Ahhhhh . . . " I cry out.

"Breathe, Shelby, you're doing great."

As the contraction fades, Belinda says, "I can see the top of the head. You're almost there."

A voice calls out from the other room, "Don't rush it. Let her take her time."

"Did you hear Dr. Sam?" Belinda asks. "We're going to go nice and slow. You'll have less problems that way."

"And my baby?"

"Doing fine, everything is as it should be."

Time seems to stand still as contraction after contraction engulfs me. Finally, Belinda tells me it's time to push.

I lean back against Grant, capturing his strength with mine.

"You're doing great, Shelby," he says.

Pain, Belinda's voice, and the beating of Grant's heart against my back are all there is as everything else fades away.

"You're doing it, Shelby. Here we go . . . okay, you've got this. He's out. I mean, she's out. It's a girl."

"A girl! We have a girl," Grant says, rubbing my arm.

I sink back into him. "A girl. How does she look?"

"She's beautiful," Belinda says, tears running down her face. "Kelley, can you take the baby for a minute while I make sure Shelby's okay?"

Our baby lets out a wail as Kelley takes her, wrapping her up. "Here she is," she says, moving our daughter toward us.

I hold out my arms to take her. I gasp. "Oh, she's so beautiful."

"She is," Grant says. "She looks like you."

We spend many minutes cuddling and admiring her.

"So what do you think, Mom?" Grant asks. "Does she look like a Hannah?"

"Oh, yes. She does. Hello, Hannah, my sweet girl."

"What a wonderful name," Kelley says.

231

"Beautiful," Belinda agrees.

"We found it in the baby book, the one you loaned us," I say. "One of the meanings is the grace of God."

"That's very fitting," Kelley says.

"God has been so good to us," Grant says. "Even when I turned my back on Him, He never let go of me. And before Shelby— "

"Before I even knew Him, He was guiding me toward Him," I say. "By the grace of God, we ended up here, safe and having Your help for the birth of our baby, of our beautiful Hannah."

From the other room, Dr. Sam says, "Thanks be to God."

The Bakerville saga continues in *Pestilence in the Darkness: Havoc in Wyoming, Part 6.*

New to the *Havoc in Wyoming* series? Start the journey with *Caldwell's Homestead: Havoc in Wyoming, Part 1.*

Thank you for spending your time with the people of Wesley, Wyoming.

If you have five minutes, you'd make this writer very happy if you could write a short Amazon review.

I appreciate you!

Join my reader's club!

Receive a complimentary copy of *Wyoming Refuge: A Havoc in Wyoming Prequel*. As part of my reader's club, you'll be the first to know about new releases and specials. I also share info on books I'm reading, preparedness tips, and more.

Please sign up on my website:

MillieCopper.com

Now Available

Havoc in Wyoming

Part 1: Caldwell's Homestead

Jake and Mollie Caldwell started their small farm and homestead to be able to provide for an uncertain future for their family, friends, and community. They have tried to plan for everything, but they never imagined this would happen.

Part 2: Katie's Journey

Katie loves living on her own while finishing up her college degree, working her part-time jobs, and building a relationship with her boyfriend, Leo. When disaster strikes, being away from family isn't quite so nice, and home is over a thousand miles away. Will she make it home before the United States falls apart?

Part 3: Mollie's Quest

Two or three times a year, Mollie Caldwell travels for business. Being away from her Wyoming farmstead is both a fun time and a challenge. They started their farm to be able to provide for an uncertain future for their family, friends, and community. The farm keeps the entire family busy, meaning extra work for her husband while she's away. This time, while on her business trip, terrorists attack. Her weeklong business trip becomes much longer as she tries to make her way home.

Part 4: Shields and Ramparts

The United States, and the community of Bakerville, face a new threat . . . a threat that could change America forever. As the neighbors band together, all worry about friends and family members. Have they found safety from this latest danger?

Part 5: Fowler's Snare

Welcome to Bakerville, the sleepy Wyoming community Mollie and Jake Caldwell have chosen as their family retreat. At the edge of the wilderness, far away from the big city, they were so sure nothing bad could ever happen in such a protected place. They were wrong. Now, with the entire nation in peril, coming together as a community is the only way they can survive. But not everyone in the community has the people of Bakerville's best interest at heart.

Part 6: Pestilence in the Darkness

Surrounded by danger, they band together with the community of Bakerville to move to a new defensible location. But they weren't prepared to have to give up so much for the security they so desperately need. And they quickly learn trust must be earned, not freely given.

Part 7: My Refuge and Fortress

When Jake and a group of hunters return to Bakerville and find their former neighbors slaughtered, they realize there is a new, even more deadly threat. Will their reinforced location be secure enough? And what about the radio announcement from the president? Will his promise of help arrive in time?

Find these titles at MillieCopper.com

Acknowledgments

Thanks to:

Ameryn Tucker my editor, beta reader, and daughter wrapped in one. I had a story I wanted to tell, and Ameryn encouraged me and helped me bring it to life.

Dauntless Cover Design for the amazing cover.

My husband who gave me the time and space I needed to complete this dream and was very patient as I'd tell him the same plot ideas over and over and over.

Two more daughters and a young son who willingly listened to me drone on and on about story lines and ideas while encouraging me to "keep going."

My amazing Beta Readers! An extra special thanks to Tim M. for his expertise in firearms and all things that go boom, Ginger B. for her for all her valuable feedback, Marian G. for giving me a fresh perspective, and Judy S. for always saying, "I can't wait to find out what happens next!"

And to you, my readers, for spending your time with the people of Wesley, Wyoming. If you have five minutes, you'd make this writer very happy if you could write a short Amazon review. I appreciate you!

About the Author

Millie Copper, writer of Cozy Apocalyptic fiction and practical preparedness manuals, uses her homesteading, preparedness, and off-grid living experience as a guide to writing her 39 (and counting!) Christian Post-Apocalyptic fiction books, including the Amazon bestselling series Havoc in Wyoming.

Millie has penned nine nonfiction, traditional food focused books, sharing how, with a little creativity, anyone can transition to a real foods diet without overwhelming their food budget.

She has also authored hundreds of articles on her Homespun Oasis blog about traditional foods, alternative health, homesteading, and preparedness—many times all within the same piece.

Find Millie at www.MillieCopper.com
Facebook: www.facebook.com/MillieCopperAuthor/
Amazon: www.amazon.com/author/milliecopper
BookBub: https://www.bookbub.com/authors/millie-copper
Instagram: https://www.instagram.com/cozyapoc
YouTube: https://www.youtube.com/@MillieCopperWrites